DEATH OF A NOVICE

DEATH OF A NOVICE

A Reverend Mother Mystery

Cora Harrison

This first world edition published 2018
in Great Britain and the USA by
SEVERN HOUSE PUBLISHERS LTD of
Eardley House, 4 Uxbridge Street, London W8 7SY
Trade paperback edition first published
in Great Britain and the USA 2019 by
SEVERN HOUSE PUBLISHERS LTD

British Library Cataloguing in Publication Data
A CIP catalogue record for this title is available from the British Library.

ISBN-13: 978-0-7278-8783-2 (cased)
ISBN-13: 978-1-84751-906-1 (trade paper)
ISBN-13: 978-1-78010-961-9 (e-book)

Typeset by Palimpsest Book Production Ltd.,
Falkirk, Stirlingshire, Scotland.

For my son, William, whose medical and scientific knowledge helped me immensely in working out the details of this death of a novice nun. I am also very grateful for his empathy and kindness when answering cries for help with computer problems.

ACKNOWLEDGEMENTS

Thanks are due to my creative, erudite, knowledgeable, sympathetic and speedy agent, Peter Buckman of Ampersand Agency; to my editor, Anna Telfer, who combines enthusiasm with the patience necessary to deal with an author incapable of keeping days of the week or hours of the day in her head; to copy editor, Holly Domney, who goes through everything with a fine sieve and to all at Severn House who take such care to produce an attractive book from my efforts.

ONE

William Butler Yeats
'Being Irish, he had an abiding sense of tragedy which
sustained him through occasional periods of joy.'

Eileen stood very still and stared at the man opposite to her. Tom Hurley had once been her military commander, a man to whom she had owed instant obedience, on pain of death. Her life as a hunted and outlawed member of an illegal organisation now seemed far from her present existence as a respectable office girl, proficient with a typewriter and earning a good weekly sum which was enough to keep her mother and herself in relative comfort. The sight of Tom Hurley brought everything back, though, and she felt a slight shiver of apprehension at the sight of him. A fanatic, she thought. A man for whom the ends always justified the means. A man she had never once seen to smile and at whose frown she and the other exuberant young patriots, hiding out in a safe house, had grown silent and apprehensive. What did he want of her?

'So there you are, Eileen MacSweeney, the girl who wanted to free Ireland from the foreign enemy. So you have sunk to this, have you? Now you want to betray your past comrades. How you have changed!'

'No,' she said.

'You deserted,' he said softly. 'You deserted your fellow soldiers, you betrayed us. And now you want to betray us again.'

'Never,' she said fiercely. 'I've never betrayed anyone.'

'But you did. You left. Left knowing our secrets. Left knowing the location of a safe house, knowing where we could go to ground, knowing where guns were hidden. You knew all of that. And now this!'

She faced him. Took a step nearer. 'I never betrayed you. Not a single word about these matters ever crossed my lips.

You know that. I wouldn't be alive now if you had found that I betrayed any secrets. You know why I left. You were about to allow a man to die, a man who was dear to me. I had to save his life.'

Tom Hurley gave a snort. The sound, contemptuous and dismissive, stirred her courage. She had grown soft; she knew that. She had been living her life among pleasant people, had been going to dances, to the cinema, buying pretty clothes. Still hoping and believing that Ireland had a future, but doing very little about it. Not like the man in front of her, a man who would kill without compunction.

A man who might now, with the greatest of ease, kill her as an example to others.

Eileen had come home from her job at the printing works at her usual time. Had parked her beloved motorbike behind her mother's tiny house on Barrack Street, had tried the back door, but it was still locked. Her mother must be working late, she thought and went to walk around to the street, taking her key from the pocket of her jacket. And then her arm had been seized, a pistol put to her ribs and she had been dragged into a car, crowded into the back seat with a trench-coated man on either side of her. The car started as soon as the door slammed behind them, swung around and went flying down Barrack Street.

'Not to worry,' said one of the men beside her. 'The boss just wants a word. Be a sensible girl, now. Just sit still and keep quiet and there will be no harm done. You know the score, don't you?'

Eileen knew the score, knew the ruthless man that she would have to deal with. She said nothing, sat very quietly and when they arrived she allowed herself to be marched into a derelict cottage outside the city. And then left there, facing the man. She waited for him to speak and tried to keep her head high and her eyes steady. He studied her.

She had been taken off her guard when seized by one of his minions, but now she told herself that if he had wanted to kill her then he would have done so straight away. This was to frighten her. This was the response to the threat that she had issued to Raymond. Raymond, of course, was nothing. A playboy. In the pay of Tom Hurley. She had guessed that. It had been easy to intimidate Raymond Roche. Tom Hurley was a different matter.

'How dare you! How dare you send me a threatening message? How dare you interfere in Sinn Féin business?'

She confronted him bravely. 'So Raymond told you what I said. I thought it was you behind him. You should be ashamed of yourself. I don't care about him. I suppose you are paying him and it's worth it to someone like that. But those two innocents, those two young nuns. They don't know what they are doing. They just think that they're being brave and patriotic. They don't think about the dead bodies, about the scandal and the complete ruination of their lives if it's found out. How can they stay in the convent after that?'

'What do I care? They serve a purpose. Who are you to interfere?'

'People matter very little to you.' She straightened herself as she said the words and she glared at him. She was lost if she showed fear; she knew that. She had seen him interrogate people before and knew how he worked.

'The cause, the cause that you have betrayed, that matters to me.' His voice was very soft, now. Waiting for her to show a weakness.

She drew in a long breath and faced him boldly. 'I don't approve of the signing of the treaty, if that is what you mean. I never did approve of it. I just think that there has been enough killing. It was achieving nothing. It . . .' She hesitated for a moment, but something drove her on in an effort to explain. 'It corrupted us all,' she went on fiercely. 'We began to think that people didn't matter. First it was English soldiers, then it was civilians, those caught up in the crossfire, people who had nothing to do with it, people who just wanted to live their own lives, to keep out of trouble. We were spreading and prolonging the misery. Houses burned down, children running from bullets, men and women shot.' She hesitated a little and then said in a low voice, 'I suppose I only began to realize that when someone who was near and dear to me was in danger of death and you refused any help to him.'

'Went off to England, afterwards, didn't he? Left you in the

lurch, wasn't that right? Not a sign of him in Cork ever again.'
His sneer made his face even uglier and the gun in his hand
moved forward, moved an inch nearer to her.

She ignored it. She would not back down now. 'You're
making use of these two girls, two novices. They don't know
what they're doing. They're silly and too young to know what
they are doing.'

'About the same age as yourself,' he remarked.

'That doesn't matter. I knew what I was doing. They don't.
Anyway, they're supposed to be nuns. They'll bring shame
and disgrace on the convent, on the Reverend Mother, and I'm
not having it.'

'You're not having it.' His eyebrows raised, though his voice
remained soft and the gun in his hand never wavered.

'You're using them to carry letters, to take messages. You
knew that they wouldn't be suspected so you pulled them in,
got that Mary MacSwiney to talk them over. Making them cry
about her sainted brother. I know how it happened. I've heard
about it all.'

He was silent for a moment. She could see him turning matters
over in his mind.

'Raymond, I suppose.'

'No,' she said, telling the lie without compunction or hesitation. She had no great affection for Raymond, but she was not
going to deliver him into Tom Hurley's hands and see a report
in the *Cork Examiner* that his body had been found in the
river.

'And what are you going to do about it?' He had shrugged
aside her denial. Knew it to be a lie, but she knew by his face
that he wouldn't press the matter, wouldn't try to force the
truth from her. Raymond was valuable to him. Raymond had
money, had influence, belonged to a good family, and, most
important of all, had his own yacht moored in Cork Harbour,
just outside Cobh. Through Raymond the Republicans could
get information about the British naval troops who were still
occupying Spike Island. And that was valuable information.

It had been part of that unsatisfactory treaty, part of the
treaty which one section of rebels refused to sign, splitting
the freedom fighters into pro-treaty and anti-treaty; into those

who took up power in the new Irish parliament, *Dáil Éireann*, and those who found it unacceptable that the British should retain not just six of the counties of Ulster, but that they should also stay in possession of the three deep water ports of Cobh, just south of the city; of Berehaven in west Cork and of Lough Swilly in Donegal. As soon as Eileen saw him decide to leave the subject of Raymond, she knew that there would be something going on about Cobh and Spike Island. She saw the awareness of her guess dawn in his steely grey eyes, saw him regret, momentarily, that he had introduced Raymond's name; then saw him decide what to do with her, how to make use of her.

'You're great friends with all those young men, aren't you?' It was said in the tone of a statement, not of a question. He was looking her up and down, appraising her and now he forced his voice to sound friendlier. 'Good-looking girl. Yes, there's no doubt, you are not a bad-looking girl. And so you know that Peeler fellow, that Inspector Cashman, don't you? I've seen you talking to him on the street.'

'Inspector Cashman is a member of the *Garda Siochána*, not a *Peeler*, they've all gone. Haven't you noticed? He's an Irishman, appointed by the Irish Free State, and I speak to him because I know him, we lived on the same street when we were young. We went to the same school on St Mary's Isle. That convent that you and your men are trying to involve in some of your plots.' Eileen was pleased to hear how calm her voice sounded. Tom Hurley had lost much of his power over her. She saw the awareness of that in his face and noticed the flash of anger from the grey eyes opposite hers.

'And I suppose that the moment you walk off out of here you will head for him, or else straight for this convent of yours and try to get it out of the young nuns, you'll be warning the Reverend Mother and she will send for Inspector Cashman.' He said the words more to himself than to her. Almost as though he were coming to some decision.

She stayed very still. It was useless to deny. He was a man who suspected everything and everyone. And he was utterly ruthless. Would kill a man as easily as twist the neck of a hen, had said one of her Republican friends.

'And the third nun, novice . . .' He was watching her very carefully, watching her to see how she reacted.

She shrugged her shoulders. 'She's a bit too streetwise for you, I suppose.' Raymond had told her that, but it could have been something that she knew from her own contacts. Cork was a very small city. Had the third novice voiced any suspicions to her superior? She thought not. The Reverend Mother was not one to hesitate. If she had any inkling of what was going on she would have immediately put a stop to those outings.

He left it then. She could see by the flicker in those joyless grey eyes that his mind had moved away from the question of the third young nun and onto a different matter. There was something going on, there must be something planned; Eileen knew that. Tom Hurley was taut as a violin string. She knew him well enough to be able to assess his mood. The mention of the convent, of the name of Inspector Cashman showed that he was afraid for the success of a plan. What had those two stupid young nuns involved themselves in? Her mind flickered through the possibilities. Something to do with Raymond, something planned for Raymond, the payback for funds received, perhaps. For a young man with no job he was surprisingly affluent, continually popping over to London to attend parties. Brainless individual. An easy prey for someone like Tom Hurley.

'You know me,' he said, as though he had read her thoughts. 'You should know me well enough not to interfere. And I know you. Know everything about you. Know where you work. Know your route home.' He lowered his voice then and the threat that followed was even more effective.

'And I know your mother. Know her well, everything about her. Know where she works. Know her route home. Nice-looking woman, your mother. Shame to see a woman like that harmed, maimed for life.'

He would know that the last threat would have done the trick. Would know that now she could not move; would know that she could not take action to reveal anything to the authorities; would know that she could do nothing without putting her mother in danger. Maureen MacSweeney was the most innocent of women. Barely fifteen years older than Eileen herself, she appeared most of the time, to her daughter, to be very much the younger of the two. A trusting woman who would accept anything from a stranger, would fall for any story. Was vulnerable to such as Tom Hurley.

Tom Hurley had known what he was doing when he had issued that last threat. Eileen stared miserably ahead. There was nothing she could do. She knew that.

Those young nuns would have to look after themselves.

'What are you asking me to do?' she questioned between gritted teeth.

'I'm not going to ask you anything. I'm telling you,' he replied. 'You'll be useful to us. Nice looking girl like you. All dressed up to the nines, too. And, just you keep it in your mind, young Eileen. One wrong move and you'll be shot. And just as you are dying you'll be wondering what is going to happen to your mother.'

'Are you all right, Eileen?'

'I'm all right, Seán,' she said listlessly. Seán had been a friend, once. Someone with whom she and the others had joked and teased, had shared danger, had taken part in raids. She and he were on different sides now and she almost felt like asking how he could continue to work for such a sour, hard man as Tom Hurley. She held her tongue, however. Her own guilt was weighing her down and she could not criticize another. She tried to tell herself that no harm would come to those young nuns, that they would play their part for a day or two and then be discarded, but she could not deceive herself. Midday tomorrow, she was to be in Patrick Street, right by the famous statue of St Matthew, the meeting place for all city dwellers. Raymond would pick her up there and she would be with him for most of the day and would be delivered back to the city in the evening. She had asked no questions. It would, she knew, have been useless. She had to leave the young nuns to their own devices and hope that no real harm would come to them.

'I'll drop you off by the South Main Bridge if that's all right by you, Eileen. Don't want the car number to be noticed going a second time in the day up Barrack Street,' said Seán apologetically.

'That's all right, Seán. The walk will do me good. Clear my head.' She said no more and he said no more. They both knew that she had been given her orders and that, in the world in which they lived, failure to fulfil an order would mean a death. Eileen stepped out from the car as soon as it stopped and gave him a nod. He, like herself, would not want to attract any notice.

After he drove away, she stayed for a moment, looking down into the river and hoping that she would be able to conceal from her mother what had happened. Maureen MacSweeney was an unsuspicious woman, but Eileen, the child who was born to her when she was fifteen years old was very deeply loved and she had an instinct that told her when her daughter was troubled.

'Not thinking of throwing yourself in, are you?' The voice from behind her shoulder startled her for a minute and she wondered whether he had noticed her getting out of Seán's car. Patrick Cashman was a policeman, now an inspector. Not terribly clever she had often thought, but industrious and ambitious and certainly had enough brains to put two and two together and to come up with the right answer. Still he had been a neighbour of hers and their mothers were friends and so she turned around courageously and confronted him.

'Not likely,' she said forcing a brightness into her voice. 'Life's good for me, these days, Patrick. I've had a rise in my salary and I've bought myself a typewriter and I'm trying to start up a business at home in the evening, hoping to build up a nice little bank account for myself. Going to Irish classes, too. Who knows but I might end up in the civil service or something like that. They say that you can't get anywhere nowadays without speaking fluent Irish.'

He was looking at her in a speculative way, rubbing a finger along the length of his long upper lip.

'No bike today,' he said and her heart missed a beat. Had he seen Seán, recognized him, perhaps?

'No,' she said casually. 'I've been out for a spin with an old friend. Down the Lee Road.'

'Nice afternoon for it,' he said. 'Nice to see old friends, too. Some of them, at any rate.' He paused for a moment and then said with deliberation, 'Of course some former friends are best avoided.'

He had not seen Seán, she thought. So they know all those faces, not just the leaders, but unimportant people like Seán who mostly acted like a messenger boy for Tom Hurley. It gave her an odd feeling to think of that vast amount of surveillance going on beneath the surface of normal busy city streets.

But it gave her an idea.

'You going my way, up the *Barracka*?' she asked and was pleased to see him smile and nod. The old word from their childhood when the steep incline of Barrack Street was always the *Barracka* seemed to take some of his usual stiffness from him and he walked by her side with no trace of embarrassment. She thought that she would take advantage of his good humour.

'Tell me something, Patrick, and this is nothing to do with me or anything that I might do, but I've been wondering whether the houses of known anti-treaty fellas would be watched.' She had been about to say 'freedom fighters' but hastily changed it. Even so, he looked at her with suspicion.

'You're not getting yourself in with that lot again, are you?'

She resented his tone, but swallowed her grievance. She needed his co-operation. She widened her eyes at him and did her best to look innocent. 'I'm finished with all that sort of thing, Patrick. I've a job now and I'm a respectable office worker. I just think about money all the time. That's respectable, isn't it?'

He gave a grin, but didn't comment on the printing works where she worked, although he undoubtedly knew that its main purpose was the printing of anti-treaty pamphlets and literature. He was, she thought, looking more relaxed than usual. Despite the shortness of her skirt, he didn't glance at it with disapproval, but seemed content to stroll along by her side. She thought that she would try again.

'Come on, Patrick,' she coaxed. 'You're off duty now. Just tip me a wink. I'm thinking of writing a book about all this. All my sources will be secret of course. That's the way these things are written – I'll just say "I've been given to understand".'

He laughed aloud then. 'Well, let's say that I would be amazed if the houses of known criminals were not watched very carefully indeed,' he said.

'I thought so,' she said endeavouring to sound careless. Those two stupid young nuns. She had always imagined that it would be something like that. How on earth had they allowed themselves to get involved? She daren't say anything, though. Her mother's life was in danger. She must distract Patrick from her question before he got too curious.

'Tell us, Patrick,' she said. 'Do you remember the time that we had the midnight bonfire up on top of *Barracka* Hill on midsummer's eve and that old tree caught fire and the Peelers came and told us that they would throw the lot of us in prison? You never thought that you would join them when you grew up, did you?' And then, when he didn't answer, she added with some curiosity, 'Are you glad that you joined, Patrick?'

She thought that he might be offended at that question, might give her an unfriendly response, but he turned a face filled with astonishment on her.

'Of course, I'm glad,' he said vigorously. 'I get £360 a year, Eileen. That's what an inspector is paid. That's not to be sneezed at, you know.'

'Goodness,' she said. 'As long as you don't feel that you've sold your soul for a mess of potage.'

He didn't take offence at that, just shook his head at her and smiled. 'You've been studying Irish,' he said. 'Don't forget that a Garda Siochána means a guardian of the peace. You might be glad of me one day.' He stopped. They had reached the spot where her mother's house was located and he knew it well. She wouldn't ask him in, she decided. That would be going too far. Would be downright dangerous. She just nodded and smiled and put her key into the front door. He came up close to her and said very quietly in her ear, 'For instance if someone is threatening you, or trying to get you to do something you don't want to do, well, that might be a time when you would be glad to get help from a Garda Siochána.'

TWO

W. B. Yeats
'Out of the quarrel with others we make rhetoric; out
of the quarrel with ourselves we make poetry.'

Raymond had often invited girls onto his yacht. That was obvious to Eileen. He instantly produced a pair of snowy white plimsolls and a cosy Aran-knit jumper, both of which fitted Eileen as though they had been made for her. He had tried to be casual when she came on board, but his eyes were anxious and she guessed that he was worried about this expedition which would involve him and his expensive yacht in serious trouble if it failed.

It was interesting, she had often thought, that Raymond, a man about town, a lover of jazz, a person who spent lots of his free time in popping across to London for a Louis Armstrong concert or to visit the latest nightclub, had remained with the Republicans when so many of the others, so many of his friends, like Eamonn, had given up the struggle. Raymond, of course, unlike Eamonn, had no real ambition to be a doctor or a teacher or a scientist. He was the spoilt, only child of a rich family. Raymond had hung around university in order to enjoy the friendships and the social life rather than to achieve any qualifications. She wondered now whether he was just a paid spy, rather than a patriot, like she, Eamonn and the others had been. Still, she had a part to play so she thanked him prettily and kissed his well-shaven cheek.

'Don't want you skidding on a wet deck,' was all that he said as he handed over the shoes, but his voice was nervous. He waited without comment as man after man slipped on board the yacht and went down into the hold. Eileen watched also, trying to keep her eyes away from Tom Hurley who was lurking beside the mooring post, dressed for the part in a smart yachting blazer. Where had he got that blazer? Stolen, or 'requisitioned', no doubt, thought Eileen. The Republicans had a habit of appearing in shops, guns in hand and pointing to any goods which they desired. She couldn't imagine Tom Hurley paying for something as expensive-looking as that blazer. She averted her gaze from him, though she knew that he would be looking at her and she had seen how one hand was slipped inside the pocket adorned with two yellow stripes. There would be a pistol in there, she knew. She could see the slight bulge and guessed that it was pointing straight at her. She didn't feel frightened though. She had made up her mind to go along with this. The threat to herself and to her mother was too real. The British soldiers on Spike Island had to look after themselves. After all, they were professionals. This plan of Tom Hurley's could go either way.

In any case, she thought, the moment to interfere for the sake of the two young nuns and for the sake of the convent, which had educated her, and above all for the sake of the Reverend Mother who had been so good to her, that moment had passed. The nuns had played their role, hopefully were now safe, and the result was this crowd of hard-faced men who had assembled in the small harbour town of Cobh by various means, mostly by bicycle and by train. No lorries. Tom Hurley would not have risked drawing the attention of the Free State soldiers. Cobh was watched carefully for any trace of paramilitary activity.

This plan might work, thought Eileen as she lounged nonchalantly against the rail and pretended to scan the water for fish. The men were coming on at irregular intervals, looking just like sailors. Already six had boarded. Raymond was whistling a tune and she forced herself to smile at him and to look like a girl on a day out with her rich boyfriend.

Two deckhands came on next, nodding to Raymond and calling him sir. Might be authentic but probably not, thought Eileen, noticing the bulge in one pocket of the loose sailor trousers. A deckhand carrying a pistol, she thought and then shrugged her shoulders. Why not. Here was she, a respectable office girl, and she was playing her part in this affair.

And then Tom Hurley stepped neatly onto the boat. Didn't look at her, gave Raymond a nod and then disappeared down into the hold. He wore a cap pulled so far down his face that it obscured most of his features. His face would be in every post office and bank, would feature on street corner notice boards with the word WANTED in large black letters beneath it. It had done so for years, but still he moved around the city, organized raids, reprisals and attacks on police and army barracks.

'Well, let's be off,' said Raymond in a voice that he strove to make sound normal. 'OK, Jim, weigh anchor; cast off, Pat. Let's show the lady Cork harbour. You all right, Eileen, hold tight now.'

Eileen felt the wind blow her hair. She wished that she could enjoy this. It could have been fun if only Raymond had taken herself and some of the other lads out on his boat at the time when they were all friends, but the group had dispersed and now everything seemed darker and more sinister. The whistle had died from Raymond's lips and he stared grimly ahead as he steered the yacht adroitly in and out of the other yachts moored in Cobh Harbour. She saw him look back from time to time at the still figure of Tom Hurley and knew that both he and she would have to play their part as a carefree young couple out for a day's sailing.

'You know this is the oldest yacht club in the world, Eileen,' called out Raymond. 'They say that it was started by Murrough O'Brien, Lord Inchiquin, in the time of King Charles I. Known as the Royal Yacht Club from the time of King William IV.'

'Thanks for the history lesson,' shouted Eileen. 'Where's that gramophone I saw you carrying on board?' She didn't think that she could keep up this casual conversation for too long, but a young man and his girlfriend, singing the latest songs at the tops of their voices would present a carefree appearance. She saw Tom Hurley give a quick nod and one of the men who was coiling rope on the deck left his task and went below, returning with the portable gramophone. The motion of the boat would probably ruin the 78 inch vinyl record, as the needle slid with the motion of the waves, but that was tough luck. Raymond could afford to buy a new one. She watched the man wind it up and waited for the first words of 'I'm Wild about Harry' before she began to join in, using all the lung power that she possessed. She had a good soprano voice and Raymond a nice light baritone, so together they sang and the voice on the gramophone rang out, with the occasional screech when the needle slid over a track as the yacht bobbed in the water.

A good sailor, Raymond. Despite the singing, he found time to issue a few commands about the sails, even sang a couple of them to the tune of 'I'm Wild about Harry' and he steered the boat competently. Eileen had guessed where they were going and she could see that she was right. With the wind in their sails they made straight for Spike Island where the British Navy had their Irish headquarters. Within minutes of going towards it she could see that a few men in uniforms had emerged from the building and were standing on the pier.

'Sing up,' said Raymond. His voice was tense, but he handled the steering wheel well. Eileen sang until she felt that her voice was cracking and her throat rasped as though with sandpaper. By now they had come quite near to the Spike Island pier. She took hold of the safety rail and executed a few neat jazz steps to entertain the men while she rested her larynx. *You're acting in a play*, she told herself, as her rubber-soled plimsoll beat out a rhythm on the wooden deck. This is a play about a young man and a girl, out for a day's sailing. A comedy, not a tragedy, nor even a nail-biting drama, just a light comedy, like a Gilbert & Sullivan musical, she told herself as she twirled and pivoted. They were now near enough for her to see the faces of the men on the pier, the British army officers. All of them smiling, she noted and redoubled her efforts.

'Evening, Raymond,' shouted one. Definitely an officer by the look of the uniform. 'Coming to take us for a spin?'

'If you like,' shouted back Raymond. His voice was nonchalant, his accent, due to his schooling in England, was as posh and as British as the officer's own. 'But I have a favour to ask. You wouldn't let my girlfriend have a peep at the tunnels, would you? I've been telling her all about them and she's wild to see them.'

'Thought she was wild about Harry.' The man guffawed and the other three officers on the pier laughed politely in appreciation of the joke. Eileen hammered out a few more steps as the anchor was lowered and a rope flung across.

'That's better,' she cried enthusiastically as the yacht slowed to a stop. 'Put the record on again, Raymond. I can dance properly now.'

No point in rushing. Now that she was committed to this enterprise, she might as well carry it out as cleverly as she could. Her own safety might depend on it. She let go of the bar and moved to the centre of the deck and began to dance.

'"I'm just wild about Harry and Harry's just wild about me",' she sang as loudly as she could and whirled around. And then she got such a fright that the words dried within her throat. Behind where she stood, through the hole leading down to the hold, she glimpsed the stairs, crowded with men, those six men who had come aboard at Cobh, and each one of those men was stark naked, smeared all over with black soot and each was carrying a small waterproofed bag. Of clothing, she thought. And a gun wrapped up in the clothing. More than likely. Well-camouflaged. Ready to swim ashore? That was certain. But to do what?

'"He's sweet like sugar candy. Just like honey from the bee" . . .'

She smiled at the men as widely as she could stretch her mouth and twirled around, knowing that her short skirt would rise up in the breeze and reveal the tops of her stockings.

There was an enthusiastic sound of applause as the men on the pier clapped their hands loudly.

'"She's sweet like sugar candy. Just like honey from the bee" . . .' sang one of the soldiers and the others joined in.

Eileen stopped dancing and went over and slipped her arm inside that of Raymond. She smiled appealingly at the officer who looked to be in charge.

'Please, please, please,' she said imploringly. 'I beseech you!'

'Oh, well, come on, just the two of you, none of your men, Raymond. You'll get me shot, you know.'

But the officer was smiling and he held out his hand to her and carefully took her weight while she stepped from the yacht onto the solidity of the pier.

So this was Spike Island. A small flat island, crowned with a row of army buildings, arranged roughly in the shape of a hexagon. Packed with soldiers. She wondered how they liked living here, on this small island, knowing that they were disliked and unwanted. Or perhaps she was just judging by die-hard rebels, by those Republicans who had influenced her thinking from an early age. Perhaps the people of Cobh did not really care, might even welcome the presence of the army just off their shore; might find that they were monied purchasers of goods and services. The dance halls and the cinema in Cobh were swamped with soldiers; her friend Aoife had told her that. Lonely, said Aoife, with that compassion for needy people which had caused her to leave a comfortable home and take up residence with a gang of rebels. Certainly, thought Eileen, looking around her, the men appreciated visitors; by now there were dozens of them who had emerged from the buildings and were smiling at her admiringly.

Behind them the gramophone played on.

> And he's just wild about.
> Cannot do without,
> Harry's just wild about me.

Eileen held her breath. Was it going to work? She looked sideways at Raymond, taking care not to move her head, but to peep at him from beneath her eyelashes. He was smiling too. Very much at his ease.

'Come and see the tunnels, then,' said the officer and he led the way. Now that he had made up his mind, he was a good host, showing them where everything was kept and introducing them, Raymond as a friend, and Eileen as 'Raymond's young lady'. Raymond kept him busy, talking knowledgeably about winds and high tides and Eileen relaxed. Her job was over now. Tom Hurley, despite all his faults, was a man of his word. He would allow her to go once they were back in Cork. She had played her part. Her mother now was safe. She glanced back over her shoulder at Raymond's yacht, rocking gently in the waves, the gramophone silent. Harry, like she, had now played his part.

And then her eye was caught by something, something that flashed in the sunlight. Something about halfway up the mainsail pole. A mirror? Surely not. No, she gave another quick glance. No, she thought, not a mirror. A pair of field glasses or binoculars. Tom Hurley had climbed up there and was following their progress.

'No smoking here,' said the officer to Raymond who had taken out a packet of cigarettes. 'Sorry about that. I know you would be careful, Raymond, but I make it a rule to have no smoking here. We have all the ammunition stored over there, you see.'

'Over there, really, in that shed in the centre?' Raymond indicated the building.

'That's right.' The officer was looking down at Eileen and she bestowed a warm smile upon him. 'Now, turn here, down this little pathway,' he said, returning her smile. 'Come this way, my dear, and I'll show you the tunnels. Somebody was telling the commander that they were built originally by monks, hundreds of years ago.'

As he led the way down the path, Eileen chanced another look back over her shoulder. The glint of light from the yacht was still there. Their progress was being followed. She looked apprehensively at the friendly, trusting officer and the young soldiers smiling at her – some were blowing her kisses and she blew one back and hoped desperately that no one would be hurt in this latest enterprise by Tom Hurley.

It was, she thought, a clever enterprise. Daring, but also very clever. While she and Raymond were being shown the tunnels, the men would dive overboard, swim to shore and wait until nightfall. The tunnels would make a good hiding place. And, of course, all of the ammunition was stored nearby.

'And what do you do with yourself all day, my dear?' The officer was only making conversation, but Eileen was instantly wary. Raymond had not mentioned her name, had introduced her as his girlfriend, but Cork was a small place and someone might have noticed her boarding the yacht at Cobh. Who knew whether their visit might afterwards be connected by the action that would take place during the night hours? She must make sure not to involve her employers. The printing works was already under surveillance and it was fairly well known through the city that they printed Republican anti-treaty pamphlets and propaganda as well as issuing leaflets and posters for small businesses in Cork. She would be a lady of leisure, she decided.

'Well, what's there to do?' she said in bored tones. She gave a shrug. 'Don't get up too early in the morning,' she said. 'Don't get to bed too early in the night, either. In fact, you could say that my nights melt into my mornings . . . And then there is shopping and hair appointments and my nails, of course.' She thrust her hands rapidly into the pockets of her skirt. One of the problems of being a typist was that nails had to be kept trimmed to an unfashionably short length and that nail varnish was an impossibility.

'So you're one of the lilies of the field, then, are you, my dear? You toil not, neither do you spin. Well, why should a pretty girl like you do anything but look beautiful?'

'Now, then, old man. Steady on. This is my girl, you know.' Raymond had a slightly forced note in his voice, not as casual as he would like it to be, thought Eileen. She wondered if he had sensed any suspicion in the voices or behaviour of their hosts. Once more she glanced over her shoulder. The sun was momentarily behind a cloud, but emerged as she watched. Yes, that glint of glass was still there. Their progress was still being watched. Tom Hurley was keeping an eye on everything. Out in the sea, she thought she saw something move, a seal possibly, but more likely a man swimming underwater, heading towards the far side of the island. They were taking their lives in their hands, she thought with a shiver of apprehension. If seen, they would be shot, or else arrested and hanged.

'I'll just take your arm here, my dear, if I may. Very rough ground here. Just a little further, now. At least you have nice, sensible shoes. That's it. Now here's one of the tunnels that you've come to see. The whole island is honeycombed with them. They say that this particular tunnel is a couple of hundred years old. The padre from St Finbar's came to have a look at a gold communion cup that we found. He's knowledgeable about that sort of thing. Said it would be sixteenth century. Time of Good Queen Bess. Don't know how he knew. Something about how the gold was shaped, I think.'

'Gold,' breathed Eileen, her voice reverential. She sounded, she knew, pretty empty-headed. Though, as a matter of fact, she was interested. The Reverend Mother would be interested, too; she made a note to tell her about it – that's if she got out of her present situation and did not end up in Cork Gaol.

'Let's go in,' she said. One of the officers had switched on a powerful torch that illuminated the path ahead and the stone walls. A few men had followed them in the idle way that those who had little to do would follow any distraction. It must be hard to keep the men interested and employed, she thought and wondered how long the British army would bother manning these remnants of their ownership of Ireland. Perhaps it was the memory of threat from Germany during the Great War. Otherwise she could not see the point.

Unless there was another Great War, of course.

'How much ammunition do you keep on the island?' she asked innocently. She regretted the question as soon as it had issued from her mouth. After all, she reminded herself, she had nothing to do with the rebels now. She was playing a part to make sure that she and her mother were safe and Tom Hurley had got what he wanted, had found a means to get six men onto Spike Island. She had her arm tucked into Raymond's and noticed how he had stiffened when he heard her incautious question.

'It's three o'clock in the morning,' she sang.

> We've danced the whole night through
> And daylight soon will be dawning
> Just one more waltz with you.

They all joined in and she began to relax. All she had to do now, she reminded herself, was, for the next hour or so, to play the part of an empty-headed society girl and to hope and pray that no harm had come to those two silly young nuns who had got themselves mixed up in such dangerous enter-prises. Indeed, she hoped that no harm would come to anyone. She had not missed the flicker of satisfaction on Raymond's face when the officer pointed out the pile of ammunition, nor had she missed the fact that Raymond had pointed his quickly extinguished cigarette at the place the officer indicated. Nor that he had stayed in that position for quite a number of minutes, commenting on the buildings and enquiring as to their history. Tom Hurley, with his binoculars, would have had a good long look at the location of the ammunition store. Surely that was the target. Six men would serve no purpose to attack a whole regiment of highly trained British soldiers.

But the eyes of those soldiers should be kept from dwelling on the yacht moored beside the Spike Island pier. Going down a tunnel was all very well, but it meant that the troops, who were all looking at her now, would turn their attention back to looking out to sea, and probably at the stylish yacht moored against the pier. Somehow she had to grab their attention and to keep it while those six men slipped down the side of the boat and swam silently ashore. Raymond gave her a good opening when he declared loudly, 'Well, men, you have a great little island here to live on. I must say that I envy you all.'

'Ah, but what about all the wives and sweethearts waiting for them back home,' called out Eileen. She moved away from his side and ran lightly over to the cannon, swung herself up on top of it and began to sing as loudly as she could the hit song: 'Baby Won't You Please Come Home?'

> I've got the blues, I feel so lonely
> I'll give the world if I could only
> Make you understand
> It surely would be grand
> I'm gonna telephone my baby
> Ask him won't you please come home
> 'Cause when you're gone
> I'm worried all day long.

They all joined the chorus, of course, and then she sang it through again, grateful of the experience that she had gained in the musical society at St Matthew's Hall. She had learned to enjoy an audience coming in on a favourite lyric, learned how to support and to lead those other voices, how to keep the singing going smoothly. And as she sang, she scanned her mind for a few more popular songs. 'Some Sunny Day', 'Three

O'Clock in the Morning' and then 'Yes, We Have No Bananas!' She could see Raymond looking restive. Probably thought that she was taking over from him, or perhaps he genuinely wanted to see the tunnels. In any case, she had given the men plenty of time to swim from the yacht around the corner of the island, so she ended up with another rendition of 'Wild About Harry' and then slid down from the cannon while they all clapped and whooped.

'Now, let's go and see that tunnel,' she said tucking her hand inside Raymond's arm.

Luckily the tunnels were not too extensive, and not too interesting. The objects that had been found had been taken to Cork University to be examined there and so they did not have to stay too long. When they got back to the yacht, there was no sign of the men in the hold and Tom Hurley was sitting comfortably on a deckchair, hiding his face in a widely opened, week-old edition of the *Cork Examiner*. She went over and perched on a rope coil beside him.

'Is that it, then?' she asked in a low voice.

He did not pretend to misunderstand her. 'So far, so good,' he said.

'But my part is over and done with.' She allowed her voice to harden. It wasn't difficult. She knew him to be false and treacherous, outside the very narrow parameters that he had set himself of loyalty and friendship, but he valued his reputation as a man of his word. 'You gave me a task and I did it. Far better than some.' She gave a brief nod of her head in the direction of Raymond and saw a flicker of amusement in the grey eyes so near to her own.

'You weren't too bad,' he admitted. 'Nice voice, you have.'

'And my mother,' she persisted.

He gave a business-like nod. 'You kept your word. I'll keep mine.'

'Good,' she said and left him with another business-like nod, a mirrored version of his own. She was tempted to say more, to ask some questions, to require further assurances, but she restrained herself. He would only take that as sign of weakness. She went and stood beside Raymond.

'All right, Tootsie?' he asked and she looked at him coldly.

Tom Hurley had followed her and now stood slightly behind them. She turned back and looked at him and said softly, 'It's amazing that with such a big strong he-man as this available, a fella brave enough to call me 'tootsie', that a couple of nuns had to be recruited for delivering your letters.'

And then she left them both. She had a bad conscience about those two young nuns. It had been a mistake to have brought them up, but her irritation and disgust at the part which she had played, coupled with Raymond's stupidity, had made the words slip out.

THREE

Thomas Aquinas
*Quorum alii aliud sensibile bonum aestimant esse
felicitatem, sicut avari divitias, intemperati
voluptates, ambitiosi honores*
(Some people judge happiness as belonging to one gift,
others to another. The avaricious place it in riches, the
self-indulgent in pleasures; the ambitious in honours.)

Reverend Mother Aquinas had been delighted with the new entrant to the convent. Sister Gertrude was twenty-two years old, mature enough to know her own mind, but not old enough to treat the convent as a last resort. She was well educated, had worked for years in an accounts department at Ford's Factory and had an easy sense of humour which appealed to her superior. She possessed a brisk manner, spent a minimum time in the confessional box and above all positively enjoyed setting out neat rows of figures that miraculously balanced.

And she radiated happiness.

Her only fault appeared to be an over-fondness for explaining the complexities of double-entry bookkeeping to her superior. And a great desire for sweet food which might lead to obesity in old age.

But she wasn't destined to live so long.

Not yet twenty-three!

With a rapidly beating heart and legs that seemed to have lost all strength, Reverend Mother stood for a moment and gazed down at the dead body. Incongruous. Lying behind the door of a hen shed. Slumped there, lifeless, hands outstretched, face contorted in its last agony. Lips very blue, eyes wide and staring. Death in the elderly does not come as a surprise for someone aged over seventy, but this particular death was a great shock.

And death in a hospital or a sickroom bed is decorous and full of care for the dying. This death here in a hen shed of a young and very healthy woman was an appalling shock.

The building had been donated as a summer house by the affectionate father of a would-be entrant to the convent community. That particular recruit had not lasted more than three months, but the summer house had remained, unmentioned by the Reverend Mother when the suddenly cheerful girl was tenderly borne away by her father, and afterwards allocated by her to some busy hens, who devoured scraps from the kitchen and produced nutritious brown eggs to make a lunch for some hungry children – and were a source of huge satisfaction for the Reverend Mother.

But today, when she had come out into the convent garden for a few minutes of fresh air before beginning work, she saw immediately that her hens, her pride and joy, had been disturbed. Not sitting placidly, not pecking at insects, not laying eggs as was their purpose, but rushing around the garden, perching in trees. Had their eggs been collected? It was the task of one of the novices to collect the eggs every morning and evening. The Reverend Mother remembering that the young novice had been unwell the previous evening, decided to check that the task had been done.

The door to the hen shed had been opened and now stood ajar. So someone had come to collect the eggs, had allowed the hens out. Nevertheless, the Reverend Mother, treading carefully, advanced into the sawdust-smelling shed. Eggs there were in plenty, but they lay uncollected, and gleaming in the straw-filled laying niches. That was, oddly, the first thing that she had noticed.

And then she saw Sister Gertrude. Slumped on the floor just behind the door, a black heap of clothes; hands outstretched; face buried in the sawdust and the egg basket beside her. The Reverend Mother bent down, touched the cheek and then moved a finger towards the pulse in the neck. No pulse. She lifted the outstretched hand, checked the wrist and then dropped the hand back again. The girl was dead. No sign of a wound. One cheek was cushioned in the sawdust and after clearing a space near to the mouth and the nostrils, the Reverend Mother held the back of her silver pocket watch to the lips. Nothing, no mist, no breath. She got to her feet and walked unsteadily back out into the open air and stood for a moment, breathing in the icy fog of the river air, holding onto the rough wood of the shed door while she endeavoured to subdue the tremble that ran through her body.

'"I'm just wild about Harry!"' sang a baritone voice. Incongruous, but welcome. The gardener had arrived. The Reverend Mother drew in a couple of deep breaths while she waited for him to wheel his bicycle down the path, and then, feeling her legs a little steadier, she advanced towards him, giving herself an extra minute while he stilled his song, snatched off his cap and wished her a good morning.

'Good morning, Mr Twomey. Would you be kind enough to fetch Sister Bernadette, please?'

Time enough to say more when she had recovered full control of her voice and her legs. She stood very still, not allowing herself to lean against the wall, but willing strength to flow back into her body, looking down on the one spinning wheel of the bicycle that had been dropped on the pathway. What had happened to Sister Gertrude? Had she been guilty of neglect by not sending for a doctor the night before? She had thought merely that the girl was mildly unwell, perhaps suffering from a gastric upset. No trace of a temperature, reported Sister Mary Immaculate. In any case, Dr Scher, the usual doctor for the convent, was not available as he had gone to Manchester to attend a family funeral. She bit her lip when she remembered that and realized that she desperately needed a doctor now. Her mind turned over alternatives as she retreated towards the hen shed and half-listened to the low-voiced conversation between the gardener and Sister Bernadette, the lay sister in charge of the kitchen, as they emerged from the back door.

'I don't know what she wants. "Fetch Sister Bernadette", that's what she said. Didn't hang around to ask any questions. You don't, do you, with her?' The gardener's voice faded away as he picked up his bicycle and retired to his own shed. The Reverend Mother heard a door bang and then the muted sound of more details about this 'Harry'. It seemed incongruous in the face of the terrible solemnity of the death. Rapidly she shooed a couple of adventurous hens from out of the shed and shut the door to bar them from entering again. And then, although she despised herself for doing it, she opened it again and peered into its gloom. But no, she had not made a mistake. Sister Gertrude, so brisk, so lively, so very full of life, now lay silent, crumpled and very dead on the floor of the hen shed.

Not allowing herself to stop moving, the Reverend Mother went rapidly towards the back door and accosted Sister Bernadette who, summoned in the midst of bread making, was busily rubbing crumbs of wet dough from her hands. Inconsiderate and thoughtless, the Reverend Mother told herself. *Why don't you make your own phone calls?* Her weary brain searched for an explanation, an answer to that question and then, some way of breaking the news gently. But, aloud, she said, 'I've just found Sister Gertrude. Could you phone Dr Scher's housekeeper and ask her to send whosoever is taking his calls while he is in Manchester. Oh, and send for the priest, Sister Bernadette.' And then, reluctantly, she added, 'I think that she may be dead.' The truth had to be told sooner or later. The poor girl could not be left there in the hen shed. 'And ask Sister Mary Immaculate to tell the community the terrible news.' This would occupy her deputy and keep her from arriving full of exclamations and of questions. A doctor should be got immediately, though. The matter was urgent.

Sister Bernadette had paled, but she did not flinch.

'I'll be back in a minute, Reverend Mother. And I'll send out Sister Imelda to get rid of the hens.' With that she was gone and the Reverend Mother was left alone. For a moment she thought that she should go into the shed, should not allow the girl to lie there without company, but then common sense told her that she would have to shut the door against the hens and then she would be alone in the dark. A thought of rats, numerous here around the river, crossed her mind and she mumbled a call to the convent's tabby cat while despising her cowardice. Still, she told herself, she had to gather her wits and her courage. There would be much for her to attend to once the body was removed. The nuns, professed and lay nuns, would all be in need of reassurance and opportunities to talk over the matter. The other three novices would be appalled and tearful. She would have to deal with them, especially with Sister Catherine who was a sensitive little soul. And then, of course, she would have to summon a taxi and break the news to the young nun's sister. No parents. At least, they were spared that. The mother had died about ten years previously and the father only some weeks ago. A heart attack, or was it something internal? She couldn't exactly remember. Sister Gertrude had been very upset, understandably, as she had been very close to her father. But she was a sensible girl and had soon regained her equilibrium.

Her thoughts were interrupted by a noisy spluttering of a car driven down the lane beside the convent. It drew up at the chapel gate. A last stutter from the engine and then a loud bang. For a moment the Reverend Mother thought that it must be a shot, one of those frequent Republican and Free State encounters, but then she realized that it was a backfire from the old car outside her gate. A door banged, the gate pushed open and slammed closed and then the appearance of a very young man, carrying a bag.

'I'm the doctor,' he announced in a strong North of Ireland accent. 'Where's the corpse.'

'I beg your pardon,' said the Reverend Mother icily. Young, she thought, young and brash. Tired, too. Up all night, in all probability. No excuse for bad manners, though. And he could take his hat off when he spoke to her. Her gaze went to it and was fixed so immovably on that object above his own eye level that he shifted uneasily and, after a moment, removed it, held it uneasily for a moment but then after a quick look around for a handy table or windowsill, he replaced it.

After all, it does make sense to keep his hat on; he will need both hands free, thought the Reverend Mother, trying to feel charitable and only succeeding in wishing desperately for the calm, gentle and supportive presence of Dr Scher.

'Sister Gertrude is in here, in the shed. I've been trying to keep the hens out. Come in, doctor.'

He aimed a couple of kicks at an inquisitive hen which fled, squawking its indignation. They would be back soon, thought the Reverend Mother and was pleased to see a young lay sister, one of Sister Bernadette's assistants from the kitchen, approach with some corn.

'Here, chuck, chuck, chuck; here, chuck, chuck, chuck,' she called melodiously. Sister Imelda was a country girl, the Reverend Mother remembered gratefully, and she knew how to handle hens, dropping the odd few grains of corn on the ground until she got them within reach of the gardener's shed whereupon she opened the door, waited until the gardener, looking injured, came out with a paint pot and large brush and began slapping paint on the fence. Then, in a series of rapid movements, the efficient girl tumbled out the rest of the corn over the floor, waved her apron at the hens and then shut them all into the shed.

'Thank you, Sister Imelda. Now, doctor, come with me.'

He was indignant when she set the shed door ajar and then moved aside for him to proceed her.

'Here! You're expecting me to examine her here!' He was as incredulous as though he had never seen a shed in his life, though she would be willing to lay a considerable bet on the fact that he was a farmer's son.

'Unfortunately, that is where she is, just in the spot where I found her and I haven't meddled with the body,' said the Reverend Mother dryly. 'I'll stand aside and hold the door open and allow as much light as possible to come to you.' He had already produced a powerful pocket torch but she was glad of an excuse to move away from the dead body and any violation of it. Perhaps she should have told him about Sister Gertrude's collapse the evening before, but she salved her conscience by telling herself that he had asked for no inform-ation. She rolled a stone to hold the door open and then moved a little further down the garden, ignoring the wet grass at her feet and going on until she could glimpse the river through the thick yellow veil of the morning fog. Not a healthy place, Cork city, she thought. She had often noticed the superior health and vigour of girls like Sister Imelda who had come from the countryside, as compared with girls of the same age who came from what, in Cork, was called 'the flat of the city'. Of course, nowadays, it was mainly the poor who lived here near to the river and who were subjected to the flooding and the bad sewerage system and to the almost constant choking fogs. The wealthy and even the moderately well-off had moved out to the suburbs. Montenotte and Blackrock for the wealthy. Turners Cross and Ballinlough for the office workers.

Sister Gertrude, she thought, came from Turners Cross. Her father had been the accountant in Ford's motor factory which was turning out tractors and now cars. Her father had started as an office boy in a shop, gone to night classes to learn the skills of typing and bookkeeping and eventually qualified as an accountant. A hard-working man, like his daughter, he had, single-handed, with only such help as his older daughter could give him, managed all the accounts and paid all the wages of the couple of thousand workers in the factory. A clever man, Mr Donovan, a man with a keen eye to profit and a knowledge of stock markets. Rumour said that he had accumulated a tidy fortune by buying shares in the Ford Company at a favourable rate.

Why had Sister Gertrude, with an absorbing and interesting job, a father who thought the world of her, plenty of money for anything that took her fancy, not noticeably pious, why should a girl like that have entered the convent?

The Reverend Mother had often asked herself that question soon after the arrival of the new novice. She had even asked Sister Gertrude that question and had been glad to see that the girl had considered it carefully and had then given a sensible answer. Marriage and children did not attract her. She wanted to use her skills and to be in a position where she could do some good with her abilities. She was ambitious, but saw no future for herself, other than as her father's helper in Ford's Factory. When he retired, she had ascertained, there would be no hope that she would be appointed to his position. The managers of the company would not brook having a woman in such a senior position. On the other hand, in a convent full of women, she did see prospects of rising in the hierarchy through her skills and her intelligence. The Reverend Mother had been somewhat taken aback by that frank confession and had wondered initially how long the new recruit would endure the restrictive life of a novice in a convent. But the beaming cheerfulness, the sound of a laugh that rang the rafters of the corridor, the healthy appetite and the zest for any task that had been given to her; all these had allayed any slight concerns that the Reverend Mother might have felt initially. And then there was her wonderful way with figures and her magnificent efficiency. Sister Gertrude, she felt, could well become Superior General of the order.

But now she was dead.

The Reverend Mother turned back to face the young doctor who had emerged from the shed, stamping his feet to get rid of the sawdust and coughing noisily to attract her attention. Calmly she crossed the grass and joined him.

'Well,' she asked, feeling pleased that she now had herself under control and that her voice was steady.

'She's dead,' he replied, the harsh, clipped accent of the North of Ireland making the words sound ominous.

The Reverend Mother waited. Twenty or perhaps thirty years ago she would have said, *I could have told you that,* but old age brings patience and so she merely looked at him inquiringly.

'Looks as though it might be liver failure,' he said casually, though with the air of one who likes to display his esoteric knowledge.

'Liver failure!' The Reverend Mother was taken aback. There had been a ninety-year-old nun in the convent who had been fading away for years and eventually died of liver failure, or had it been kidney failure? She wasn't sure. 'But what could have caused liver failure?' she asked. 'She was only twenty-two years old and seemed very healthy.'

'What was her name?' He produced a notebook and pencil.

'Sister Gertrude. She was a novice in the convent. She came here six months ago.'

'Did she drink?' He asked the question abruptly and she stared back at him incredulously.

'Alcohol, I mean. Heavily,' he added in explanation.

'Doctor,' she said, just biting back the words *'young man'*, 'this is a convent. We don't drink alcohol here.' He was probably a Protestant, or a Presbyterian, she thought. Nevertheless, she would have expected him to know that.

He shrugged, looked around at the low iron fence and the laneway that ran to the side of the convent and then looked up at the windows, unbarred. His eye went to a drainpipe and despite her misery, she suppressed a smile. No doubt, he had a mental picture of nuns climbing out of their dormitory windows and seeking out some public house in order to quaff large glasses of Murphy's Stout. He saw her suppressed amusement and reacted angrily.

'I know alcohol poisoning when I see it. It destroys the liver. This city is full of alcohol. I could tell you some tales—'

She interrupted him quickly. 'But in the meantime, what is the next step?' And then, when he looked indecisive, she asked, 'When does Dr Scher return?'

'Should be back this evening,' he said, and now his manner was sulky. 'Won't say any different, though. I can assure you of that. I see enough of that sort of thing in this city. Terrible place for alcoholic poisoning, Cork. You'd be surprised.'

'And Sister Gertrude's body?' Definitely a Presbyterian was her thought. There had been a note of almost hysteria in his voice when he spoke of the evils of drink.

He glanced towards the small chapel next to the lane and then appeared to think the better of it. He sighed heavily and looked exasperated.

'I suppose that you'll want an autopsy. Won't take my word for it. I'll send an ambulance. Dr Scher will probably do it tomorrow morning.'

'And you'll send the ambulance immediately, won't you? It isn't suitable for her to stay here. I'm sure that you can understand that,' she said quietly and noticed that he looked a little shame-faced. Young, she thought. Young and insecure. Trying to cope without the reassuring presence of the deeply experienced Dr Scher.

'It will be here in ten minutes. I promise you that,' he said in more subdued tones and she thanked him.

She would keep vigil, she thought. It was the least that she could do. The hens would have to put up with the gardener's shed for the moment unless the efficient Sister Imelda could devise some way of keeping them away from her. The girl was coming out now, sent by Sister Bernadette, whose kitchen commanded a view of the road and who would have seen and heard the departure of the young doctor.

In any case, Sister Imelda was now carrying a light canvas

chair with a warm cloak, folded carefully over one arm and the Reverend Mother blessed the kind thought. Sister Bernadette, who always knew everything that was going on in the convent, would have known that she would stay with the dead body.

'I'll take it from you here,' she said as the young girl approached, but Sister Imelda shook her head.

'I don't mind seeing Sister Gertrude, Reverend Mother. And, I'd like to say a little prayer.'

So Sister Bernadette had told the lay sisters. For a moment she felt contrite that she had not included them in the instructions to Sister Mary Immaculate, but then dismissed the thought. Sister Bernadette was practical and sensible and not one to take offence needlessly. The distinctions between 'choir nuns' and lay sisters didn't trouble her unduly. In any case, Sister Bernadette might make a better job of telling the young lay sisters the tragic news. Sister Imelda didn't seem distressed.

The girl offered the cloak to her superior and arranged the chair with its back to the shed wall, quite near to the body, cleared away some soiled sawdust, scattered a fresh supply just where the Reverend Mother's feet would rest and then, quite unselfconsciously, she made a sign of the cross and murmured a prayer.

The Reverend Mother felt ashamed. She had not prayed yet. More of a Martha, than a Mary, she reflected with a sigh. *But Martha,* she thought, remembering her bible, *was cumbered about much serving and came to him, and said, 'Lord, dost thou not care that my sister hath left me to serve alone? Bid her therefore that she help me.' And Jesus answered and said unto her, 'Martha, Martha, thou art careful and troubled about many things: But one thing is needful: and Mary hath chosen that better part, which shall not be taken away from her'.*

All very well, and a typical reaction from a man, the Reverend Mother had often thought while listening to sermons on that theme. The Lord and his followers would probably have been rather shocked if no meal had been put in front of them after a busy day preaching. However, now was a moment for prayer and the well-practised words came fluently to her lips: '*Requiem aeternam dona ea, Domine: et lux perpetua luceat ea . . .*'

Nevertheless, once she'd finished the prayer, her busy mind could not leave the matter of this strange death. What had happened to Sister Gertrude? She had been unwell yesterday at supper. And then a terrible thought came to her and she trembled slightly. Could she have been poisoned? And if so, were others in the convent at risk. Her mind went to the boxes of rat poison that she kept to hand out to desperate parents of the school children. She always made sure that the poison was safely concealed within a sealed tin and that the opening was big enough for a rat, but too small for children to get at the deadly substance. An obliging hardware merchant made these up for her and only charged a small sum for the service. But what if one of them had become flooded and the substance had contaminated the food in her kitchen? Sister Bernadette kept a spotlessly clean environment, but, nevertheless, always had a tin of rat poison in the pantry. It was kept on a top shelf, well away from food. However, an accident might have happened. She would have to nerve herself to check the pantry. Something she must do herself. It was not a message to give to the young lay sister and perhaps spread panic through the congregation.

And, at that moment, Sister Imelda, as unselfconscious as a young child, bent down, signed the dead girl's forehead, lips and breast with her thumb and then rose up and turned back.

'Reverend Mother,' she said. 'Sister Mary Immaculate has told everyone what has happened. Sister Catherine is ever so upset. She's crying and Sister Mary Immaculate is being very angry with her. She'll throw a fit of hysterics in a minute.'

The Reverend Mother admired the accuracy of the prognosis. The convent kitchen, she thought, was a place where all was known. Many a discussion there would have been about Sister Mary Immaculate and her effect on the sensitive young. She suppressed a nod of understanding and said quietly, 'Please send Sister Catherine to me, Sister Imelda.' She would not be able to stir from here until the ambulance arrived to take away the body. But in the meantime, she thought, the time could be well spent if she might manage to calm Sister Catherine and listen patiently to whatever was upsetting the girl.

FOUR

St Thomas Aquinas
*. . . impossibile est felicitatem humanam consistere
in delectationibus corporalibus, quarum praecipuae
sunt in cibis et venereis*
(. . . it is impossible for human felicity to consist
in bodily pleasures, the chief of which are those of
food and venal.)

Sister Catherine took some time to obey the summons. The priest arrived before she did and was in the middle of the last rites when she came hesitatingly to the door of the shed. Her face still bore the traces of tears and she gulped noisily as she stood at the entrance. Unlike Sister Imelda, she did not offer to say a prayer, but stared, white-lipped, down at the body. And then, predictably, she burst into violent sobs. The elderly priest, chaplain to the convent, flinched perceptibly, but forced himself to go on anointing the dead girl's hands and feet with the holy oil, murmuring the Latin words: '*visum, auditum, odoratum, gustum et locutionem*' as an undertone to the violence of the tempestuous weeping from the fellow novice. When he stood up with a creaking of stiff joints there was a look of relief on his face. The Reverend Mother hesitated for a moment. Her sense of propriety dictated that she and the priest should accompany the body to the ambulance, just as they would escort it to a hearse, but she did need to hear what Sister Catherine had to say. And all in all, it would probably be best to hear it in private.

'Thank you, Father,' she said gently, allowing him to depart before readying herself to listen to Sister Catherine. There was a moment's silence after the priest departed, but then the sobs broke out again.

'I should have told you. I might have saved her. Oh, I'm sorry! I'm sorry!'

'Calm yourself, my child,' said the Reverend Mother wearily. She seemed to have said those words about a thousand times to this girl. When would Sister Catherine be brought to realize that convent life was not suited to a nervous and scrupulous nature? She got to her feet, brushed the sawdust from her skirt and moved the canvas chair invitingly. 'Here, sit down, sister, and dry your eyes. Let's say a rosary together.'

The immense length of that prayer, with its repetition of same prayers, fifty times the 'Hail Mary' and then numerous 'Our Father' and the 'Glory Be . . .' all of these prayers, recited over and over again, would, she hoped, lull Sister Catherine into a comatose state, but to her alarm, the girl gave a slight shriek and shook her head violently, repudiating both chair and prayer.

'I can't pray, Reverend Mother. I'm not worthy. Sister Gertrude prayed, but it did her no good. She dwelt too much on worldly matters. And now she has been punished.'

Oh, bother! The Reverend Mother closed her lips firmly so that the words could not escape. Wearily she sat down again on the rejected chair. Why waste Sister Bernadette's kindness? The chair was a support and she was feeling her age. She stared ahead and with difficulty suppressed a sigh. *Why on earth did I give into the bishop and accept this unfortunate child into the convent?* How many times had she said those words to herself? Sister Catherine had been a niece of one of the bishop's chaplains and both he and the bishop had been determined that Reverend Mother Aquinas was to have the honour of receiving this saintly soul into her community. The bishop enquired about Sister Catherine every time he saw the Reverend Mother and on every occasion, the Reverend Mother voiced apprehensions about excessive piety and an unhealthy addiction to confession. And, every time, the bishop expressed hearty reassurance and rapidly changed the subject. 'Nice little girl' had been his summing up of her reports. The Reverend Mother looked wryly at the innocent, child-like and tear-stained face that gazed at her confidingly and decided that the life of a hermit would have its compensations.

'May I tell you something, Reverend Mother?'

'I am always ready to listen,' said the Reverend Mother

cautiously. 'Would you set the door ajar, sister, please?' The air in the little shed was pungent with the smell of hen droppings. In any case, she wished to listen for the sound of the ambulance driving down the little laneway and her hearing was not as acute as it had been.

The request took the girl aback. She swallowed another sob, went to the door and opened it, gazing out at the fog-misted gardens. The river smell now seeped into the little shed, but it was a smell that all Cork inhabitants, from cradle to grave, were accustomed to and it seemed to calm Sister Catherine somewhat for a moment. In any event she stood very still for a few moments. Perhaps the worst was over. But then she gave another hysterical sob and turned back to the Reverend Mother.

'Sister Gertrude was a blackmailer,' she announced dramatically.

The Reverend Mother frowned. She said nothing, just passed her beads through her fingers. There was, she thought, something very soothing about the motion and she allowed a certain amount of time to elapse. Time, perhaps, for Sister Catherine to bite back her words, or to offer an explanation for them. The girl's figure, outlined by the grey light through the door, was tense and her breath was audible; gasps and a slight hiccup.

Oh, Sister Catherine, please go away. The words had no sooner gone through her mind than she felt ashamed of herself. If the girl had come to her from Sister Mary Immaculate, then she would have been thoroughly scolded already. Sister Mary Immaculate, surprisingly unsympathetic to one who shared her temperament, had already reduced Sister Catherine to tears, according to little Sister Imelda. Patience and understanding, the Reverend Mother told herself.

'Tell me about it,' she said aloud and endeavoured to make her voice as calm and as soothing as she could.

Sister Catherine gave another couple of sobs, looked over her shoulder anxiously and even then lowered her voice to a whisper.

'She was blackmailing Sister Brigid and Sister Joan,' she said.

'Really.' The Reverend Mother allowed that one word of doubt to stand unaccompanied and she waited for a response.

Sister Catherine, she thought wearily, would now burst into tears and sob that no one ever believed her.

It didn't happen that way, though. For once Sister Catherine held her tongue and stayed there at the door, standing very upright and staring out towards the river. The tears had stopped and there was almost an ugly look on the child-like face. Could it be triumph? The Reverend Mother sighed, pushed up her glasses and rubbed her eyes. I'm getting too old for all of this, was her thought and then, with shame, she banished that piece of selfishness and turned her attention back to Sister Catherine.

'I don't think that you mean blackmail, sister,' she said gently.

'Yes, I do.' This was an unexpected answer from Sister Catherine, but at least she had stopped wailing.

'Did she get them to pay her money?' asked the Reverend Mother wearily. That, of course, was an absurdity. None of the novices had any money at all. Parents and relatives could bring small gifts of cakes or sweets, but traditionally these were shared with all. Money was definitely not allowed. The Reverend Mother waited with interest to see what would be said.

'She got power over them,' hissed Sister Catherine and then hastily, with a scared look at the corpse on the floor, she crossed herself hurriedly.

'And you,' enquired the Reverend Mother. 'Did she have power over you?' She had not missed a note of venomous dislike in the girl's voice.

But there was no answer to her question. She could not even be certain that it had been heard. Sister Catherine was now looking up towards the boarded roof of the shed. Was that a rat hole up there, wondered the Reverend Mother, following the direction of the eyes that looked heavenwards. A rat hole, or was it just that the roof had been made from cheap, thinly cut pine and a knot had fallen out? For a moment she pondered a letter of complaint and then remembered that she, personally, had not purchased the shed.

'May I tell you something, Reverend Mother?' Sister Catherine's voice was full of suppressed excitement as she gazed at the roof. Funny, thought the Reverend Mother, how we always think of heaven as above the sky, not deep down in the earth. And yet the earth is the producer of all that man needs to maintain life. Why shouldn't heaven be down there? Why do we look down at the earth when we speak of hell and up to the sky when we speak of heaven?

'Yes, sister,' she said wearily.

Sister Catherine seemed to have gathered courage and inspiration from her study of the small hole in the roof, because now the sobs had ceased and her words came fluently.

'I have felt for some time,' announced the novice, 'that the Holy Ghost has put a shield around me, that a mantle has descended from heaven and that it wraps around me; something that keeps me isolated from all evil and wrong-doing. No matter what was going on among sinful souls, I was kept protected from it.'

'But you thought that something was going on?'

Sister Catherine bowed her head and assumed a saintly expression. All traces of tears had vanished from her eyes and her cheeks were now slightly pink. The Reverend Mother tried to subdue feelings of dislike and breathed a prayer for Christian charity.

'You overheard something?' She would have to get rid of this girl. The bishop considered that Sister Catherine would prove to be a marvellous teacher and a wonderful influence on the older girls of the school. The Reverend Mother, not for the first time, felt herself in total disagreement with the bishop.

'She had a very loud voice,' said Sister Catherine with a glance at the silent figure on the floor. 'May God have mercy on her soul,' she added piously.

'And what did you overhear, Sister Catherine?'

'I heard her threaten to inform you unless they gave her what she wanted.'

A fate worse than death. The Reverend Mother managed to suppress the words. It was no time for joking.

'And what was that?' she enquired.

'I'm not sure,' said Sister Catherine, reluctantly. 'She lowered her voice just then. But I heard Sister Joan shout at her. She said, "We can't possibly do that. You're just an officious busybody. You have no patriotism, no love for your own country." That was what Sister Joan said.'

This sounded a little odd. What had been going on? The Reverend Mother frowned.

'And Sister Brigid?' she enquired. 'What did she say?'

'Something that I would not like to repeat,' said Sister Catherine primly.

The Reverend Mother waited. What on earth was this business of patriotism to do with her novices? Sister Catherine bit her lip but still said nothing. She fidgeted uneasily, moving her feet, turning each shoe edge in turn to the ground and then back again. Her fingers began to pluck at her sleeve cuffs, an almost invariable precursor of a fit of tears. She would have to be distracted, and quickly or else a full blown fit of hysteria would ensue. And then, to her relief, the Reverend Mother heard the sound of an engine, the banging of vehicle doors and the crash of iron gates pushed open to their fullest extent. The puzzle about Sister Joan's and Sister Brigid's relationship with the dead girl would have to wait.

'That sounds like the ambulance,' said the Reverend Mother, rising to her feet. 'You'd better get back to your duties, Sister. Tell Sister Mary Immaculate that I kept you.' She walked to the door and held it open for the girl, not looking at her, but peering through gaps in the bushes for a glimpse of the white roof of the ambulance, giving, she hoped, an appearance of one who is no longer interested or waiting for an answer.

It worked. Sister Catherine was not much more than a child, after all, and, like all children, she could resist entreaties and commands to reveal a secret, but immediately yielded to bored indifference. As she passed her superior, she stopped at the doorway and hissed dramatically.

'Sister Joan said that she would kill Sister Gertrude. And Sister Brigid said that she would help her!' With a hunted glance of horror at the silent corpse on the floor behind her and another at the ambulance which was now visible, Sister Catherine moved quickly away, exchanging her usual small demure footsteps for something which was almost a run.

The doctor from Northern Ireland had not accompanied the ambulance. There were three men and a driver and between them they lifted the body onto the stretcher and carried the remains of Sister Gertrude to the ambulance.

The Reverend Mother walked beside the stretcher, passing her beads through her fingers and praying aloud in Latin. The ambulance men were respectful, and slightly over-awed and she waited until the body had been placed within the vehicle before she spoke.

'Dr Scher will be back tonight,' she said, as much to comfort herself as to gain information.

'Don't worry, Reverend Mother,' said one reassuringly. 'He'll be back. No one was to touch anything while he was away. "Don't let no one lay a finger." Them were his words to me.' He paused, but when she said nothing, he visibly summoned up courage. 'I'm Pat, Reverend Mother,' he said looking at her expectantly.

'Goodness,' said the Reverend Mother, rising to the occasion nobly and smiling at the tall figure that addressed her. It was not the first time that some fully grown man or woman had said something similar. Her past pupils generally assumed that as she looked the same to them, then they must be recognizable to her and that, of course, she would remember their names. 'I would never have known you, Pat,' she said. 'How you have grown!'

That was enough for Pat who looked confused and embarrassed while his friends looked from her to him respectfully.

'Well, I'll wish you all a good day,' said the Reverend Mother, realizing that it was up to her to take charge since Dr Scher was not here to give orders. Pat, she thought – and she did wish that she remembered him – had got himself a good job as an ambulance attendant. There was a very high death rate in Cork city. What between victims of shooting, suicides, fatal fights and starvation, there must be bodies to be taken to the hospital on a daily basis. The young man looked cheerful and competent and she hoped that his early education in her school had proved to be of benefit to him in this useful life of his.

Meditatively, she returned to the convent and went into her study. The fire was burning brightly and there was a pot of tea in the hearth and a plate of scones on the table. She welcomed Sister Bernadette's care of her and forced herself to taste a scone. The cup of tea she swallowed thankfully and then unlocked her desk and took a file from the middle drawer. It was marked 'Novices' and she skimmed through it until she came to the present day. Yes, the address of Sister Gertrude's next of kin was there. The father's name and address had been struck out after his unexpected death a few weeks previously and the sister's had been substituted. The full married name and address. A terrace of houses in Turners Cross. No telephone, though, and that was a shame. She would have to go out there and take a chance on finding Sister Gertrude's nearest relative at home. It would be unforgiveable if rumour, always rampant in the city of talkers, would have notified her of the fatality before she had been informed of it officially.

She took a bite from the scone and concealed the rest behind a pen stand on her desk. Some bird would welcome it later on when she disposed of it on the windowsill. The tea, however, she drank with appreciation. And then she rang the bell for Sister Bernadette.

'How very kind of you to leave me something to eat and to drink,' she said when the lay sister appeared. 'I did so enjoy your delicious homemade scone.' She had long decided that white lies which ironed the paths of daily intercourse with her fellow men, were no sin to be confessed in the convent chapel. In her mind, they were wholly justified and they smoothed and made pleasant relationships.

'I have to go and see her sister,' she said. 'I understand that she lives in Turners Cross.' She held out the book to Sister Bernadette, an authority on the streets of Cork city, who nodded sagely.

'I'd go now if I were you, Reverend Mother. Not too far, and you should find her in at this time of the morning. A bit early for shopping. She's quite pleasant. Wouldn't think that she'd blame you in any way. Not too much love lost between them, anyway. So I've heard tell,' added Sister Bernadette in tones that absolved her from such an uncharitable verdict on the relationship between the two sisters. 'I'd take a taxi, Reverend Mother. It's very wet on the streets and the trams will be full of people coughing. Not healthy. Where would we be if you were to get ill?'

'You're probably right,' admitted the Reverend Mother.

Modesty should have elicited a denial, but common sense told her that Sister Bernadette had spoken the truth. If anything happened to her, then the convoluted financial affairs of the convent would be exposed to the unfriendly gaze of the bishop's secretary. Really, she needed an efficient deputy who understood how the whole show worked and who could carry on the various schemes and projects once her superior had shuffled off her mortal coil. Sister Mary Immaculate would not be equal to the task.

There had been times, when during the last few months she had played with the thought of bringing Sister Gertrude into her own office as a secretary and gradually confiding in her how to run the whole concern so far as the money aspects went. The girl was fitted to be a business woman.

But was she interested in the children?

The Reverend Mother had thought not. Perhaps it would come, but there appeared to be little sign of it so far. Figures were not everything. The whole organisation had to be run for the children and because of the children.

In any case, the girl was dead.

She was roused from her melancholy thoughts by a knock on the door. She knew the knock and knew that she needed to deal with this matter before she left the convent to see the sister of the dead nun.

'Ah, Sister Mary Immaculate,' she said.

'I just popped in, Reverend Mother, not wanting to delay you in any way, or to take up your valuable time, but just to say that I've seen all the novices and have told them about the terrible death of Sister Gertrude. I've sent them all to pray in the chapel now, all that is except Sister Catherine who has gone to bed with a sick headache. Don't you worry at all, Reverend Mother. I shall see to everything in your absence. They are all being very sensible.'

'You are very good,' said the Reverend Mother. She ran her mind through the day. No teacher was ill, thank goodness. The classroom lessons would go on like clockwork. Sister Bernadette could be relied upon to see to the hot lunches, eggs and potatoes from the convent garden for those children who stayed in school during the midday break. And she herself had no class to take in the afternoon. And then she remembered why her timetable had been cleared. Of course. It was accounts day.

'One thing, Sister Mary Immaculate, would you see the bishop's secretary for me? He will be coming for those accounts. They're all here, ready for him. I'll put them into an envelope for him. It shouldn't take long.' But it would, of course. He and Sister Mary Immaculate would have a long confidential chat and consume lots of tea and of Sister Bernadette's fruit cake. The Reverend Mother was conscious of a feeling of benevolence as she thought of how much pleasure she would be giving to these two people.

'I would be most grateful,' she said aloud.

From a drawer she lifted out some neatly filled in sheets of squared paper. Last handled by Sister Gertrude and left in perfect order. Everything balanced beautifully. Everything that should be hidden from the bishop's secretary, like the sweets which she bought for the children, was expertly concealed among the necessary expenses. A wave of intense sadness swept over her. The young novice had been gifted in a way that had not come to her experience before – gifted in the necessary, though prosaic, skills of organization and adminis-tration. She had seen the convent as a business – a business whose end result for the Reverend Mother was the education and the happiness of slum children and her comments on the efficiency needed to deliver the aim had been novel and thought-provoking.

The Reverend Mother placed the documents in a large envelope, thought about sealing it and then decided not to bother. She handed them over to Sister Mary Immaculate, heaved a sigh, dusted some stray crumbs of sawdust from her warm cloak and made her way heavily to the front door. Sister Bernadette had gone to the gate and was exchanging a few lively comments with the taxi driver, but little Sister Imelda was standing politely holding the door open for the Reverend Mother. She did not look her usual cheerful self and the Reverend Mother stopped and looked at her with concern. There were traces of tears on the lay sister's cheeks and her mouth trembled slightly. The Reverend Mother knew a moment of compunction. After all, the girl was very young, barely fourteen, she thought and perhaps she should have been shielded from the dead body of the novice, lying on the soiled floor of the hen house.

'My child, what is wrong?' she asked.

The tears sprang into the young eyes and overflowed. 'It's nothing, Reverend Mother,' she said and tried to smile.

'Nonsense, of course it is something. You are always so cheerful. Tell me. Was it Sister Gertrude? No need to be ashamed. It was a very upsetting sight. I felt it and I am five times your age.'

The girl shook her head. 'No, it wasn't that, Reverend Mother. It's just that there's a tin of treacle missing from the pantry and Sister Bernadette thought that I might have taken it. But it's all right. She believes me now.' Sister Imelda brushed the tears from her eyes and did her best to smile cheerily.

'I see,' said the Reverend Mother. It wasn't for her to interfere in the affairs of the kitchen. Sister Bernadette was a very kind person and the young lay sisters were all very happy under her rule. She was, however, an impulsive woman who often spoke before she had time to think. No doubt she would arrange a little treat for Sister Imelda and then all would be cheerful again in the kitchen.

It was odd though, she thought as she made her way into the taxi. Why should a tin of treacle suddenly go missing? Sister Bernadette, she had gathered once, used a teaspoonful of treacle in her fruit cakes. It was, she seemed to remember, a very infrequent order on the weekly grocery list, usually featured at the end of November or the beginning of December. Dreadfully sweet stuff. Would anyone steal a whole tin of it?

And then she dismissed the matter from her mind and thought of how to break the news of that untimely death to Sister Gertrude's nearest living relative.

FIVE

Garda rank structure in descending order
Commissioner
Deputy Commissioner
Assistant Commissioner
Chief Superintendent
Superintendent
Inspector
Sergeant
Garda (constable)

Inspector Patrick Cashman opened the door to the police barracks and came quietly in. Although he had been a member of the Garda Siochána for quite a few years now and had risen rapidly through the ranks of constable, sergeant and inspector, he was still conscious of a slight thrill when he came into these hallowed surroundings. It had been worth the hours of study and the daily intense concentration on doing the job well, in order, for him, a boy from the slums, to be able to wear the uniform and to hear the officer on the desk, a man old enough to be his grandfather, respectfully greet him by his title.

'Any news of Dr Scher, inspector?' Tommy loved a gossip and always found a line of conversation that would detain a transient police officer for a few minutes.

Patrick shook his head silently and lifted some envelopes from the counter. Three of them for him. By rights, Tommy should by now have delivered these to his office but the man liked to finger through them first.

'It's just that the Mercy Hospital have been on to me, inspector. Got a body that they want him to look at. A young woman. Dropped dead.'

Patrick nodded. The trick with Tommy in the morning was to say nothing. Give him no words to hang another sentence onto. He began to make his way to the door.

'Heard the news? About the explosion?'

Tommy had saved the best for the last. Patrick stopped abruptly. More trouble?

'Spike Island,' said Tommy dramatically. 'Some of these Republican boys must have got onto the island. No one knows how. A whole shed full to the brim of explosives. The whole thing blown up. They could feel the heat of it right over in Cobh. Got them all out of their beds. You can read all about it in the *Cork Examiner*. The superintendent has got it now, but he'll pass it onto you when he's finished with it. God only knows how these IRA fellows organize these atrocities, what with the city crawling with spies and informants and a posse of soldiers at every street corner. I know for a fact that they'd have every one of that lot watched like hawks until they get enough to pop them into prison. They've been watching their doors, checking every visitor, checking their letters. You wouldn't know this, I suppose, inspector, but there is a list of suspects in every post office in the city and any letter that arrives for one of them is checked before it is delivered.'

Patrick nodded silently. He knew that, of course, but he didn't grudge Tommy his snippets of information. A military matter, this blowing up of the ammunition on Spike Island. Nothing to do with him. Just as well. He had enough on his plate. Three cases of violence, eight robberies, including the theft of lead from the roof of a Protestant church, and then there was a missing twelve-year-old girl and a complicated case of possible blackmail that involved a local publican and a friend of the superintendent. It was all very well for Tommy to talk about the surveillance of known anti-treaty dissenters. In Cork, the rebel city, as it was well known by police and army, there would always be found some innocent to deliver a letter, a newspaper boy or someone like that. Still nothing to do with him, he thought.

'Joe in?' he asked and moved on towards his own room without waiting for an answer. Joe would be in. He was very reliable and would always be at his desk once the hour of nine struck.

'Ten people on the phone looking for you,' said Joe as soon as Patrick entered his own room. Everything neat and ready for the day's work. A schedule of appointments lying on the snowy-white blotter on his desk, his inkwell would have been newly filled, pen nib checked and a packet of new nibs in the drawer. Patrick nodded to him, glanced at the schedule, placed the letters on the folders and then saw one of the names on the notebook by the telephone and looked up at Joe with surprise.

'Dr Scher phoned. He's back then.'

'Dropped in, too. Came to the window and tapped on it. Wanted to see you. Didn't want to get held up by Tommy. I told him that you would be late, that you were going over to Union Quay before you came in. Came across just a few minutes ago. You just missed him.'

'What did he want? I'd have thought he would be sleeping off his journey. He had enough to say about it before he went. Terrible ordeal, those boats, that was what he said. Said he's always seasick and that he would take days to get over it.' And then Patrick stopped. There was a piece of paper tucked into the corner of the blotter. Joe had, in his usual efficient manner, made a note of the conversation with Dr Scher. He picked up the piece of paper and read it through again. 'A young nun from St Mary's of the Isle Convent. Dead!' he said incredulously.

'That's right,' said Joe. 'That's what he wanted to see you about. He's over in the morgue. You should catch him if you get over there straight away.'

'Oh, there you are, been looking for you, inspector.' The superintendent stuck his head in through the door. Patrick silently instructed himself that in future, he should be sure to come into the barracks before doing other jobs. Everyone was acting as though he were out amusing himself and had arrived a couple of hours late for work complete with a hangover.

'Union Quay,' he said briefly and looked enquiringly at the superintendent.

'I've had one of the soldiers at Victoria Barracks on to me about that blowing up of the gunpowder on Spike Island,' said the superintendent. 'He says that a crowd from North Main Street were mixed up in it. Someone in Cobh recognized them. Wants to know why we're not keeping an eye on them.'

'Yes.' Patrick turned his attention to this new problem that was being landed on his shoulders. He did not contradict the name of Victoria Barracks, although the military barracks on the hill at the top of Wellington Road had been renamed Collins Barracks for some time. The superintendent was a leftover from the old regime, from the Royal Irish Constabulary and he hadn't much patience with all the renaming that was going on where George Street was turned into St Oliver Plunkett Street and Great George's Street was rechristened Washington Street and many more changes were in the pipeline. 'Is that our job,' he asked aloud and then told himself that he shouldn't bother. He knew better than the superintendent. And he knew that it wasn't their job unless the men had committed some crime.

'Well, we're all on the same side,' said the superintendent obscurely as he prepared to return to his perusal of the back pages of the *Cork Examiner*. 'I've got to go to a funeral,' he said over his shoulder as he opened the door to his office. 'Old Ted Murphy has died eventually. Won't be missed. Ted, I mean. Odd fella. Dr Scher's been looking for you,' he added and then shut the door firmly behind him.

Dr Scher was still in the morgue when he went across. Looking very tired, he thought. Tired and discouraged. Must be a bit wearing, the amount of dead bodies that turned up in Cork.

'Joe tells me that you're up to your eyes in work,' he said briefly. 'Wouldn't have troubled you, Patrick, but there is something very strange about this. I'd better warn you that I think we'll probably have to have an inquest.'

SIX

Thomas Aquinas
. . . nullius boni sine consortio iucunda est possessio.
(. . . there is no delight in possessing any good things,
without someone to share it with us.)

The door to the house on Friars Walk was opened instantly to the taxi driver's knock. The Reverend Mother, obeying Sister Bernadette's instructions, stayed in the car until the door had been opened and until he came back to hand her out and escort her to the front door. The face awaiting her was not familiar. Not the sister of the young novice, that was sure. This was a woman in her late forties, at least. Perhaps, now that she approached, there was something slightly familiar about her. Yes, this was the aunt. She remembered the face from the day when the funeral of Sister Gertrude's father took place. The mother's sister, she thought, as the woman came rapidly down the path.

'Oh, Reverend Mother, you won't remember me. I'm Sister Gertrude's aunt. Mrs O'Sullivan.'

Is anything wrong? Her worried face asked that question as she escorted her guest up the garden path. Everything very neat. Very well-cared for garden, white net curtains in the windows. Comfortable, though not monied. Still, very much more than a normal, newly-married couple in Cork could afford. No garage, so probably no car. Or not yet. A shed with a widely opened door showing a long shelf filled with what looked like about twenty tins of paint and various bottles of cleaners and below them a two-bicycle rack, now empty.

'My niece will be so sorry to have missed you.' Mrs O'Sullivan was still puzzled, but she ushered her guest into the immaculate front room and rapidly put a match to the fire that had been set, but was probably only lit when the parish priest made a visit. The Reverend Mother wished that she could be entertained in the kitchen or living room. Mrs O'Sullivan was wearing a lightweight cardigan and already began to look cold. To her relief, the chimney began to pour out smoke to the extent that there was little possibility of staying in the room. She gave a few coughs to encourage the invitation to come into the kitchen.

'It's the fog,' said Mrs O'Sullivan apologetically. 'It gets into the chimney and blocks the smoke. I'm sure that Betty had it swept. Denis is most particular about getting the sweep every year. You know Denis, don't you, Reverend Mother?'

'Yes, indeed, I met him. Just before they were married. And at the funeral of Sister Gertrude's father, of course.' But her memory was more distinct of him at the former occasion. He had hung back at the funeral; but she had a clear picture of him in the convent parlour. A devastatingly handsome young man, who had been dragged by his fiancée to the reception tea party always held by the convent to welcome a new recruit into the ranks. Looked intelligent and efficient. She was sure that Denis had done his best with the chimney, but this was a common Cork city problem. Chimneys that were not used soaked up the prevailing fog and moisture. So Sister Bernadette had told her and they had decided, despite the cost of coal, that it was more efficient to light fires in unused parlours rather than let the damp seep into walls, floors and furniture.

But this room was going to be uninhabitable for the next few hours. The Reverend Mother gave another few coughs and this time Mrs O'Sullivan, with a despairing glance at the fireplace proposed that they would go into the kitchen until the fire 'had a chance'.

'What a lovely room,' said the Reverend Mother as she was ushered in. Partly, she had to admit to herself, the comment was evoked at the sight of the glowing range, but the kitchen was a very pleasant place with a well-scrubbed pine table, two bentwood easy chairs beside the fire and a pine dresser between the two windows. She crossed the floor to examine the wedding photograph that hung on the wall, while Mrs O'Sullivan plumped up the cushions and refolded an open copy of the *Cork Examiner*.

'So they were married in February,' she observed. 'That

must have been just after Sister Gertrude entered the convent.'
She had noticed the novice's date of entry this morning when
looking for the address of a family member.

'That's right, caused a lot of trouble that did,' said Mrs
O'Sullivan cheerfully. 'It had all been arranged, you know.
Betty was dead set on her sister being bridesmaid and she
even changed the wedding from Easter back to the sixteenth
of February to accommodate her. Patsy, I mean Sister Gertrude,
was going to enter the convent in April originally. Not a nice
month, February, to get married in. I said that at the time.
"But that's the last day, Aunty. Shrove falls on the sixteenth
of February and then it's Lent, so what can I do?" That's what
she said to me.'

'Yes, of course,' said the Reverend Mother sympathetically.
The Roman Catholic Church did not permit marriages to be
celebrated during Lent. She had never quite understood why.

'But then Patsy wouldn't wait, after all the fuss and the
bother. Had to rush into the convent before the wedding took
place. Never understood it myself.' The girls' aunt shook her
head. More than a year later the puzzlement remained and her
brow was creased.

'Nor do I,' admitted the Reverend Mother. 'I hadn't known
about that,' she added. She, too, was surprised at the decision.
Very unlike Sister Gertrude who had struck her as a very
sensible and calm young woman who knew her own mind
and, she seemed to remember, had some practical reason for
the change in her entry date. Why avoid her only sister's
wedding day?

'And then poor Betty had to get a school friend to stand as
bridesmaid.' Mrs O'Sullivan was still pondering on the
wedding day and the Reverend Mother judged that the time
had come when she had to break the news.

'When will Betty be home?' she enquired, making her way
to the fireside seat and choosing the chair with its back to the
window.

Mrs O'Sullivan sat down opposite to her, shaking her head.
'Don't expect her back for the day,' she said. 'She went off
to spend the day with a friend, down Crosshaven way. Took
her bike. Careful of the fog, I said to her, but she was sure

that it wouldn't last beyond Douglas. "First time that I've had a day off since his little lordship was born and I'm not going to give it up for a bit of fog." Always knew their own minds, the two of them. That's the way that their father, God have mercy on him, brought them up. And how is Sister Gertrude anyway, Reverend Mother?'

The moment had come. The news could not be postponed. If Betty wasn't going to return until the end of the day, then she couldn't possibly delay the news until then. Far better, anyway, that the news of her sister's death should be broken to her by an affectionate aunt, than by a stranger.

'I'm afraid that I have some very bad news for you, Mrs O'Sullivan. Sister Gertrude died this morning. It looks like some sort of poisoning. Perhaps she ate something. I will have more news for you tomorrow when our own doctor returns. In the meantime the ambulance has taken her body to the hospital.'

It was the best that she could do, though she was conscious of it sounding rather lame and improbable. There were lots of questions that could be put to her. How could a nun be poisoned while eating the same meals as everyone else in the convent? Why take a dead body to a hospital, rather than to a mortuary or an undertaker's place of business? She braced herself to give satisfactory answers, but the woman was weeping silently into a handkerchief. After a moment, the Reverend Mother got up and took a glass from the dresser, a rather ornate one, meant to be displayed rather than used, she noticed. Nevertheless, she filled it with water and carried it across to the woman.

'I'm very sorry,' she said sincerely. 'There's no easy way to tell of a death, is there?'

The woman sipped the water, shaking her head, but her tears ceased and after a moment she put the glass aside and said sadly, 'Would you like me to tell Betty? I'll have to wait for her to come home. Don't even know the name of this friend of hers. And I don't suppose that she'd have a telephone or anything like that.'

'I would be grateful,' said the Reverend Mother. 'No easy task, I know,' she added. 'I suppose that she will be terribly upset.'

'Well, I don't know,' said the woman after a moment's thought. 'They weren't that close, the two of them. A bit of jealousy between them always. Nothing to it, of course, but there you are. Sisters aren't always best of friends.'

'Both competing for their father's attention, perhaps. Their mother died when they were quite young, didn't she?'

'That's probably what began it. And then Betty was always the pretty one and always nice and slim. Didn't have a sweet tooth; not like Patsy. Funny child, she was; Betty, I mean. The only child I've known that wouldn't thank you for a sweet. Would always have Marmite on her bread, while Patsy would have hers piled high with jam. Fat little thing Patsy was, while Betty was as thin as a rake. I looked after them when they were young, you know. After the death of my sister. Didn't grudge it, still don't. Never got paid a penny for it, either. Had the two of them every day down in my house. Of course, John Donovan was full of thanks, then.'

'I'm sure that he was very grateful to you,' said the Reverend Mother. There had been a pause in the flow and she understood that she was expected to put something into the conversation. The woman gave a slightly ironic laugh.

'Grateful, well, at the time. So he said, anyway. That's the way that it was when they were young. Ever so grateful. Going to leave me something in his will. Told me that he had left me a nice little sum. Showed the will to me. Of course he was a lot older than I was, but even so . . . Not much use to me, by then, why not give something to me now. That's what I used to say to myself. Still, it would have been something. Just as well, anyway, that I was not counting on it. And then, of course, when he died, well, not a penny to me and not a penny to anyone except Betty. Well, that was a surprise, because Patsy, Sister Gertrude, well, she was always the one that he liked the best. She was the one with the brains.'

'She was a very gifted young lady,' said the Reverend Mother with sincerity. 'She had great ability to deal with figures and accounts. And a very pleasant cheerful member of the convent. She will be very much missed. A shock and great sadness for us all at the convent.' She was glad to get away from the subject of the last will and testimony of Sister Gertrude's father, John Donovan. It was obviously a very sore subject with the woman who had looked after his motherless daughters for him. 'It will be a terrible shock for her sister,' she added.

'As I say, perhaps. The truth is, Reverend Mother, well, they were quite jealous of each other. Of course, Patsy was the one with the brains and her father liked that. He'd be giving her all sorts of puzzles and asking her trick questions. Betty could never take any interest in that sort of thing, but Patsy, I mean Sister Gertrude, was always as sharp as a needle. That's what her father used to say about her. Sharp as a needle,' repeated the woman. 'But then, as they grew up, well things began to change. The balance shifted . . .'

'Betty grew even prettier and that gave her confidence, I'm sure,' said the Reverend Mother. The face in the photograph and the face that she remembered was certainly a pretty one, not classically beautiful, but sweet, with widely-opened eyes and an attractive smile. A girl with a nice figure, too, slim and long-legged; she had noticed that when watching the two walk in the convent garden together only yesterday. 'And then when Denis fell in love with Betty, that must have given a great boost to her confidence,' she added.

This business of Betty's elder sister, and the natural choice for a bridesmaid, persisting in entering the convent before her sister's wedding could take place, puzzled her slightly. It was an odd choice and did not fit with her mental picture of Sister Gertrude. Could she have been in love with this young man? It would have worried her at the time if she had known about it.

'Well, yes and no,' said Mrs O'Sullivan. There was a hesitant note in the woman's voice.

The Reverend Mother waited while the sorrowing aunt gulped down some more water. It would do the woman good to talk.

'Well, yes, she did meet him there, but it was not her that he came to visit in the first place when he came to their house. Of course, you see, Reverend Mother, Patsy was the one that knew Denis first. He worked in the paint room in Ford's Factory, was in charge of it and he'd be in and out of Accounts, because he would have been responsible for all of the ordering.

You knew that she worked in Accounts, didn't you, Reverend Mother? Of course, it was her father who got her the job. Straight out of school, she was, but he went to the manager and told him that he had been training her up for years. And, of course, he had lots of influence in Ford's.'

'Yes, of course,' agreed the Reverend Mother. 'I remember his funeral. There was a good turnout of senior men from Ford's at the funeral, wasn't there?'

'That's right.' Mrs O'Sullivan crossed the room to the dresser and took out a yellowed newspaper clipping. 'Betty kept the obituary notice. Look at that, Reverend Mother. That will show you how highly respected he was at Ford's.'

It was indeed an impressive list of heads of departments from Ford's and included the name of the managing director. The Reverend Mother scanned it for a respectful few minutes and then, just as she was about to hand it back, something caught her eye.

'Mr Donovan was not an old man, though, was he? Only fifty-eight. One would not have expected such an early death.'

Mrs O'Sullivan gave a deep sigh. 'No, indeed. And he hadn't a notion of retiring, not to mind ending his days so soon. Poor man. Liver, it was; that's what killed him,' she explained.

'Liver!' The Reverend Mother was immediately on the alert. That had been mentioned by the young doctor. Odd that daughter and father should have died of the same condition within weeks of each other. 'What caused that?' she asked.

Mrs O'Sullivan hesitated a little. 'Well, I wouldn't know,' she said. Then with a burst of confidentiality, she said in a whisper, 'Liked the drop of whiskey. You know what men are like, Reverend Mother. Always had a glass of it every night. I'd say it would have been that. That's what my husband thought, anyway.'

'I see,' said the Reverend Mother. She was puzzled though. A glass, or even two glasses of whiskey in the evening didn't amount, she thought, to a sufficient intake to damage the liver. Her cousin's husband, Rupert, regularly consumed a couple of glasses every evening judging by what Lucy related. And yet he was fit and healthy, played golf every Saturday, ran the foremost legal practice in Cork, was alert and trim in appearance.

And, after all, Mr Donovan, also, from her memory of him, was slim and healthy in appearance and doubtless was capable for an onerous and responsible job, one that would require a sharp brain – if he were not, she doubted whether the managing director, who had the reputation of ruthlessness, would have kept him on. It was unlikely that he consumed enough alcohol to damage his liver, while at the same time being responsible for the accounts of a big, prosperous business like Ford's Factory. Nevertheless, she decided that she might have a chat with someone at Ford's about the possibility of raising money to resurface their playground. A good project for a prosperous firm. Showy enough to warrant a few paragraphs in the *Cork Examiner*. It would, she thought, be easy then to lead the conversation around to the recent death of one of their staff.

'He was attended by his own doctor, I suppose,' she said aloud.

'Well, to be honest, I don't think he ever went to the doctor, never known him to do a thing like that. Never missed a day's work, anyway. This was a Saturday night. He just fell ill, was vomiting and then, he just died. A terrible shock for poor Betty. He was alone in his house. She hadn't seen him for a few days. He was just able to stagger into the house next door and get someone to run down to Turners Cross and find the doctor there. They got him into hospital but it was no good. He died in a couple of hours. The doctor told Betty that it was his liver. Signed the death certificate.'

It would, of course, be feasible that a middle-aged man had a bad liver. Middle-aged men living alone might well be prone to drinking too much. The unlikelihood of a nun drinking heavily had forced the young doctor who attended Sister Gertrude to agree to an autopsy, but a bewildered and sorrowing girl like Betty would hardly have argued with a doctor. Especially if the word 'liver' and not the word 'alcohol' had been mentioned.

The coincidence, however, set the Reverend Mother's brain working actively. Father and daughter both dying from liver problems. It did seem strange and unlikely. She turned her attention back to the loquacious aunt.

'So once Sister Gertrude left school her father persuaded the manager of Ford's to give his daughter a job,' she remarked.

'That's right, but it wasn't long before she was making her own way. Doing really well, too. Lots of compliments. Her father was ever so proud of her. He was telling me all the nice things that people were saying about her. Calling her efficient and saying that she never made a mistake. He said to me that she halved his work, started a new filing system and went around to all of the departments and gave them a typed-out sheet for their orders. None of this popping their heads around the door and asking for this or that. Her father said she was a boon to him.'

'Sister Gertrude was a talented girl.' But already the Reverend Mother, mentally, was calling the girl by the name of Patsy. Patsy the clever, though plain, one of the two sisters, the one who was valued the most by the widower, the one who went to work with him every day. And the one who knew the handsome Denis first of all. The Reverend Mother knew little about the running of a factory, but guessed that there would be lots of contact between the paint stockroom and the accounts department.

'Patsy had her father's brains,' said Mrs O'Sullivan thoughtfully, 'but Betty was more like her mother, more like my sister. Nice girl, but not interested in figures. Worked in one of those houses in Newenham Terrace, looking after the children, she liked that, was sorry to give it up after she married, but there you are, now she's got a darling little fellow of her own, fast asleep now.' And Mrs O'Sullivan sent a glance up to the ceiling.

The darling little fellow would probably wake up soon and make all further conversation impossible, thought the Reverend Mother, and quickly phrased a question.

'And so, Sister Gertrude, Patsy, knew her sister's fiancé first,' she remarked.

'That's right. Great friends, they were. She brought him home for tea one day. I was there. To be honest, Reverend Mother, I thought that there might be something going on between them at that stage. My brother seemed to like him very much. I wouldn't have been surprised to hear of an engagement being announced between the two of them. Great friends, they were. Of course, that was all that there was to it. Just friends.'

'But Betty was the one who took his eye.' Prettiness would, of course, win over mathematical intelligence, thought the Reverend Mother. She got to her feet. Time to be going. She hoped that this Denis was a good husband to poor Betty. The girl had lost her mother at an early age, had been brought up in a household where her sister was valued by her father more than she. And now both father and sister were dead. Aloud, she said, 'I mustn't keep my taxi waiting any longer. I will be in touch, Mrs O'Sullivan, about the funeral arrangements. Please give my sincerest condolences to your niece. And thank you for your kindness and hospitality. And I am sorry that I have left you with the task of breaking the sad news.'

Still, she thought, as she took her seat in the taxi and waited while the driver hastily extinguished his cigarette and economically placed the stub behind one ear, still, she had troubles of her own. Even if a lot could be discounted from the sensitive Sister Catherine's account of the undercurrents within her novitiate, nevertheless, she would have to question Sister Joan and Sister Brigid and ask for an explanation of those cryptic words overheard by their fellow novice: 'Sister Brigid said that she would kill Sister Gertrude. And Sister Joan said that she would help her!'

SEVEN

St Thomas Aquinas
*. . . oportet in intellectualibus non deduci
ad imaginationem.*
(. . . it is important when dealing with matters of the
intellect not to be led away by the imagination.)

But before the Reverend Mother could send for the two young novices, Sister Bernadette, unsummoned, was knocking at her door. The Reverend Mother, recognizing the distinctive double knock, sighed silently. It would be another crisis. Sister Bernadette set herself very strict rules in her position as guardian of the Reverend Mother's door. Unless it was something serious she would not dream of intruding until the Reverend Mother had a chance to divest herself of her outdoor cloak, perhaps change her shoes, straighten her veil, look at her letters, communicate with God, look through the *Cork Examiner* or anything else that was appropriate to a Mother Superior who was resuming command over her little kingdom after an absence.

However, there Sister Bernadette was, hard on the Reverend Mother's heels, standing outside of the door and it was imperative to see what now required attention.

'Come in,' called the Reverend Mother in a pleasant tone. She lowered herself into her chair and turned a placid countenance towards the keeper of the convent door.

'It's Denis Kelly,' said Sister Bernadette apologetically. 'Young Denis Kelly. He's asking for you. Very upset, he is. In a terrible state, walking up and down the parlour, pouring with sweat.'

'Denis Kelly.' The Reverend Mother hesitated. Who was Denis Kelly? And why should he pour with sweat on this foggy morning? The name was familiar, but for the moment she could not place the man.

'Him that married Sister Gertrude's sister. Works at Ford's Factory. In charge of the paint department, if you please. His father was a coal man for Suttons on George's Quay. Married that daughter of the floor manager in Dowdens. Just had the one boy, Denis. Did well for him.' Sister Bernadette, like all good Cork people, not only knew name, breed, seed and generation of most of the inhabitants of the city, but was able, with a few economical words, to convey the whole history of a family. This Denis, the Reverend Mother understood instantly, was the son of a man who had married above his station and, having but the one child, had educated that boy to a degree that, instead of the back-breaking, filthy work of delivering heavy sacks of coal to households and seldom appearing in public without a coal-black face, young Denis had been sent to school, raised above his father's station in life and had got a good job in Ford's.

'He's in charge of the whole department, does all the ordering and all that, got two men and four boys working under him; doing very well for himself,' supplemented Sister Bernadette. 'Then married the Donovan girl, the sister of our Sister Gertrude. Good match that. I did hear tell that they were moving house, now. Moving out to St Luke's Cross. Of course, the word is that the girl's father was very warm, very warm indeed, and I suppose it will all go to the younger sister now. Would you like to have a cup of tea before you see him, Reverend Mother?'

Amazing how Sister Bernadette always knew everything, reflected the Reverend Mother after she had declined the tea and removed her cloak. *'The word'* was true if it told that the late Mr Donovan had accumulated a tidy sum of money during his hard-working life, all of which he had invested in Ford's as soon as he had found out about the move from Southampton to Cork. Had lined up a good job for himself once the factory opened and, doubtless, had done well. Had been paid a good salary, and had seen the value of his shares rise month by month. It was indeed true that John Donovan had amassed a considerable fortune. The solicitor who had regretfully informed her that Sister Gertrude had been cut out of her father's will once she had entered the convent, had hinted that the money accumulated by the old man had been considerable and all of it had been left to his younger daughter. She and her husband were now rich young people and no doubt a car would soon follow the purchase of the house at St Luke's Cross.

Half of that money would have been very welcome to the convent and would have made the task of feeding, clothing and educating the slum children to be a little less 'hand to mouth' as Cork people said. Nevertheless, she thought as she called an invitation to enter, it was very understandable that the late John Donovan should want his fortune to go to a daughter, and grandson, rather than to an institution such as her convent.

'You've heard the sad news,' she said to the young man as he entered, cap in hand, well-dressed, she thought. A very white well-starched shirt, a good black suit, trousers neatly narrowed with bicycle clips and a pair of well-polished black leather shoes. Shoes, not boots, she noted. This was a young man on the rise, a young man who might well aspire to a managerial position in Ford's. Especially if he followed his father-in-law's example and invested in the company.

'My wife's aunt sent a message to me at work,' he said. 'She wanted me to find Betty and tell her. I thought I'd come here first. Come and find out what had happened to her.' To her surprise, his voice cracked on the last words and he sank down onto a chair and hid his face in his hands. His shoulders were trembling and sobs seemed to shake his whole frame. The Reverend Mother thought about sending for tea, but then decided against it. A young man like that would not want a weakness exposed. She just sat very still, relaxed and allowed herself to think of Sister Gertrude, not as a problem to be solved, but as a tragedy. A young life, a life of promise, suddenly and abruptly snuffed out. Someone to mourn. To her surprise she felt tears well up into her own eyes. She would miss the girl. And she caught herself thinking of all the elderly and bedridden nuns to whom death had showed its face for many a long year, but still lingered over the final blow. Sister Gertrude had been vibrant with life and with energy. Her brain and her body had been bubbling with youth and vigour. Her laugh rang out in the corridors. Quickly she banished thoughts of her own loss and set herself to deal with his.

'We will miss her terribly; we were very fond of her,' she said with sincerity and saw him struggle to control himself. He took out a well-laundered handkerchief and mopped his eyes.

'I loved her. Loved her very much.' The words came out in a sort of wail, slightly shocking the Reverend Mother and making her feel glad that she was the only witness to this outbreak of sorrow. What, she wondered, would the pretty, rather childish-looking Betty think of her husband's declaration of love. A sister-in-law, yes, but not a true sister. A wife's sister, but not a wife. There was something about those sobs, those words that almost seemed to negate that relationship; seemed to hint at a warmer and more intimate one.

Young Denis Kelly, thought the Reverend Mother, sobbed as though he had lost a wife or a mother. How close had they been? Worked closely with each other, the aunt had said. The older sister had worked in a prestigious position, worked in a man's world, while the younger girl, Betty, just had a job as a nursemaid, something that was often handed over to a girl from an orphanage. What was it that the aunt had said? She had hinted at a certain amount of tension, jealousy, perhaps. *They weren't that close, the two of them. A bit of jealousy between them always.* These had been the words of a woman who knew both girls very well, had probably been a mother to them during childhood and through their adolescent years, after the death of their own mother. Patsy, Sister Gertrude, the clever one, the favourite of her father and Betty the pretty one. Would that have been the first time that a young man had favoured Betty over her elder sister? Or was the elder sister used to giving into her appealing younger sister. She scrutinized the young man carefully, and hoped that her silence was sufficient to calm the atmosphere.

'I'm sorry, Reverend Mother. I'm sorry. It's just . . . Well, it's just come over me that I'll never see her again. I just can't believe it.' The young man was struggling for control, his handsome face distorted, blotched dark red and white, his eyes still streaming.

'Don't make any apologies.' The Reverend Mother purposely made her voice matter-of-fact and slightly detached. Nevertheless, she offered no condolences. It was time for him to pull himself together. After all, he couldn't sit there and cry for ever. He would have to go and break the terrible news to his wife. Presumably that was why Mrs O'Sullivan had sent for him.

'You would have known Sister Gertrude very well, of course,' she added. 'Now tell me what you would wish to know. I don't want to detain you too long. There is, in fact, little that I can tell you,' she went on as he still sobbed and still wiped his eyes. 'As I said to Mrs O'Sullivan, we here at the convent are mystified as to the reason for Sister Gertrude's death. She had complained of feeling unwell last night, of feeling dizzy and nauseous but she had no temperature and the sister in charge of the novices felt that there was little more than a good night's sleep needed to restore Sister Gertrude to her usual happy and healthy self. Unfortunately, there must have been something more wrong with her and at the moment I am awaiting the examination by the convent's doctor.' She rose decisively to her feet and was glad to see that he followed her example.

'I'll send a message over to your house as soon as I have more positive information,' she said briskly. 'In the meantime, I can only convey my most sincere condolences to Sister Gertrude's sister and I hope that you will assure her that she, as well as her sister, will be remembered in the community's prayers today.'

He gulped a little, shook his head sadly, but said nothing while she rang the bell to summon Sister Bernadette. She didn't feel up to showing him out herself. There was something about this almost unbridled show of sorrow which slightly alarmed her.

Even after the young man had silently followed Sister Bernadette to the door, she did not take up her paper knife and deal with the correspondence which had been neatly piled on her desk. Two things stuck in her mind and made her feel uneasy. She hoped that the young man managed to master his excessive grief by the time that the burial of Sister Gertrude took place and she hoped that there had been nothing significant about Mrs O'Sullivan's recollection of the bridesmaid question.

But then Patsy wouldn't wait, after all the fuss and the bother. Had to rush into the convent before the wedding took place. Never understood it myself.

Nor I, she had commented at the time, but really, it was not difficult to understand. What if the original love affair had been between Denis Kelly and the older daughter of John Donovan? What if it had been only temporarily terminated by the pretty face of the younger sister? Perhaps, after a few months, he had reverted to his first love and the eldest sister had fled to the convent in order to avoid breaking the heart of Betty.

And then she remembered something else.

Betty had visited her elder sister on the afternoon before she became ill. The Reverend Mother had a sudden vision of the two of them walking in the garden. They had seemed friendly enough. She had heard a peal of laughter as Sister Gertrude had displayed the hens which were her special responsibility, bestowed upon her by Sister Mary Immaculate who had not wanted the young novice to get above herself because of all the time she spent in the holy of holies, the Reverend Mother's own room. They had seemed friendly enough then, but had there been any hidden dislike, any memory of passionate words spoken by that handsome young man to the wrong sister? Was he, wondered the Reverend Mother, one of those people who like to load their sins, whether sins of commission or sins of desire, on to the shoulders of others? Had he confessed to his young wife? And if so, what had Betty thought about her husband's feelings for her cloistered sister?

The Reverend Mother thrust the image of the two sisters walking in the convent garden from her mind and rang the bell once more.

'I'm sorry to keep disturbing you, Sister Bernadette,' she said apologetically, 'but I wonder whether you could send someone to find Sister Joan and Sister Brigid and ask them to come here. I want to have a word with them.'

The fact that Sister Catherine was an attention-seeking

nuisance did not absolve her superior from enquiring about a threat to kill a girl who died shortly after the reported quarrel. She did, at least, need to ask the two young novices about the reasons for the quarrel.

They had entered the novitiate on the same day, Sister Joan and Sister Brigid. Had been born in the same hospital to mothers who were near neighbours, had known each other in their prams. Had gone to school on the same day and had been friends right through their school life.

Two nice girls, the Reverend Mother had thought. Fond of the children, interested in the theories of teaching, willing to expand their own education.

A certain fanaticism about the resurrection of the Irish language, a tendency to exclude older nuns by happily chattering in Gaelic to each other, well, the Reverend Mother had been willing to tolerate this. After all, she was old and probably very out-of-date, and perhaps it was important for a new country to disinter a language which had not been spoken by most Corkonians for many generations, even if it had been still in use in remote districts in the west of Ireland. Moreover, if jobs in the future were to depend on a fluency with the Irish language, then she was all for her new teachers to be drilled in this. Even if it meant a certain amount of head-tossing from Sister Mary Immaculate who resented the number of evenings when the girls were missing Benediction because they had gone to attend an Irish class on the other side of the city.

They came quietly and demurely into the room and stood waiting.

The Reverend Mother looked at them. Something very tense about both of them.

'You've heard the news?' They both nodded. Sister Brigid half-suppressed a sob. Her very sensitive mouth quivered. She took out her handkerchief and dabbed her cheeks. But above the snowy whiteness of the linen, her dark brown eyes were fixed upon her friend. Tentative, unsure, waiting for a lead.

'We heard that she may have eaten something. That she might have been poisoned.' Sister Joan, like her namesake,

St Joan of Arc, was courageous and forthright. The Reverend
Mother appreciated this quality. She would have preferred to
say nothing until after Dr Scher had seen the body and had
given his opinion, but doubtless the convent was seething with
rumours sparked off by the loud and tactless observations
voiced by the young doctor from Northern Ireland. Sister Joan
would have to be answered and would have to have as full an
answer as she could provide. Not pretty like her friend, nevertheless, Sister Joan had a pair of forthright, honest, pale blue
eyes that compelled a similar honesty from her superior.

'I don't know yet; I'm waiting to see Dr Scher, but that was
said,' admitted the Reverend Mother. Odd, she thought, how
faces can differ. The two girls sitting opposite to her, same
age, in what way did the arrangement of mouth, nose, cheek-
bones and eyes ensure that one was strikingly pretty while the
other was downright plain?

'But we all eat the same food. And the same amount of it.'
The pale blue eyes opposite hers were intent upon her. 'I just
don't understand, Reverend Mother. How could just one person
in a convent be poisoned and no one else show any signs of
illness?'

'I think that we are all puzzled, all in the dark at the moment,'
said the Reverend Mother and added pointedly, 'I won't
speculate until I've spoken with Dr Scher. At the moment, none
of us knows why poor Sister Gertrude died.'

'She was ill after supper yesterday.' Sister Joan was refusing
to take the hint. The thin lips had firmed and the blue eyes
were staring ahead, with a hint of belligerence. 'She got up in
the middle of the night and I heard her vomit. She went to the
window and threw it open and I heard her vomit through
the window, right down the ivy.'

The Reverend Mother sat up very straight. This was unexpected. Surely Sister Mary Immaculate, in her role as Mistress
of the Novices, should have known if one was ill during the
night. She said nothing, but saw her thoughts mirrored in
the face opposite. Sister Brigid gave a slight whimper but there
was no surprise in those childlike brown eyes. Apprehension,
perhaps, but certainly not surprise. She, too, had known of this
attack of vomiting.

'Anyone else disturbed in the night?' she asked. Currently there were just four novices, but the divisions between the novices' dormitory and Sister Mary Immaculate's room was only marked by heavy curtains. It was pointless, she thought, to ask the competent Sister Joan why she had not summoned the mistress of novices. The Reverend Mother tried hard to be fair to the young and not to ask them stupid questions. After all, if she were ill, she acknowledged to herself, the last person that she would want to see would be Sister Mary Immaculate who would pass from exclamations to cross-examinations.

'No, no one,' said Sister Joan. 'Sister Catherine slept through and no one else heard. Sister Gertrude and I have the two beds nearest to the window, and I probably disturbed Sister Brigid when I jumped out of bed, to see what was wrong.' The girl's lips were very firm, rather compressed, accentuating the length of the over-long upper lip but her eyes were anxious. Sister Brigid slid her eyes between her friend and her superior and then looked towards the door. Convent life was ruled by bells and soon the summons to the midday dinner table would sound and would release the two from further questioning. And why was she questioning them in the first place? A novice had died. Quite unexpectedly. A brash and rather ignorant young doctor had declared his opinion that she had died from alcohol poisoning. That, most surely, must be incorrect. But why had Sister Gertrude fallen ill yesterday, vomited in the night and then died the following morning? All novices in her care had a three-monthly check-up. And a full medical examination before they were allowed to enter the convent. The dreaded tuberculosis disease was rife among the population of this wet and foggy city and the Reverend Mother guarded against allowing it entry to her flock.

'Did Sister Catherine tell you that we, Sister Brigid and I, had a quarrel with Sister Gertrude?' Never one to shirk her fences, Sister Joan faced her courageously.

'Did you? Have a quarrel with Sister Gertrude?' The Reverend Mother disliked betraying confidences and resolved not to be stampeded by this confident young lady. A very steady gaze met hers. Sister Joan was trying to decide whether

Sister Catherine had said anything or not. Beneath the heavy, dark brows the blue eyes were speculative and then became hard. The pair of lines that ran from nostrils to upper lip flattened out as the mouth tightened.

'Well, I suppose that she did. It wouldn't be like her not to.' The words were addressed more to herself than to either the Reverend Mother or to her friend, but Sister Brigid flinched noticeably. Sister Joan, however, did not look at her. She stood very straight and there was a determined lift of her head and the firm chin jutted forward. 'She told you that I had threatened to kill Sister Gertrude.'

'Sister Gertrude made no complaint to me,' observed the Reverend Mother.

'Well, she wouldn't, would she? She's . . . she wasn't stupid; bossy, yes, but not stupid.'

'And you would prefer not to tell me what it was all about . . .' The Reverend Mother allowed her unfinished observation to hang in the air. Sister Brigid fastened her pearl-white teeth on her lower lip and looked up apprehensively at her taller friend.

'Just schoolgirl stuff.' The words were decisive, but Sister Joan's rigidity betrayed her unease.

'School.' The Reverend Mother seized on the word. 'Something to do with the classes that you two attend at St Ita's, at *Scoil Ide*?'

And that had been an inspired guess. Tears brimmed Sister Brigid's brown eyes and she turned so pale that for a moment she looked as though she would faint. Sister Joan's face whitened also, but courage came to her rescue and she lifted her head and stared blankly at the Reverend Mother.

'Scoil Ide?' she queried.

'Yes.' The Reverend Mother allowed the monosyllable to stand without explanation or modification. There was something very odd about both girls' reactions.

St Ita's School, Scoil Ide, in Irish, was a small, private school for girls, run for the monied children of rich and liberal-minded families with republican leanings. It had been opened about eight years ago by the two sisters of Terence MacSwiney, former Lord Mayor of Cork, who had died of a hunger strike in an English prison. Mary MacSwiney had been a teacher in St Angela's Convent, a fee-paying Cork school for girls, but had been dismissed from her post due to her notoriety in Republican matters. She and her sister, Annie, had set up a school in their own house where the instruction of the pupils was carried on completely in Irish. A very successful school, so the Reverend Mother had heard. Mary and her sister were well-educated, well-qualified, had both been trained as teachers in a college at Cambridge. The pupils were well taught; they were, she had heard, carefully educated with an unusual degree of respect for their opinions and priority was put on learning for interest rather than by rote or through fear of punishment.

So far as her school was concerned, the Reverend Mother had a respect for Mary MacSwiney, but on a personal basis she found her shrill and dogmatic, one whose opinions were very black and white and never did admit the slightest shades of grey. The woman bitterly opposed the Anglo-Irish Treaty, which despite its limitations had brought a certain measure of peace to the troubled country of Ireland, calling it 'the grossest act of betrayal that Ireland ever endured'. Her speeches were among the most powerful in the Irish parliament, calling on the members in the Dáil not to commit 'the one unforgivable crime that has ever been committed by the representatives of the people of Ireland' by accepting a treaty which required an oath of allegiance to the British monarchy, and which divided the country of Ireland, placing a border that made six counties from the nine counties of Ulster to belong to Britain. She may well have right on her side, but she had, suspected the Reverend Mother, little thought for the young lives that were still being lost amongst those who followed her dogma.

Nevertheless, Mary MacSwiney had been one of the founder members of the Gaelic League and was passionate in her love for the ancient language, so when two of her novices expressed an earnest desire to attend evening classes at Scoil Íde, the Reverend Mother instantly gave permission, despite Sister Mary Immaculate's whispered confidences about young men attending these lessons. It was no part of her philosophy to immure these novices within the convent walls. Better for them to see as much of the world as possible before they made the decision to take their final vows. After all Mary and Annie MacSwiney were middle-aged women in their forties who should be able to ensure decorous behaviour among a crowd of young people. As a precaution she had persuaded Sister Gertrude to accompany the two younger girls.

But perhaps she had been mistaken, perhaps it had been a bad idea. The late Sister Gertrude had been no prude, no convent schoolgirl. She had been out in the world, had held her own in the very masculine atmosphere of Ford's Factory and had forced men there to accept her ability and her status. Had been, by all accounts, very happy at her workplace. She would not have issued a threat to report the girls to the Reverend Mother unless she had felt something serious was going on.

'So why do you think Sister Gertrude was worried about you two?' she queried.

Sister Brigid's brown eyes overflowed with tears and Sister Joan was white-lipped, almost looking like her namesake, St Joan of Arc, when faced by the flames. Something was badly wrong.

'I don't know.' The tone was almost rude, but the Reverend Mother decided to ignore this.

'I'd prefer to know all that had been said, rather than hearing from a third party,' she said in a detached manner. This, she hoped, gave a non-judgemental opportunity for a confession. Some silly flirtation, giggles on the road back from Wellington Street, possibly young men assisting the two young novices on those break-neck steps descending the steep hill to Patrick Street.

But why and how had the older and more sophisticated Sister Gertrude come to be so concerned about that. And would she have been even interested? The Reverend Mother thought not. Sister Gertrude, the one-time Patsy Donovan, had been interested in figures, in puzzles, but not particularly in people. She had shown bare tolerance of the other novices who were all four or five years younger than she, had not appeared to be friendly with any of them.

'But you're not a schoolgirl, either of you, are you? And yet you used that very extreme expression. That is correct, is it not? You threatened to kill Sister Gertrude.' The Reverend Mother slid her eyes sideways to look at the silent Sister Brigid. The girl was very white and there was a bead of blood glistening on the deep pink of her lower lip.

'She was interfering in something that was none of her business.' Sister Joan faced her superior bravely, but her eyes were beginning to look frightened.

'Had Sister Gertrude any grounds to be concerned? Why did she threaten to tell me?'

Silence greeted this. Sister Brigid once again caught her trembling lower lip between her teeth, glanced at Sister Joan, but Sister Joan stared stonily ahead.

'And neither of you deny the extreme language that you used to Sister Gertrude, is that true?'

There was no answer. But something had changed. This time it was Sister Joan who looked at her friend, looked tentatively and almost as though seeking permission. And this time it was Sister Brigid who gave a half shake of the head and then looked straight ahead of her.

'I would think that your vow of obedience must now come to your mind,' remarked the Reverend Mother. 'I have asked you why such extreme language was used by both of you to Sister Gertrude. I have asked why this occurred. And now I am waiting for an answer. You do realize that you are putting your future in this convent in jeopardy?'

Both stood there, stiff as martyrs and neither answered. That surprised her, but now she had played the most formidable card in her hand and she was left with no other threat.

The Reverend Mother began to lose patience. She would have a word with Mary MacSwiney, she decided. If necessary she would suggest to Sister Mary Immaculate and some other of the teaching nuns that they, too, should attend these evening classes in the Irish language. That would scotch all occasions for scandal, she thought. However, in the meantime, she had other matters to occupy her attention.

'Perhaps you two should go away now and think about this matter and then come back when you are happy to tell me about it,' she said evenly and turned her attention to her correspondence.

It was only when the door closed behind them that she lifted her head and stared at the opposite wall.

Alcohol poisoning? How on earth could a novice in her convent be suffering from alcohol poisoning? She just couldn't understand it. She would have to curb her impatience until Dr Scher had time to examine the dead girl.

EIGHT

St Thomas Aquinas
*Praeterea, sicut potential se habet ad bonum et malum,
ita et habitus, et sicut potential no semper agit,
ita nec habitus. Existentibus igitur poetentiis,
superfluum fuit habitum esse.*
(Moreover, as power possesses both good and evil, so
also does habit. And just as power does not always
achieve, nor does habit. Given, therefore, the existence
of power, habits become superfluous.)

D r Scher arrived at the convent early the next morning.
The Reverend Mother had been listening absent-
mindedly to Sister Mary Immaculate's views on the
importance of strict formation of good habits at an early stage in
a novice's career in the convent. Apparently, Sister Catherine,
with her mind on higher things, continually forgot to change
her outdoor shoes for indoor slippers on coming back from
chapel. And as the pious Sister Catherine spent every spare
moment that she possessed praying earnestly in the convent
chapel, situated across the garden from the convent itself, then
the opportunities for trekking mud back indoors and on the
highly-polished floor were manifold. Or so Sister Mary
Immaculate had decided. Surprising how much she disliked
the girl whom, privately the Reverend Mother considered to
be a junior version of the Mistress of Novices.

'I think that we need to shame her, make her think, make
her more considerate to others,' said Sister Mary Immaculate.
'I propose lining up all the children by the door and sending
her over to the chapel and have them watch while she
changes into her slippers when she comes back. If she has
to do that ten times, it should impress the importance of
obedience upon her.'

And humiliate the girl and drive her into a state of hysterics,

Cora Harrison

probably, thought the Reverend Mother, reflecting on the thought that neither she herself, nor Sister Mary Immaculate, nor any of the professed nuns, ever changed into slippers after a visit to the chapel or to the gardens. There was a perfectly well-gravelled, well-raked path kept in good order by the gardener. What, after all, was the function of the doormat? Who on earth dreamed up that stupid rule about slippers for novices? And why hadn't she done something about repealing it? She made a mental note to review the rules for novices and to formulate her thoughts on what they needed to learn and to experience in order to assist them to determine whether they had a vocation for a life as a nun. After all, the acquisition of good habits often led to a dull and pedestrian mind. Much better for novices to meet each day with fresh minds and new resolves.

It was at that moment she heard Dr Scher's cheerful voice telling Sister Bernadette that it rained in Manchester almost as much as it did in Cork. She turned back to the Mistress of Novices with renewed energy.

'No, better still, tell her that she must only visit the chapel when all of the community go,' said the Reverend Mother firmly. 'And then you will be present to remind her if necessary.' This would perform the dual role of frustrating Sister Mary Immaculate's humiliating punishment and of cutting down on Sister Catherine's excessive visits to the convent chapel. Without waiting for an answer she went straight out into the hallway, holding out both hands to Dr Scher.

'Welcome home,' she said. He was, she thought, pleased, though slightly overwhelmed by her effusiveness. She was so relieved to see him, though, that she did not care. Now she would know the truth. A tiny prayer flashed through her mind that this chalice should pass from her and that the doctor would find that the unfortunate Sister Gertrude had died of some disease which had not shown up in her medical examination, only a month or so previously. Let no scandal touch my convent, she prayed, as she led the way back to her room. Let no talk of alcohol or young men or wrongdoings mar the work that we do here. Please God, give no opportunity for an episcopal visitation.

'Come in, Dr Scher,' she said, ignoring Sister Mary Immaculate's sulky face and leading him into her room and towards a chair by the fire. To her relief she had heard him refuse Sister Bernadette's offers of hospitality. She waited for the door to close and braced herself. Now she could hear the worst without further delay.

'Yes,' she said, taking a chair opposite to him.

'She died of poison, alcohol-based,' he said bluntly.

She said nothing. He would go on, she knew. He had never yet left her in ignorance or glossed over the truth. She could hardly believe it though. Where, on earth, had the girl obtained alcohol? And yet Dr Scher would not have spoken unless he was sure. And if he was sure, he would, she thought, be correct in his assertion. She had absolute trust in him. She bowed her head and tucked her hands inside her sleeves and waited for the rest of the communication.

'Tell me what she was like the last time when you saw her,' he said.

The Reverend Mother struggled for a moment with the feelings of despair. And then she raised her head bravely. Somehow, no matter how often she had told herself that the young doctor might be mistaken, there was something within her that told her the man probably knew what he was talking about. 'She appeared ill that evening at supper,' she said steadily. 'She was dizzy when she got up from the table. She stumbled; knocked over her chair; her speech was slurred; she was nauseous. She vomited when she was brought upstairs. And again during the night, apparently.' She stopped then, feeling an absurd sense of protectiveness towards the dead girl and any secret that she may have had. But only with complete knowledge could Dr Scher be enabled to form a correct verdict. 'I have since found out,' she said, endeavouring to make her voice as calm and as dispassionate as she could, 'that the novice who sleeps in the bed next to her in the novices' dormitory had observed her get out of bed, open the window and vomit out through it. Doubtless,' said the Reverend Mother dispassionately, 'the very thick ivy on the wall concealed the vomit and her fellow novices did not inform on her. It may have happened before.' Surely, she thought despairingly, no one dies of alcohol poisoning unless they are of a habit of imbibing the stuff. But where could Sister Gertrude have found a source? She, like the other nuns, had no personal money, only what might be doled out to her for a special purchase, or for a fare for a taxi or the tram.

'And she would have eaten the same food as the others.' Dr Scher was frowning to himself, puzzling over the problem.

'Exactly the same, and the novices are ordered to hand over any gifts of food or such from relatives to the sister in charge of the novices; that is Sister Mary Immaculate. The usual practice is that such gifts are divided among the whole community.'

'So there would be no way that she could get hold of, or be fed, a substantial amount of alcohol. Would have to be spirits, I think, judging by the fatal effects. Something concentrated. Some sort of whiskey or brandy. You don't keep anything like that in the convent? Nothing to administer to fainting nuns after long services, anything like that? Something to sip after a hard day. Any little secret supply that she might have got hold of. You have no little secret hoard hidden here in your room.'

'No,' said the Reverend Mother curtly. Her mind went guiltily to the secret drawer where she kept a box of illicit sweets used sparingly to reward excellent work or to console badly traumatized children. Still, even if Sister Gertrude had gorged the entire contents, it would have been unlikely to have killed her. And sweets did not contain alcohol.

'Any possibility that she could have got out of the convent secretly, smuggled in some spirits?' His mind was running on the same lines as the doctor from the north and she sent a mental apology to the young man for doubting him.

'Three of my novices attended a class, attended twice weekly classes for Irish language lessons in the early evening. They took place at St Ita's school on Wellington Road, run by the two MacSwiney sisters, owners of St Ita's. I suppose that it would be about a half an hour walk there and they would, of course, have passed public houses and bars on the way. But they would not have money, just a small sum for emergencies. They were supposed to take a taxi if it rained, but they usually returned that money as they seldom bothered. None of them seemed to mind the walk and they enjoyed the classes.' She stopped but then forced herself to go on. There was some mystery here and all facts to do with the dead girl had to be relevant. 'To be honest,' she said, 'I was the one who encouraged Sister Gertrude to join, almost put pressure on her. She didn't have much interest in the Irish language; mathematics, accounts, all that sort of thing, these were her interests and I think that she had little to learn in that field. However, she was about four years older than the other two and I meant her to be, to a certain extent, a chaperone, a responsible person who would make sure that these two young novices were discreet and sensible, but who was yet not too old to spoil their evening out with other young people.'

'But now you are worried about those Gaelic language classes, is that right?' Dr Scher was watching her closely.

'Something was wrong,' said the Reverend Mother. 'I was informed by another novice, well, between ourselves, it was Sister Catherine; you remember her, the nervous hysterical one.' She thought that with Dr Scher she could be honest. He had dealt with Sister Catherine and could assess her story for what it was worth. 'Apparently, according to Sister Catherine, who was probably eavesdropping, Sister Gertrude threatened to tell me about something, and Sister Joan, forthright young lady that she is, told her that she would kill her if she did so, and Sister Brigid, you know the one with the big, innocent brown eyes, Sister Brigid said that she would help her.'

'Goodness, what very holy novices you have here, Reverend Mother. Blackmailing each other, if you please. Now don't frown at me. It's quite funny, really.' He looked amused, but the Reverend Mother, ignoring him, continued to frown thoughtfully.

'But you see,' she said, 'Sister Gertrude, the one that I would have sworn was mature and sensible, she's the one who, according to you, had taken enough alcohol to kill her. And yet I could have sworn that my judgement of her was correct and that she was the last person to sneak a bottle of whiskey or gin into the convent and to drink its entire contents . . .'

He looked at her for a moment and then he nodded.

'Well, let's turn matters inside out. Let's say that you are right. Let's say that we are both right, but remember that I am a man of science. When I say that someone died of alcohol poisoning, I do not necessarily mean that they have swallowed a couple of bottles of Paddy Whiskey, though that is the easiest solution. Some of those chemicals that they use in mixtures for cleaning windows or polishing brass, silver, furniture, anything, really – Windolene, Brasso – a lot of that sort of stuff that my housekeeper uses, or even paint solvent, for instance, all of these have alcohol bases and all of these could cause the same symptoms.'

'So what you are saying is that Sister Gertrude could have died from drinking some chemical, but surely—'

'Has been known. So drinking whiskey or brandy is probably by choice, probably done for pleasure, to enhance a moment or to forget your troubles. But it's a different matter when it comes to window cleaner or anyone of those other things that I have mentioned. Then you are on to accident, suicide or murder.'

The Reverend Mother thought about that. 'Sister Gertrude would not have been involved in any cleaning or painting within the convent. The lay sisters do the cleaning, the gardener would do any odd painting jobs, and once every five years we have the painters in to do the windows and the doors. In any case she was the last person to do something so incautious as to swallow some cleaning liquid. So an accident would be unlikely, almost impossible. Suicide, I would feel, knowing the girl very well, better than I know other novices since she worked in here, in this room, on the accounts with me – well, I would deem suicide to be extremely unlikely, impossible, in fact, if anything is really impossible.'

'And murder?' queried Dr Scher.

The Reverend Mother paused and thought about this. 'There are those words reported by Sister Catherine,' she said as calmly and as dispassionately as she could. Recalled there in the room, they sounded even more ridiculous than when voiced by the hysterical Sister Catherine.

'You don't seriously think that one of your other novices could have murdered her for fear that she might report some

silly breaking of the rules?' he said, looking almost amused.
'Two nice girls, Sister Joan and Sister Brigid. Can't see them
doing something like that? And how would they feed the stuff
to her?'

'Tell me about these chemicals,' said the Reverend Mother,
ignoring his questions. 'What would they taste like?'

'To be honest, I'm not sure,' he said. 'But you do get
ethylene glycol in window cleaners and that's a form of alcohol.
It's a sort of syrup, thins out paint, and liquefies solids. They
use it in lots of factories. I don't suppose that it does any
harm, though, unless you drank half a bottle of it. I seem to
remember reading that it tastes quite sweet, but that is
something that I can find out. Yes, now that I think about it,
there was the case of a child, child of a painter, drinking
some. We had to pump his stomach, poor little fellow. Yes, it
would be sweet and so could easily be disguised in a drink,
well sugared tea or something like that.'

The Reverend Mother thought about this. 'I think,' she said
decisively, 'that you need a cup of tea.' Without waiting for
an answer, she reached across and pulled the bell rope.

'Oh, Sister Bernadette, I'm sure that our visitor would like
a cup of tea,' she said when the nun came in beaming.

'I've the kettle just on the boil,' said Sister Bernadette
with the air of one who had been expecting this summons.
She bestowed a smile on Dr Scher that promised more than
a bare cup of tea.

'Dr Scher has been admiring your windows,' said the
Reverend Mother and was pleased to hear that there was no
note of embarrassment in her voice. 'He wondered how you
keep them so clean. I said that you probably buy a bottle of
something, some sort of cleaner or polish.'

'Never would bother my head,' said Sister Bernadette
emphatically. 'Why waste money on something expensive
when the *Cork Examiner* will do the job just as well. Just run
the paper under the tap and then polish the window, Reverend
Mother; that's how I clean windows. I teach all the young
sisters how to do it the same way, just crumple the newspaper
and wet it. And a little vinegar in warm water for some of the
outside ones if the smuts and the soot gets on to them.'

'Interesting,' said the Reverend Mother light-heartedly when the lay sister had gone hurrying back to the kitchen. 'Well, I must say that the *Cork Examiner* is well worth the three pence that we pay for it. It gets read from cover to cover by everyone in the convent and then the old copies are used to light fires and to clean windows.'

'You are relieved that there are no dangerous cleaners lurking around your convent kitchen, aren't you? You sound relieved. You think that this murder has nothing to do with your community. Is that right?'

The Reverend Mother thought about this comment. Was she relieved? Perhaps. Nevertheless a life had been lost, a young woman, who had enjoyed her existence; had loved her work; that young woman was now lying dead in the mortuary. A girl who had been under her care. Almost an unbearable thought. She turned back to the question of chemical poisoning.

'Well, now that I come to think of it, I don't think that Sister Bernadette buys much other than soap and vinegar for the cleaning,' she said. 'I never remember seeing any strange names like Windolene or Brasso or anything like that. Though I must say that I hardly notice the kitchen accounts, just take it for granted that we need what she writes down. But I will check, now that you've told me that some of these cleaners can be lethal.' All the time that she was talking, though, she kept running the three faces of the novices through her mind. Who amongst them could have hated Sister Gertrude enough to kill her?

Or was this crime nothing whatsoever to do with convent life, but had its seed in the previous existence of that strong-willed, self-possessed Sister Gertrude who had led another life previously as Patsy Donovan, the darling of her father and a valued employee of Ford's Factory. Her mind went back to the trim kitchen which she had visited in Turners Cross. Cupboards, well-polished, well cared for, drawers and shelves. Crockery in some, food in others, but then there was one, over under the window. One door not quite closed. Garish tins, ranged on a shelf, just glimpsed inside and a basket with dusters and cloths. Would that newly married Betty Kelly, sister of the late Patsy Donovan, wife of a man with a very good job, have used the modern polishes, rather than be content with news-paper and vinegar? Probably. A modern young housewife. Of the generation that slightly despised the *mores* of their mothers and their aunts. Even the young girls that she taught, though not well-off like Betty, had this instinctive rebellion against their elders. There would have been no shortage of money in that household. Certainly not since the death of the father and probably not even before it. Sister Bernadette seemed to think that Denis was in charge of the paint department. Ford Factory paid very well. Even an ordinary factory hand was earning five pounds a week at that time. Excellent wages for men who were used to part-time and irregular casual work. A man like Denis would be comfortably well off.

'Your mind is moving onto murder. Is that right? Don't think that it was an accident?'

'No, I don't,' said the Reverend Mother miserably. 'What about you? Are you going to ask the police to open a murder enquiry?'

'It goes automatically to the coroner as I can't certify it as a natural death. And yes, it will end up on the police desk if neither of us can think of a plausible reason for Sister Gertrude to consume one or another form of alcohol in sufficient quantities to poison and kill her.'

The Reverend Mother thought about this and then shook her head. 'No, Dr Scher,' she said. 'You will have to inform the police. This death needs to be properly investigated.'

'I'll do that, then.' A yawn escaped him. He would still be tired after his trip on the ferry between Cork and Liverpool. She rose to her feet.

'You're tired,' she said. 'Don't work too hard today, but I wonder whether, on your way home, it would be possible for you to drop into the printing works and ask Eileen MacSweeney whether she could come and see me. I shouldn't ask you when you are so tired, but . . .'

'Only three minutes around the corner from me.' He said the words in an absent-minded fashion, visibly curious about this request. 'What was the name of those women that held those classes?' he asked.

'Mary and Annie MacSwiney. Nothing to do with Eileen

MacSweeney,' she said, replying to his unasked question. 'The name is spelled differently. No, no relation to Eileen. Mary MacSwiney was born in England. Her mother was English, though her father had Irish connections.'

'But she runs those classes for the Gaelic League. That's right, isn't it? Now that I come to think of it, I believe that I have heard of the lady. Odd, isn't it, brought up in England and an Irish fanatic.' His eyes were very shrewd as they looked at her and she had the feeling that he was reading her thoughts, understanding her fears and her doubts. She gave a nod.

'We have a saying here in Ireland, Dr Scher, "*hiberniores hibernis ipsis*" – more Irish than the Irish themselves. It was said hundreds of years ago about the first Norman/English settlers in Ireland, people like the Earl of Desmond who loved everything Irish and ran into conflict with Queen Elizabeth. It's been seen down through the ages and Mary MacSwiney, despite her birth and heritage, despite her early education in England, despite her English mother, despite the fact that she trained as a teacher at Cambridge University, taught in an English school, speaks, still, with what sounds to us like an English accent, nevertheless, I would deem her to be a fanatical Republican, obsessively opposed to the treaty that was hammered out by Michael Collins and his men.'

'And you are a little worried that your novices might have got themselves caught up in some Republican business.'

It was, she thought, a valid speculation on his part. After all, why did she want to see her former pupil Eileen MacSweeney? The girl might have given up her active involvement in the illicit activities of the rebellious Republicans, but she still knew many of them and would still have plenty of information. The struggle still went on and only recently there had been an attack by the Irish Republican Army on British troops in Cork harbour. Mary MacSwiney made little secret of the fact that she was strongly on the side of the anti-treaty Republicans and completely against the present government in Ireland. Had she been stupid to allow her novices to attend these classes? And yet perfectly respectable and law-abiding people in Cork had entrusted their precious children into the hands of Mary MacSwiney. There had never been any attempt to indoctrinate the pupils in the school. She had heard that from many sources.

'Don't trouble yourself too much,' said Dr Scher struggling to raise his bulk from the comfortable easy chair. 'It will probably prove to have nothing to do with Republicans, nothing to do with those Gaelic League evening classes. Girls sometimes swallow strange stuff, to clear their skin, to make themselves lose weight.'

'She wasn't like that.' The Reverend Mother, also, rose to her feet. 'She was hardly a girl. She was twenty-two years old, mature, sensible, cheerful and well-balanced, I would have said. I relied on her good sense and on her judgement.' And then, suddenly, she remembered the missing tin of treacle. Had that ever turned up in the convent kitchen? Could it have anything to do with Sister Gertrude's death? She would speak to Sister Bernadette before she said anything about it.

'Well, I'll send your little favourite Eileen to you,' said Dr Scher, injecting a note of cheerfulness into his voice. 'She's got a bank account now, did she tell you? She's getting a little sceptical about this promised golden dawn of Patrick Pearse when "all children of the nation shall be cherished equally" and so the girl has bought herself a second-hand typewriter and is busy earning money in the evenings to send herself to university. Great little typist. Beautiful work. Persuaded me into writing a book about Irish silver. Nags me for the next bit every time that she sees me.'

'And I suppose that you pay her double what she is worth.' Despite her worries, the Reverend Mother felt a smile lift her spirits. It would be good to discuss the whole matter with Eileen. Perhaps these Gaelic League classes had been innocuous and Sister Gertrude's death due to some terrible accident which could not have been foreseen and could not be the fault of anyone.

'When you see Patrick, tell him that I shall be here and ready to see him any time,' she said. 'He'll want to take a statement from the novices and other members of the community, also and I will arrange for him to have one of the parlours,' she added. In general, novices should be chaperoned by another nun when in the presence of a man, but she decided that she would conveniently forget that rule. There were some odd undercurrents here and the priority had to be to uncover the truth as soon as possible.

NINE

St Thomas Aquinas
Sic ergo summum gradum in religionibus tenent quae ordinantur ad docendum et praedicandum.
(Thus the highest place in religious orders is held, therefore, by those who are dedicated to teaching and instructing.)

When Dr Scher had left, the Reverend Mother did not turn immediately to her letter writing, *begging letters*, she thought ruefully. She had been planning a new and original project to touch the heart and purse of the managers of insurance companies, something about cutting the rate of crime, of reducing burglaries in the shops of Cork and thereby increasing the profits of insurance companies; something about the future; something that would sound well and could form a good headline on the *Cork Examiner*, with, of course, a list of businessmen who had generously contributed to that worthy cause. Well-educated children tended to get jobs; that was her theme, or to go to England, she admitted privately to herself. Surely it would be to the advantage of insurance companies if these potential young criminals did well in school, as they might do if she could afford an extra teacher to give special attention to those with difficulties in learning to read. Her experience was that if a child had not learned to read by seven, then they would continue to fail throughout the rest of their time in school. A dedicated teacher, one especially trained, Montessori or Froebel, perhaps, someone who understood how young minds worked, someone who would give extra lessons to these children with difficulties – if only she could afford to hire someone like that. She would think up a catchy title for the project – Insuring the Future. That sounded good, sounded like something that would appeal to hard-headed businessmen, she thought and cheered by her brainwave she set to work.

'Dear Mr O'Callaghan,' she wrote. 'I remember how generous you have been to us in the past . . .' She held her Waterman fountain pen poised in the air for a second and then put it down with a sigh. Sister Bernadette again.

'I'm sorry to disturb you, Reverend Mother.' Sister Bernadette paused in the doorway, looking hesitant and unhappy.

'Come in, sister.' The Reverend Mother replaced the cap on her new pen, a present from her cousin Lucy and turned an attentive face to the lay sister. It was unusual to see Sister Bernadette look so troubled.

'I'm sorry to disturb you, Reverend Mother,' repeated Sister Bernadette. She came in and shut the door carefully behind her and placed a lidded basket on the table by the window. 'And I don't like bearing tales, but I think that you should know about this.' And then she opened the basket, removed a duster and took from the basket two small boxes, bearing the legend 'For the Foreign Missions'.

The Reverend Mother looked at the boxes with bewilderment. Surely Sister Bernadette was not about to suggest that she stop collecting money for the poor of Cork and concentrate on the Foreign Missions instead.

'I just thought since I had a bit of time on my hands that I would give a good going-over to the novices' dormitory,' explained Sister Bernadette. 'I know they are supposed to keep it clean and neat themselves, but you know what young girls are like, Reverend Mother. Dust balls by the legs of the bed, cobwebs behind the curtains, grime at the back of the washstands . . .'

'And you found these.' The Reverend Mother nodded towards the collecting boxes.

'That's right.' Sister Bernadette was having to think now before proceeding. A very practical woman with lots of common sense, she had, as long as the Reverend Mother had known her, completely and without resentment, accepted the differences between lay sisters and the ordained nuns. That did not stop her from a certain motherliness and decided indulgence which she bestowed upon the young of both sectors. The fact that she had brought these two boxes to the Reverend Mother showed that she recognized the serious implications for her find.

'One under Sister Joan's bed and the other under Sister

Brigid's. Tucked right up next to the bed leg, between it and the wall. No one would notice if they weren't down on their hands and knees.'

The two women stared at the find with shared dismay. Two flimsy cardboard boxes, oblong, lidded, six-sided, made with a slot for a coin on the lid. Would be used by orders of nuns such as the Missionary Sisters of St Columban who made periodic visits back to their home country in order to organize nationwide collections to fund their work in Africa or China.

'What on earth have they been up to?' breathed the Reverend Mother.

Sister Bernadette shook her head sadly. She had too much common sense to put forward some religious explanation. She went to the window and peered out through the fog, taking the opportunity to swab the moisture with the duster that was permanently tucked into the belt around her broad waist. She kept her back turned and allowed the Reverend Mother some time for her thoughts.

'You'd better send them to me,' said the Reverend Mother, recovering herself. 'Take your basket, but leave the boxes.'

'Yes, Reverend Mother,' said Sister Bernadette, obediently. But as she turned to go, the Reverend Mother suddenly thought of something. Something sweet, Dr Scher had said. This alcohol which was not real alcohol, not beer or whiskey or anything like that, this ethylene glycol which was a deadly poison. A syrup which could be hidden in something sweet.

'Oh, Sister Bernadette,' she enquired, 'has the tin of treacle turned up?'

Sister Bernadette blushed. 'I suppose Sister Imelda told you about that. I blamed her without thinking. Poor little thing. Such a nice little girl. Best little helper that I've ever had in the kitchen. Cheerful and willing. I've said sorry to her, but I'll have to find a little treat for her, as well. No, it wasn't her at all.'

'No?' queried the Reverend Mother.

Sister Bernadette hesitated. 'Well, I wasn't going to say anything about it to you, Reverend Mother. After all, she's only young and she does a lot of praying. Takes the energy out of you, too much praying,' stated Sister Bernadette, looking anxiously at her superior. 'I dare say that she meant to return it. She'd be waiting for an opportunity. Found it under her bed when I was cleaning the novices' dormitory. A nervous sort of girl. I wouldn't like to get her into trouble with Sister Mary Immaculate. It doesn't matter that much. I'm not going to miss the odd spoon of treacle.'

A nervous sort of girl. Wouldn't like to get her into trouble with Sister Mary Immaculate. The Reverend Mother restrained her eyebrows from moving up towards her wimple. 'Do you mean Sister Catherine, Sister Bernadette?'

'That's right. No harm done, though, Reverend Mother. A few tablespoons gone, but plenty left. I always order those big tins and they last me through the year. Don't worry about it, Reverend Mother. These young girls, they miss the little treats of home, you know,' said Sister Bernadette compassionately.

'I suppose so,' said the Reverend Mother slowly. 'Perhaps you had better send her to me, also. Tell them I want to speak to all three of them. Don't worry, I'll just enquire whether any of them know anything about these things found in the dormitory. I won't say much about the treacle, but I must deal with it.' There was, she thought, something very puzzling about this last find. As the lay sister was on her way to the door, she said, casually, 'Did you notice at any time before now that Sister Catherine had a sweet tooth, Sister Bernadette?'

'Well, no, I didn't, not like Sister Gertrude, God have mercy on her. Now she was a one that liked her pudding, used to have jokes with me about it. "Any second helps, Sister Bernadette," she used to say to me. Joking, you know. Full of life and fun, she was. Poor girl. We'll miss her!'

'Yes, indeed,' said the Reverend Mother gently. 'We'll miss her.' A novice to be missed, certainly. Confident and happy, quite unlike Sister Catherine. She sat for a moment thinking about the oddness of that theft.

'Strange,' she said aloud. 'Sister Catherine, of them all. I could never have imagined her doing something like that.'

'Well, she's a poor little *pisáin*, though, isn't she,' said Sister Bernadette compassionately. 'Very religious, of course, but that was the way that she was brought up. Wanted to be special. That would be it. A mammy's girl. I couldn't help feeling sorry for her. Mind you, no speaking ill of the dead, or anything, but

I think that Sister Gertrude was a bit hard on her. Mocking her, you know. Pretending that she would tell the bishop something terrible about Sister Catherine. All a joke, of course, but Sister Catherine wouldn't be one to take a joke. Crying she was. All upset. Only child, isn't she? Mother a widow, a very starched sort of person, so the butcher was telling me once. And, of course, Sister Gertrude was a bit like that. Would have been brought up in a different way, very close to her father, she was, and men do like to tease, don't they? She'd have picked it up from him. Meant no harm, but that was her idea of fun. And working there in Ford's Factory, well she would have had a lot of argy-bargy with the lads working there. She wouldn't realize that the poor little thing would take it all so seriously. All this talk about telling the bishop, just a joke, I suppose, that was what Sister Gertrude would think, but of course, frightened the life out of little Sister Catherine. Well, don't you worry about the treacle, Reverend Mother! A little goes a long way, ever so sweet it is. And when all's said and done, there's probably only a few spoonfuls taken from the tin. I'll go and send them all to you now. I'll just say that you want a little chat . . .'

And then Sister Bernadette took herself off, leaving the Reverend Mother rather ashamed of herself. Had she hardened over the years? Had her compassion for the poor and down-trodden denizens of the slums robbed her of sympathy for a novice under her care? And was the competent, self-assured and humorous Sister Gertrude a little too fond of ruling the other girls. Perhaps she was at fault in valuing the cheerful common sense and undoubted maturity of her latest recruit, over and above the more spiritual qualities of Sister Catherine.

She would not, she thought, labour the point about the strangeness of Sister Catherine's theft of a tin of treacle. One glance at the girl's thin frame would be enough to reveal that this was a person who had no love of sugar. So why had she stolen a tin of treacle?

Or had she?

Very easy for a novice to place something under a bed that was not her own. They had unrestricted access to their own territory and no one would question or even remember a visit.

When they arrived in her room, at first glance she saw that

only Sister Catherine looked serenely unaware of any significance for this summons. Sister Joan's small eyes were wary
and apprehensive. A courageous girl, though. When the Reverend
Mother's eyes met hers, she lifted her head and stared bravely
back. Her heavy brows began to knit and the resolute mouth,
with its protruding lower lip, slightly trembled before she
tightened it into a narrow line. She had immediately guessed
the significance of the summons. Brigid looked sideways at
her friend, her dark brown eyes filling with tears and her small
white teeth biting into her lip.

'I wanted to have a talk with you,' said the Reverend Mother
cautiously. 'There is one serious matter and one that may not
be at all serious, so, perhaps, I'll start with that affair. But first
of all, I must say to you that Sister Bernadette who works so
hard for us all should not feel that she had to clean your
dormitory. I want you to take that seriously and to be sure
that you clean everything, under the beds, the tops of the
cupboards, everything like that.' She ran out of ideas then, but
kept her eyes fixed on the three girls.

An immediate reaction from two out of the three. Sister Brigid
turned scarlet, her cheeks flushing to a poppy-like shade. She
pressed her hands against them and stared at the Reverend
Mother. Sister Joan paled and then stiffened. Sister Catherine
looked bewildered, darting tentative glances from one to another.

'Sister Bernadette, unfortunately, feels that she has to clean
your dormitory, though, goodness knows, she has enough to
do, otherwise. And when doing so, she discovered that a large
tin of treacle, which had been missing from the kitchen was
under one of your beds.' She stopped there and looked keenly
from one face to another. There had been, she noticed, an
immediate slackening of tension. Sister Catherine looked
bewildered and the other two relieved.

'It was under one of your beds.' The Reverend Mother
looked from face to face. Sister Catherine assumed a self-
righteous expression, Sister Brigid stifled a giggle and Sister
Joan looked somewhat scornful.

'It's very easy to put something under someone else's bed,
Reverend Mother.' Her voice was quite steady and she met her
superior's eye courageously.

'Indeed,' agreed the Reverend Mother. 'Children play those sort of tricks, don't they?'

'It was probably that lay sister in the kitchen, the small one. Sister Imelda,' said Sister Catherine triumphantly.

'Why would she do something like that?' enquired the Reverend Mother.

'To get us into trouble,' responded Sister Catherine instantly and looked at the other two novices.

'I don't think that she would,' said Sister Joan. She looked at Sister Brigid and then said defiantly, 'Neither of us thinks that she would do a thing like that.'

'And the collecting boxes for the Foreign Missions,' asked the Reverend Mother. This time she looked directly at Sister Catherine. Was it some private enterprise, some effort to speed her on the way to sainthood. All three girls were shaking their heads, though.

'I wonder whether they could have belonged to Sister Gertrude,' said Sister Joan. Her tone was calm and her manner as self-possessed as normal. 'She told me once that she had thought of joining the Foreign Missions. She said that it would be a great way of seeing the world.'

'Yes, I remember.' Sister Brigid looked relieved. 'It was that day when it was so foggy.'

'We were coming down the hill from Wellington Road and we could hardly see Patrick Street, just a few flashes from the trams, and a glow from the gas lamps.' Sister Joan picked up the story in an animated fashion while Sister Catherine looked from one and then the other of her fellow sisters in a bewildered fashion. 'It was very interesting, Reverend Mother. Sister Gertrude started talking about America. She said an American came over to Ford's Factory when she worked there and he was telling her about Arizona and how hot it was and how—'

'Thank you.' The Reverend Mother, conscious of all that she had to do, thought it best to terminate the conversation. It really didn't explain either the presence of the tin of treacle or of the two Foreign Missions' collecting boxes, but now that the name of the dead novice had been introduced there was a shadow of doubt over whether the articles had been placed there by some or all of the three girls facing her, or whether a fourth person had been responsible. 'You may go,' she said aloud.

Once they had left the room, she sat back and thought about the matter. And then she scribbled a note, put it in an envelope, printed on it: 'MISS EILEEN MACSWEENEY' and put the words 'BY HAND' in the top left-hand corner. It might be hours or even a day before Dr Scher could find the time to contact Eileen and she did want to see the girl, urgently. She left the note upon her desk and then she rang the bell for Sister Bernadette.

'I wonder could Sister Imelda deliver this note to the printing works off South Terrace, Sister. There is no hurry about it. She can go whenever you can spare her.'

That soul of discretion, Sister Bernadette, did not venture to enquire about her interview with the three novices. Just as well, thought the Reverend Mother ruefully when the lay sister had left the room. She would have had to admit that she had been totally vanquished by a pair of young girls. Sister Catherine, she thought, seemed guiltless. The tin of treacle could have been a joke, a prank, though whether committed by the two girls of her own age, or by the completely mature Sister Gertrude, that she could not tell. And the more she thought of it, the less likely either alternative seemed. After all, why do it? It was not particularly funny, especially as Sister Catherine was noted as someone who ate very little and was certainly an almost painfully thin girl.

And then she sat back in her chair and stared fixedly at the window opposite, now, despite Sister Bernadette's efforts, once again, streaming with moisture.

Yes, Sister Catherine appeared guiltless, but what was it she had said? The girl's words came back to her mind. *I've felt for a long time that the Holy Ghost has put a shield around me, that a mantle has descended from heaven and that it wraps around me; something that keeps me isolated from all evil and wrong-doing. No matter what was going on among sinful souls, I was kept protected from it.*

What if this magical shield had also the properties of shutting off unpleasant or unwelcome memories? What if Sister Catherine was serenely unaware of any act which she would prefer not to remember?

TEN

St Thomas Aquinas
Unde non dicitur bonus homo, qui habet bonum
intellectum, sed qui habet bonam voluntatem.
(Hence a man is said to be good, not by his good
understanding; but by his good will.)

'I tried to put a stop to it, Reverend Mother. I tried and I failed.' Eileen looked earnestly into her former teacher's eyes. 'I'm really sorry, but I did try. I was threatened. Not myself. I could have looked after myself. My mother. You know my mam, Reverend Mother. She's an innocent. She'd talk to anyone, fall for any story. Some of these fellows are very ruthless. I couldn't chance it. I had to go along with it. I had to keep quiet. In fact . . .' Eileen stopped as the Reverend Mother shook her head at her. Just as well to say nothing to anyone of the part she had played on Spike Island. Oddly, and to her great relief, there had been nothing said about the young man with the yacht and the girlfriend who had danced and sang and kept all eyes upon her, during the afternoon before the Spike Island explosion. No doubt, she thought shrewdly, the commanding officer had decided not to mention this to the military authorities. It would make him look a fool and might even have been a court martialling offence. The story seemed to be that a party of men swam over from Cobh and landed on the island after dark.

'I did hear that two young nuns from the Gaelic League classes were delivering letters,' she said aloud. 'I thought I could put a stop to it, but I couldn't. But, in any case, I would have been too late to save Sister Gertrude.'

'Don't worry about it, Eileen. You are not responsible for others' evil deeds. Your first duty is to yourself and to your mother. It's important to keep both of you safe. Now, Eileen, tell me about those classes at Scoil Ide, St Ita's, the MacSwiney school, those Gaelic League classes. Something strange has been going on, I think, and I am quite worried about it.' The Reverend Mother watched the girl's face and saw her nod.

'Dr Scher told me about Sister Gertrude. But I didn't think that she was involved. It was the two younger ones that I was worried about.' Eileen frowned in a slightly puzzled way and then said quickly, 'Unless, Sister Gertrude had found out something. Was a threat to them . . . I don't mean the young nuns, the young novices, I mean. You see, Reverend Mother, Sister Gertrude was different to Sister Joan and Sister Brigid. She hadn't fallen for the propaganda, she wasn't interested, so she became a threat to *them*; well you know who I mean, Reverend Mother. You've heard me mention Tom Hurley, and . . .' Eileen stopped and looked at her appealingly. The Reverend Mother felt a surge of compassion. Eileen had sacrificed her future, had abandoned any plans that might have raised her from the slums where she had been reared, had foregone the chance to go to university and to carve a new and bright future for herself. And all for the chimera of a bright new future for Ireland, for the dreams that were, in many cases now, peddled by hard and ruthless men such as '*them*' such as Tom Hurley. She looked at the girl compassionately. It was a shame to have to involve her, but she needed to know what had happened to Sister Gertrude.

'Tell me what you know – that's if you are not sworn to secrecy or anything like that.'

Eileen, the Reverend Mother reminded herself, had no obligation to her and the ties to old comrades might still be of great importance to the girl. Ireland, like England in the time of the civil war, was split, brother against brother, cousin against cousin, and neighbour against neighbour. For Eileen, the struggle had been of huge importance, had promised a bright new future where all would be equal. It must have been difficult for her to make the break with her former comrades.

However, the girl was shaking her head. There was, thought the Reverend Mother, something new about her. Almost as though Eileen had aged, had been forced to confront some unwelcome truths.

'I've finished with all that stuff now,' said Eileen emphatically.

'Just banging our heads against a brick wall and no one bene-fiting. The poor are getting poorer. There are no more jobs around than there were before all the fighting started. And,' she finished rather bleakly, 'in every graveyard in the country there are a lot more graves filled with young people than there used to be. I've known four boys that were killed and I don't know what good their deaths did to Ireland.'

The Reverend Mother bowed her head. 'At least no one was killed by that explosion on Spike Island,' she said.

'You guessed that was it, did you?' Eileen looked at her with an admiration that amused the Reverend Mother.

She shook her head at her former pupil. 'Don't tell me anything about the explosion,' she warned. 'I would not put either you or your mother in the slightest danger. Just tell me about those Gaelic League classes at Scoil Ide. You weren't present, were you?'

Eileen shook her head, one of those quick, impatient move-ments that reminded the Reverend Mother of the bright little girl who was always three steps ahead of anyone else in the class. 'No, I'm busy in the evenings now. I'm trying to earn some extra money for university by doing typing at home. But I know someone, his name is Raymond, and he went there. I got it out of him. He told me that Miss MacSwiney took a great fancy to Sister Joan, your novice. She knew a lot of Irish and she was very patriotic. That's what Raymond told me. He said that Miss MacSwiney started to give her private lessons, conversation lessons, they were supposed to be, down in her sitting room.'

'Raymond,' queried the Reverend Mother slowly. Someone had been talking to her recently about someone called Raymond. Who could it have been? And then she remembered. Her cousin Lucy had been talking about her granddaughter. Something about an unsuitable young man. Aloud she said, 'What's this young man's name?'

'It's Raymond Roche,' said Eileen. 'He's very posh. Got pots of money.'

'Raymond Roche,' repeated the Reverend Mother. Yes, that was the name. The Roche family would have 'pots of money' and would, she thought, certainly be deemed by Eileen to be 'posh', but according to her cousin Lucy the young man himself had no money at all. However, Lucy would be visiting her tomorrow and so she put the question about this young man to one side and went back to the private lessons given to Sister Joan.

'So Miss Mary MacSwiney gave lessons to Sister Joan by herself. Sister Brigid and Sister Gertrude were not present?'

'No, not them. They stayed with the rest of the class. Raymond said that Sister Gertrude wasn't very interested in learning Irish and that she kept asking what was the point and Miss Annie MacSwiney got very annoyed with her and told her not to bother coming if she felt like that. Mind you,' said Eileen sagely, 'I don't know what Raymond was doing there. He doesn't know a word of Irish, even went to school in England, so I don't know what on earth he was doing there. I expect it was a recruiting job. Tom Hurley sent him there to recruit some new people for the cause. Raymond does everything that Tom Hurley tells him to do. He'd be in his pay is what I reckon.'

The Reverend Mother compressed her lips with exasperation. If only she had made some searching enquiries about these Irish classes. She had been too busy with raising funds to employ a teacher specially qualified in the teaching of reading. That had been a driving ambition for her during the past weeks and she had just absent-mindedly seen the young novices off and then welcomed them back, expressed vague hopes that they had enjoyed themselves and had found the classes interesting. Looking back over it now, she remembered that Sister Gertrude had been hesitant over her answers and would no doubt have opened up if questioned.

'I was always too anxious to get onto money matters with her,' she said half to herself and then when Eileen looked at her in a slightly startled manner, she said, 'I relied on Sister Gertrude to keep an eye on the other two. She was a good four or five years older than them and she had been out in the world. I could not have imagined that she would have condoned any business like pretending to collect for the Foreign Missions. They had boxes under their beds, you know. Perfect replicas of the real thing. No money in them.'

'No, of course,' said Eileen. 'They were only a front.' As usual, Eileen's mind had worked fast and she had jumped to the right conclusion. 'No one would ever worry about a couple of nuns collecting for the Foreign Missions,' she continued. 'Even if they were calling at houses that were under suspicion, no army spy or guard would take any notice at all of nuns.'

'What were they really doing?' asked the Reverend Mother, but she knew the answer to her own question. 'Delivering notes, instructions, I suppose,' she said.

Eileen nodded. 'Yes, of course,' she said. 'It was a perfect cover. Tom Hurley had to gather a gang together for the Spike Island attack. He has to stay under cover. Most of these men were under surveillance so he dared not visit them or be seen in their company. These silly girls, all dressed up in their nuns' uniform, carrying boxes, going to houses on their list, knocking at the door and delivering a letter, or giving a message. I suppose Raymond set it up. He does all that sort of thing. Tom Hurley would have sent him to those Irish classes to get hold of someone and a pair of nuns would be more than they would have hoped for. They looked such a pair of innocents,' said eighteen-year-old Eileen with a world-experienced air.

'So you think that they were inveigled into working for the rebels.'

Eileen nodded. 'They were just a godsend to Tom Hurley and their gang. No one would ever have noticed them. These nuns from the Foreign Missions; they are forever collecting. I remember them even from away back, when I was a child. I remember my poor mother saying to one of those sisters, "I've only got sixpence in the house for myself and the child." You'll excuse me, Reverend Mother,' said Eileen apologetically, 'but it really annoyed me when the nun said, "The unfortunate pagans in Africa need that sixpence more than you do." I was only ten years old at the time, but I remember shouting at her, "At least they get lots of sun in Africa; they don't have to put up with the rain and the fog!" It was pouring rain that day and we had no turf for the fire and I was really cold. The nun didn't know what to say and so I whipped out, right in front of my mother and shut the door in her face.'

The Reverend Mother smiled. 'I remember you at ten years

old, Eileen,' she said. She could imagine the scene, remembered the ten-year-old Eileen, brim-full of confidence and
already showing all the signs of a girl who might have a bright
future ahead of her. She sighed. Perhaps she had failed there,
also. Something should have been done for Eileen. She should
never have been allowed to leave school and to throw in her
lot with those misguided patriots.

'You couldn't have stopped me.' Eileen had read her mind.
'I had to learn my own way. But I am sorry about your novice.
I don't know what happened. Sister Joan was the one that had
been picked out. The one that they depended on to deliver the
letters. Raymond told me that. Sister Brigid was just a nonentity
and the other one, Sister Gertrude, was just going to be kept
out of the way. Raymond said that Miss MacSwiney, Miss
Mary MacSwiney, was going to take care of Sister Gertrude.'

The Reverend Mother thought about the matter. There were
three personalities to ponder. Sister Brigid didn't matter. She
would do what her friend, the strong-minded Sister Joan, would
instruct. But there was Sister Gertrude, clever and decisive,
used to making her way in a man's world, used to trusting her
own judgement. She had thought that Sister Gertrude would
have influence over those two young girls, barely out of school.
But she had been wrong and it had been stupid not to have
checked on how matters were progressing. Perhaps if she had
done so, Sister Gertrude might still be alive. And then there
was the enigma, there was Mary MacSwiney, the patriot, the
woman who had challenged Michael Collins and his treaty
with Britain, had even challenged Eamon de Valera himself.
The woman who was always certain that she was right. What
part had she played in the tragedy of a wasted young life?

'Miss Mary MacSwiney?' she said aloud and introduced an
interrogative note into her voice.

Eileen looked across at her, slightly unsure. 'Raymond said
that Miss Mary MacSwiney was going to take care of Sister
Gertrude; I overheard him say that to another man, another
member of the Sinn Féin party. He said *Máire*, that's what
they called her, he said that Máire, would take care of Sister
Gertrude,' she repeated and there was a note of hesitation in
her voice, almost as though an unwelcome thought had made

its way into her mind. 'I thought that he meant that she would delay her, or send her home without the others, something like that. I don't think he meant . . . I don't think that she . . .'

And then she stopped, chin propped between thumb and first finger, thinking hard.

'Miss Mary MacSwiney has never been involved in any violence, not that I know of, Reverend Mother,' she said eventually. 'A great talker. Words are her weapons. So far as I know,' Eileen ended on a slightly unsure note. Her grey eyes were troubled as she looked across at the older woman. 'But I've learned to know that for some people the end will always justify the means,' she said after a long moment. 'She's a funny woman. She has a way of talking, of staring into your eyes. She forces people to do things, she makes them feel that they are selfish, lazy, cowardly and without principles; I've seen her at it and she has great influence over people.'

The Reverend Mother nodded. 'I understand. Now, Eileen, I won't detain you any longer. It was very good of you to come in the middle of your working day. I hope that it did not put you out in any way.'

'No, I was delivering some leaflets to Beamish & Crawford Brewery. It's only a few minutes on my bike from there to here.' Eileen's tone was lighter now, but there was something slightly hesitant about her expression. She picked up her leather helmet and tucked her long hair neatly inside, put on a pair of sheepskin gauntlets, checked her appearance in the mirror, but still she hesitated slightly, turning around when she reached the door.

'You will take care, Reverend Mother, won't you,' she said. 'Some of these Sinn Féiners can be very funny people. You want to be on your guard with them.'

The Reverend Mother bowed her head and tucked her hands into her sleeves.

'I will take the greatest care, Eileen, and thank you for your concern.'

A half an hour after Eileen had left the convent, the Reverend Mother was sitting in a taxi and on her way to Wellington Road. The words, Scoil Ide, were enough for the man and he drove up the steep incline of St Patrick's Hill and swept along Wellington Road without hesitation until he reached Belgrave Place with its terrace of houses set back from the road and within iron railings. The school was held in a three-storey terraced house set in the middle of a row of eight houses. 'Belgrave Place,' said the taxi driver and the Reverend Mother looked out of the window as the taxi went through the gate. There was a lawn in front of the houses, and a gravelled path around the outside of it, skirting overgrown bushes that grew unchecked between wall and road and curving around the plot of some badly-cared-for grass in the centre. The taxi swept up to number five and then slowed to a stop.

'I won't be long,' said the Reverend Mother, accepting the hand to help her out, but refusing the offer to ring the bell. She would like to be the first to see Miss MacSwiney's face, once she realized the identity of her visitor. She went to the door, pressed the bell while the taxi driver went back to his seat and almost immediately it was opened to her.

'And what can I do for you, Mother Aquinas?'

The words were abrupt, unwelcoming, unnecessarily so, thought the Reverend Mother. It would not hurt the woman to greet her politely, to ask her to come in from the heavy fog that cast a pall over everything and, in a ghostly way, seemed to cut off the tops of the terraced houses and the crowns of the bushes that dotted the communal garden behind her. She waited on the doorstep, and said nothing for the moment. A girl dressed in the St Ita's brown gymslip and carrying a heavy bag of books was coming down the hallway. The Reverend Mother waited until she murmured a farewell in Gaelic and slipped past them, with a quick smile for her headmistress. Even after she had gone on her way, though, there was a silence between the two women. Eventually the Reverend Mother broke it.

'May I come in, Miss MacSwiney? I don't think that this is a matter to discuss on the doorstep, do you?' The Reverend Mother was pleased to hear how firm her voice sounded. After all, she said to herself, age has its privileges. She was a good thirty years older than the woman in front of her.

Strange-looking woman, Mary MacSwiney. Dressed all in

black. Had done so ever since the death of her brother four years ago. A terrible death. Terence MacSwiney had starved himself to death in a British prison, had spent seventy-four days voluntarily denying himself of food and the enormity of those seventy-four days of agony was something that could barely be contemplated, even by someone who had never known the man. For his devoted sister, who had supported him in his iron-hard resolution, it had become the central part of her life and had filled her with a terrible bitterness and an overwhelming desire to create the Ireland for which her brother had died.

But not by using my novices as tools, thought the Reverend Mother as, still uninvited, she stepped into the narrow hallway and closed the door behind her. A narrow strip of drugget led towards an uncarpeted wooden staircase and on the right hand side there were two closed doors, painted white, painted a long time ago, judging by the scuff marks. As the Reverend Mother hesitated, still waiting for an invitation, the first door opened and a woman came out. Annie, she thought. The younger sister. Very much in Mary's shadow. Copied her in every way. Dressed in the same funereal black. She gave a brief, slightly hunted glance at the Reverend Mother, inclined her head and then hurried down the back passageway, towards the kitchen, probably.

'Shall we go in here?' enquired the Reverend Mother. The door had been left ajar and she could see that a small fire burned in the narrow grate. This must be the sitting room for the two sisters and, perhaps, for the teachers in the school. The table by the window was weighed down by copy books, essays for marking, no doubt. A good school, she reminded herself. Parents spoke highly of the MacSwiney sisters, of how they made learning interesting, inculcated a love of poetry, of Shakespeare, an appreciation of art and of music. The girl who had been leaving had been respectful, but not subservient in any way, had smiled almost affectionately at her headmistress. And by all accounts the pupils were happy in the school.

Nevertheless . . . She said the word silently in her mind and waited for the reluctant invitation to take a seat by the fire.

'You hold the Gaelic League classes here, or upstairs?' The

stony face opposite to hers did not encourage genial conversation, but the Reverend Mother was determined to get to the bottom of the matter. *Mary MacSwiney knows all about it.* The words came to her mind and she knew them to be true. There was a defensiveness about the woman that was revealing.

'Not that it matters,' she went on smoothly when an answer did not seem to be forthcoming. 'What bothers me is that two of my novices were recruited to act a lie, to bring collecting boxes to houses when they were not authorized to do so.'

'No money changed hands.' The lined face opposite to hers wore a flush of anger.

'So what was the purpose of equipping Sister Joan and Sister Brigid with those very authentic-looking boxes with Foreign Missions written on them?'

There was no answer to this and she did not expect one.

'Do you deny that my novices were used to deliver letters for the purpose of organizing a crime? And that you talked Sister Joan into acting a lie by carrying those collecting boxes for the Foreign Missions. You agree that you organized that, don't you?' She did not really expect an answer and did not wait long for one. '*Qui tacet consentit,*' she said sharply. If the sentence was good enough for Sir Thomas More to assume that *he who is silent gives consent*, it was good enough for the Cambridge educated woman sitting opposite to her, but Mary MacSwiney still preserved her silence. The Reverend Mother felt a rising tide of anger well up within her and decided not to control it.

'By Heaven, if I don't get an answer to my questions, Miss MacSwiney, I shall go straight to the bishop himself,' she said angrily. 'You are used to defying the civil authorities, but I don't think that you will defy the bishop. This was an abominable thing to do and you know it. You involved two very young girls, two young novices, in nefarious doings where they could have been shot or imprisoned. You did not consult me or ask my permission, did you?'

'Younger than they have been involved in the struggle to free Ireland from Britain.' The woman had broken her silence at last and there was a contemptuous note in her voice. She shrugged the thin shoulders beneath the black silk shawl that she wore over her black dress. Black upon black, black from shoulders to feet, just as though she were newly widowed. A virgin widow, mourning for a brother, living off his memory, using the sacrifice of his life as a means to extract money from America and devotion and service from the young of her own country. What had been said to those two silly girls that had made them consent to that lie? 'She has a way of talking, of staring into your eyes,' had said Eileen. 'She forces people to do things, she makes them feel that they are selfish, lazy, cowardly and without principles; I've seen her at it and she has great influence over people.'

Well, thought the Reverend Mother, *you can stare into my eyes as much as you like, but I'm too old a bird to be influenced by a narrow zealot such as you, Miss MacSwiney.* She made no answer to the comment from the woman, just waited quietly.

'If you want to, you may withdraw them from the classes,' said the woman, angrily. 'I suppose that you have supreme authority over them. You can take Sister Gertrude, too, if you wish. She has neither interest nor aptitude.'

'Sister Gertrude is dead,' said the Reverend Mother. And then she said no more. She watched the woman narrowly. That last comment had been a surprise; the woman had started; one involuntary movement, perhaps, but perhaps not. Was it a subterfuge? Was she as ignorant as she pretended or had she known of the death of the young nun? Had she heard the news? Possibly. In any case, after the first movement, there was no reaction to her words. The straight mouth had not opened, and the stony grey eyes were still expressionless. The woman sat very still for a few moments, sat as though turning over the matter in her mind.

'You sound almost as though you are blaming me for that death, Reverend Mother,' she said eventually. 'I am, naturally, very sorry to hear it but it can have nothing to with the classes which Sister Gertrude attended here.'

'That, of course, will be a matter for the police to decide,' said the Reverend Mother. It was interesting, she thought, that Miss MacSwiney had not enquired into the reason for the death, had not exclaimed in horror or in surprise, but had immediately switched into defensive mode. 'She fell ill shortly after her return from your premises.' Not even that assertion caused any change to come over the immobile face opposite to her.

'I cannot see that can have anything to do with our classes. We do not make a habit of providing refreshments. She ate nothing here. I really cannot see, Mother Aquinas, why you have come to me.'

'I came to find out what had happened. You managed, neatly, to separate the two younger girls from the older one on whom I relied. You kept Sister Gertrude back, kept her here in your sitting room. You made sure that the younger girls were released well before Sister Gertrude could chaperone them on their way back to the convent, sent them on their way with collecting boxes for the Foreign Missions and, of course, letters to be delivered to certain houses. You subverted my novices, involved them in a dangerous game.' The Reverend Mother leaned back into her chair and allowed her four sentences to hang in the air. She had delivered them as shots from the barrel of a gun, she thought with satisfaction.

And then she thought of the woman's words. *We do not make a habit of providing refreshments. She ate nothing here.* This would be the truth. Mary MacSwiney would not lie over a matter so easily disproved by a simple enquiry . . . but the word that she had used was *ate. She ate nothing.* Refreshments. Eating and drinking.

The Reverend Mother's eye went to the heavy old-fashioned sideboard placed against a side wall. On top of it was an unlocked tantalus and snugly arranged on it were three decanters, labelled in ornate copperplate lettering. *Raspberry Cordial, Cherry Cordial* and the third was *Elderberry Cordial.* The decanters matched exactly, except that the red liquid in the raspberry cordial and the cherry cordial reached right up as far as the stopper, but the purple syrup in the third decanter was barely at the shoulder of the glass container. It looked as though a drink or two had been poured out from the elderberry cordial. Yes, she was sure that no lie had been told, that Sister Gertrude had not eaten while she was here at St Ita's school.

But had she taken something to drink?

'A sweet flavour,' had said Dr Scher. An alcohol used in factories to thin liquids, used in window cleaning products and other polishes, used in various fluids, almost caused the death of a young boy, poor child, who had relished the sweet taste and who had to have the deadly liquid pumped from his stomach. The sweet flavour would disguise the poison, would be easily hidden if introduced to something similarly sweet. Sister Bernadette made elderberry cordial for a Christmas treat, sending her young helpers out into the nearby lane to pick the fruits in early September. The Reverend Mother did not care for it much, but took a ritual few drops every Christmas morning. Yes, it had always been intensely sweet. There was no doubt in her mind that elderberry cordial, innocuous though the non-alcoholic liquid would seem, could conceal any other similarly sweet liquid. How easy it would be to offer a glass to Sister Gertrude, a girl who loved anything sweet and had confessed that the hardest thing she found about life in the convent was the deprivation of her previous daily indulgence in sweets and chocolates. She would be unable to resist it.

The Reverend Mother removed her gaze from the sideboard. She would say nothing, ask no further questions. The enquiry into Sister Gertrude's death would, by now, be in the hands of Inspector Patrick Cashman. It was not for her to meddle and to risk the destroying of evidence. She got to her feet decisively.

'I think, Miss MacSwiney, that you will not be surprised to hear that I am about to withdraw permission for any of my novices to attend the Gaelic League classes here. If they need to study Irish, then they will have to make do with books for the moment, until they attend their regulation teacher training classes. I make the strongest possible complaint to you about the use of these young girls to carry out nefarious and illicit activities, but will say no more now until the police enquiry is completed. And now I wish you good day. Those Foreign Missionary boxes will be burned. And I hope that never again will you make use of young and innocent girls, or boys, in order to carry out errands which might place them or others in danger of death.'

ELEVEN

St Thomas Aquinas
*Ad tertium dicendum quod omnia studia humanarum
actionum, si ordinentur ad necessitatem praesentis
vitae secundum rationem rectam, pertinent ad vitam
activam, quae per ordinatas actiones consulit
necessitati vitae praesentis.*
(All the occupations of human actions, if directed to
the requirements of the present life in accord with
right reason, belong to the active life which provides
for the necessities of the present life by means of
well-ordered activity.)

'Goodness, gracious, Reverend Mother, nobody would ever think that you are a holy nun. You forever have your head stuck in columns of figures or sheets of bank statements. You should be praying and leaving all that sort of thing to God, shouldn't she, Sister Bernadette?' scolded Lucy as she came in, looking her usual well-groomed, well-dressed self, carrying an elegantly tied cake box in one hand and an expensive handbag in the other.

'What's the cake for?' asked the Reverend Mother, ignoring the criticism, hoping that Sister Bernadette would not be offended if Lucy took to bringing her own cake when she arrived for tea. The lay sister had looked somewhat flustered as she hesitated at the doorway before proffering the usual refreshments and had hovered, looking rather uncertain. But that may have been just because she was embarrassed at the very idea that she should comment on how the Reverend Mother should spend her time.

'Emergency provisions,' said Lucy. 'I'm not staying. My granddaughters are giving me a surprise party. They're doing all the cooking themselves; apparently it's going to be all the things that I used to make for them when they were little girls.

Oh, Sister Bernadette. Such fun! A surprise party for my wedding anniversary. I've come to persuade your Reverend Mother to come with me. Do tell her that she must come.'

'How do you know about this party if it's supposed to be a surprise?' The Reverend Mother cast a look at her bank statements. It would, she thought, be tempting to abandon them for a few hours. Sister Bernadette was now happily beaming encouragement, but stopped short of telling her superior what to do. The decision had to be hers. The figures wouldn't silently steal away just because she abandoned them, but perhaps a fresh mind would make matters seem more possible.

'Because my daughter Anne is sensible enough to know that surprise parties are something that should be inflicted only on one's greatest enemies,' said Lucy tartly. 'Now do come. They are expecting you, too. Anne told them that I would be collecting you for an afternoon visit so at this very moment, they will all be flying around, setting the table and getting everything ready. If things are too bad then we have this to eat afterwards.' She dangled the cake daintily from one fingertip.

'Well, if I can't make ends meet, I shall refer the bishop to you,' said the Reverend Mother, putting back her pen on its stand and rising to her feet. She did want to talk with Lucy about that unsuitable suitor for her granddaughter's hand. No doubt, once justice was done to the girls' efforts, then they would be able to have a private conversation.

The prosperous suburb of Montenotte, where the wealthy of Cork built their mansions, was placed on a hill high above the city and on this day, as on many others, the fog thinned as the chauffeur drove up the steep road. When they reached Lucy and Rupert's home the sun shone on its stone walls and its well-groomed garden and the Reverend Mother sighed with pleasure as she accepted the chauffeur's supporting arm to lever herself out of the car.

'What a lovely place to live,' she said. 'The air feels so different.'

'Look at the heads in the window,' said Lucy, hastily bestowing her cake box upon the chauffeur with a murmured instruction. 'Now, Reverend Mother, put on your most surprised expression.'

Lucy had six granddaughters altogether: three from her daughter Susan and three from her daughter Anne and all were there, peeping from the window. As soon as the Reverend Mother and Lucy came through the front door, they swarmed around, calling out congratulations and good wishes and expressing, slightly to the Reverend Mother's surprise, great pleasure on seeing her, also. There were, she noticed quickly, several young men in the background and she wondered whether one of them was Raymond Roche.

'Anne is so worried about her youngest, Charlotte,' said Lucy. 'That awful young man, Raymond Roche. Nothing wrong with the Roche family, of course. Would have been very suitable if it had been one of the other boys, but not Raymond.'

At the time the Reverend Mother had listened absent-mindedly. She had, she considered, more to trouble her than worries about suitable young men for Lucy's granddaughters, but now, after Eileen's words, she eyed the line of young men with interest. All of them well-dressed, well-groomed, hair well-smoothed down with a lavish use of pomade and hands well-manicured. Under the instructions of the eldest grand-child, Angela, all were singing a Happy Anniversary version of the 'Happy Birthday' song before ushering them both into the dining room. Lucy, who was an actress, swooned into her husband's arms at the sight of the table. The girls all laughed, one of the young men clapped a tribute and the Reverend Mother began to be glad that she had come.

The table was wonderful, all set with the memories of their childhood when their grandmother used to have parties for them. Colourful balloons tied to each chair, plates of iced fairy cakes, glass jugs of pink milk – from the queen of the fairies' very own pink cow, Lucy used to tell the little girls – and dishes piled high with jelly and with trifle. On a side table, she noticed, that there were a few bottles of pink champagne and she guessed that Rupert, like his wife, had sneaked in his own provisions for the feast.

'The Reverend Mother must sit at the head of the table,' said Lucy when the singing and the clapping had finished.

'No, indeed, certainly not. Your place is there. I shall sit here next to this young man.' It might not be Raymond, but after Eileen's story about the yacht, she had swiftly chosen the most tanned of the young men. Charlotte, Anne's youngest daughter, was on his other side, so she thought that she was probably right even before the girl had murmured an introduction. A good-looking young man, bronzed from sun and wind, brown hair with gold tints in it and an athletic frame. He very politely pulled out a chair for her and she sank down into it and eyed the tiny sandwiches with amusement. Lucy, she thought, must be a very beloved grandmother if the girls had remembered every detail of their childhood parties.

'I think that I have heard of you, Mr Roche,' she remarked. 'Some young novices of mine have surely mentioned your name, if I am not mistaken. They were attending some Gaelic League class at St Ita's School. And I believe that you were there, also.'

This took him aback. He gave a hasty glance around, tossed two tiny Marmite sandwiches into his mouth, did an unnecessary amount of chewing over them while he thought about an answer to her comment. She surveyed him with interest. He was demonstrating, she thought, a degree of alarm and discomfort, which, surely, such an innocuous pastime as learning the Irish language would not have warranted. His eyes darted around the table as if in hope of some escape.

'Irish!' exclaimed Charlotte. 'What on earth are you learning Irish for, Raymond? I thought that you said that was a complete waste of time.'

'Are you really going to Irish classes, Raymond?' Angela looked at her sister's boyfriend with an incredulous stare. 'But you were the one that laughed at the very idea of that, didn't he, John?'

The Reverend Mother sat back and enjoyed the clamour. Everyone seemed to have some recollection of a sweeping criticism voiced by the unfortunate Raymond. The interesting thing was that he appeared confused and indeed angry as past remarks of his were thrown back at him. She would have expected that a young man of his breeding and background would have had the confidence to invent some reason for his attendance at Irish classes in the MacSwiney school. Surely he could have pretended an interest in some girl, or said that he was only doing it to please his mother. But nothing like that occurred to him and he kept shouting at his friends to leave him alone.

'Oh, for heaven's sake,' he said eventually, jumping to his feet and exploding the balloon on the back of his chair with a hasty sweep of his hand. 'Shut up, John. Oh, give it a rest, Charlotte, won't you? I'm off to have a cigarette.'

'You can't do that. It'll spoil the party.' Charlotte was almost in tears and Raymond hesitated for a moment. His tanned face had flushed to a deep red and he looked both confused and angry, even, she thought, a little scared. It was time to make a diversion. She was not the only one to think that. Lucy sent a glance of appeal to her husband and Rupert went smoothly to the sideboard and popped a cork from one of the pink champagne bottles and then another and advanced on the table with a foaming bottle in each hand.

'Not for me, thank you. I shall try the pink milk; I've always wanted to know what it tastes like,' she said to Rupert as he came around with his bottles. He put down one and instead picked up the glass jug and poured a glass of the pink milk for her with great ceremony and a certain flourish, which made her suspect that he had sampled a bottle of his pink champagne before their arrival. It had been a good idea to open a bottle now, though. It had distracted attention from Raymond and the pink bubbles had a very festive appearance.

'What about you, Charlotte?' he said to his granddaughter. 'Will you have pink milk? You can't be old enough for champagne, now, can you?'

'Oh, Grandpa! I daren't taste even a drop of pink milk. None of us dare. We are all scared to try it in case it doesn't taste right now that we're all grown-up,' said Charlotte, with great presence of mind. She held out a glass for the pink champagne and smiled sweetly at her grandfather.

'Quite right,' said the Reverend Mother. 'Pink milk is only for under-sevens and over-seventies.' She said the words in her most dogmatic manner and that brought her several grateful smiles from the young ladies and there was a clamour for the bubbles.

'We're going to be playing all the old games, too, Reverend Mother. Blind Man's Bluff, Charades, Pass the Slipper, The

Minister's Cat and all those old favourites,' said Charlotte, leaning across Raymond, her hand on one of his shoulders, and nestling close against his chest. 'Don't worry,' she added, 'you, Grandma and Grandpa are just going to watch. Angela has it all organized.'

'That'll be a bit of a bore, won't it? I brought along some jazz records,' said Raymond. His voice was unnecessarily loud and he looked a challenge at his hosts.

'I think not,' said Angela, through gritted teeth.

'Oh, no, not jazz, that would spoil everything,' exclaimed Charlotte. 'We just want to have it all just as it was when we were little and Grandma had those parties for us.'

'Got to play the game the way the girls have organized it, old man,' said Rupert smoothly. Champagne bottle in hand, he ignored Raymond's outstretched glass for a second helping and went to top up his wife's supply.

And very well-organized, too, thought the Reverend Mother when the feast had finished and the games began. Angela had everything well-prepared for and never allowed tedium to creep in, as all were forced into hastily changing to a new game each time a whistle blew. The girls acted the part of six- and seven-year-old children and their boyfriends and fiancés adopted their roles with enthusiasm, Annette's young man even having a sulky tantrum, stamping his foot on the floor and saying 'not fair' in a high-pitched squeak when he was beaten by her to the last chair. Lucy, the Reverend Mother saw with affection, was completely overwhelmed by this tribute from her grand-daughters and hid her face in her handkerchief to hide her tears. Rupert poured more champagne and Angela's fiancé, one of the Dwyers, organized the singing of 'For She's a Jolly Good Fellow!' and the anniversary event ended with laughter.

'What lovely girls. You must be very proud of your grand-daughters, Lucy.' The Reverend Mother paid the compliment sincerely when she and Lucy retired to the little back sitting room leaving the dining room and drawing room to the young people.

'Well, I'm a very lucky woman,' said Lucy. 'And they all seemed to have chosen such suitable and charming young men, don't they, all except Charlotte. Oh, dear, I'm so worried about her, Dottie. But wasn't it kind of Angela! She arranged it all, of course. She's grown into a thoroughly nice girl. Going to be married this summer. A nice boy, one of the Dwyers. Joined in everything.'

'And what about Charlotte?' The Reverend Mother thought that they could move on to that subject while Lucy fortified herself with a choice specimen from the Campbell cakes and a good strong cup of tea.

Lucy grimaced. 'Anne is so worried about her. We're all worried. That awful young man. Did you see him? Turned his nose up at everything. Wanted to play some of that awful jazz again and again, kept bringing it up. Anne said that he sulked a bit to Angela, but she was firm with him. "This is Granny's party." That's what she said to him. "There was no jazz around when we were little and we agreed that it was going to be just the same as the parties that Granny used to organize for us. Raymond, you will just have to do without that jazz." Told him that he could put those records back in the car. Anne told me it all.'

'One of the Roches, isn't he? Some sort of trouble with him, wasn't there?' The Reverend Mother wasn't sure of her ground, but decided that there usually was some sort of trouble in the upbringing of these young men from rich families.

'Drugs,' hissed Lucy. 'The Roches were in a terrible state. They stopped his allowance so that he couldn't pop over to London for supplies, but it did no good. He's still finding the money from somewhere. Goodness knows from where. But he's still going over there. Rupert had a strong word with Anne only the other day. "Don't fancy any granddaughter of mine being mixed up with that young man," that's what he said to her. "He's a problem to the Roches, Anne; make sure that he doesn't become a problem to you and Henry." And, of course, Anne comes crying to me. "As if parents nowadays have any control over their children." Apparently Charlotte has threatened to run away from home if she is not allowed to see him. And she's only eighteen years old. And with her looks she could marry anyone. Not that there's anything wrong with the Roches. All in all, it would be a good match if it was a different young man. One of the younger boys, perhaps, as I said to you, before. But not Raymond.'

The Reverend Mother thought about what Eileen had told her. Was it in confidence? Probably not. Anyway, she knew very little, but a hint would be enough to set the girl's grandfather on the trail. Lucy's husband, Rupert Murphy, a solicitor with a large practice, had a reputation of knowing everything that was going on in the city of Cork.

'I've heard a rumour that Raymond Roche might be mixed up with some Sinn Féin activity,' she said cautiously.

Lucy looked at her sharply. 'How did you hear that?' she asked. And, then: 'Don't tell me. I suppose it was that little girl, the one who is saving up to qualify as a lawyer. You wouldn't believe it but my husband is soft enough to give her documents to copy in the evening. I suppose she told you.'

'My source was reliable.' The Reverend Mother decided not to confirm or to deny. Eileen, she thought, was reliable and this young Raymond Roche sounded a most unsuitable husband for Lucy's granddaughter. 'Three of my novices were going for lessons in the Irish language to St Ita's School and it now appears that there may have been a connection between a harmless activity such as language learning and a less harmless involvement in passing messages for rebel activity.'

She would say no more, she thought, but Lucy was owed a warning. It would be a tragedy if Charlotte, young and silly, but with a kind heart, should get involved with a young man who might well be arrested and put on trial.

'Tell me about drugs, Lucy,' she said humbly. 'I don't think that they were around when we were young, were they? The worst that seemed to happen then was that someone got tipsy on champagne.'

'Came from America,' said Lucy dismissively. 'Like that awful jazz. Cocaine. People take it, so they say, because it makes you feel great. They get a "high", so I hear.'

'And then a "low", I suppose,' put in the Reverend Mother.

Lucy looked at her suspiciously. 'You seem to know a lot about it,' she said. 'Yes, as you say. Then they get a "low", and so they can't wait to get "high" again and so it goes on. The more they have; the more they crave. One of the Crawfords became addicted. They had to ship him off to Switzerland for a cure. Cost them a mint of money.'

'Talking of money, I presume this stuff is expensive. What does this young man do for a living?'

'He doesn't,' said Lucy succinctly. 'He's supposed to be a student. Hangs around the university. Was supposed to be studying medicine, but I don't think that he has got much further than the first year of medicine.'

'How does the young man afford to purchase cocaine, then?' The Reverend Mother thought that she probably knew the answer to her own question and so she answered it almost without a pause. 'I suppose that he could get it from Sinn Féin if he gave them good service, afforded them an easy way onto Spike Island, for instance.'

'Spike Island?' Rupert had come in, still bearing the bottle of pink champagne. 'You've heard that he was mixed up in that business.' This was a statement, though his first utterance had been a question. Rupert had a quick mind. And a multiplicity of sources of information. Now he abandoned his champagne and his glass and looked soberly from his wife to her cousin. 'This is a bit of a mess,' he said soberly. 'Anne and Henry are just going to have to put their foot down. Send that girl off to finishing school in Switzerland or something like that.'

'I'd prefer that this confidence of mine was not mentioned to the police,' said the Reverend Mother.

'Young Eileen, I suppose,' said Lucy from behind her hand to her husband.

'I wouldn't like to upset the Roche family,' said Rupert. 'Nice family. Just want to keep that young fellow away from my granddaughter. I think I'll have a word with Henry.'

'And Anne,' said Anne's mother.

'And Anne,' amended Rupert. 'And one of the Roche family, too.'

'Saying what?' enquired the Reverend Mother. 'To the Roche family, I mean.'

'Saying that I had heard a rumour that he was involved in the Spike Island affair. Saying that they should ship the young man out of the country. Send him off to Switzerland for a cure or something like that.'

The Reverend Mother considered this. If a girl had been poisoned, then her murderer should be arraigned for the crime, not shipped off to the continent, just because he belonged to a rich family.

'I'm very concerned about the death of Sister Gertrude,' she said soberly and saw the two faces swing instantly around to face hers. To Rupert, she said, 'Lucy has told you about my young novice, hasn't she?' before continuing. 'Raymond Roche may have been involved in the employment of the two younger novices to pass messages. And in that case, Sister Gertrude, who was so much older and so much more mature, might have picked up what was going on . . .' She stopped there. Without betraying confidences, from Patrick and from Eileen, she could go no further. It was enough, though. She could see that from the glances exchanged between husband and wife.

'Sister Gertrude was poisoned at some time during the evening before her death,' she said. 'She had an early supper, and then left the convent in the company of Sister Joan and Sister Brigid. She attended the Gaelic League class at St Ita's School, was delayed in conversation with Miss Mary MacSwiney while the two younger novices slipped out, equipped with collecting boxes, on their errand to deliver some secret messages. She came back to the convent, was ill that evening and died the following morning. Dr Scher has found that she was poisoned with something called ethylene glycol, a form of alcohol, I gather, though not pink champagne,' she added, but neither Rupert, nor Lucy smiled. Both faces were serious and perturbed. She looked from one to the other of them.

'Is it too far-fetched to think that Raymond, at the behest of his Sinn Féin employers, might have had a hand in that poisoning?' she asked. 'Sister Gertrude, apparently, had guessed something of what was going on and had threatened the two young novices with disclosure to me. This was overheard by a fourth novice.' She would, she thought, keep the rest of that unseemly squabble to herself. Despite her endeavour to be broadminded, it still slightly shocked her to think that death threats had been bandied about by pious young ladies.

'Stranger things have happened in this city of ours,' said Rupert. He spoke lightly, but his face was very serious, very stern.

'Now I must return to my flock,' said the Reverend Mother, getting to her feet. 'Perhaps you could ring for your chauffeur, Lucy, if you will be so kind. No, Rupert, you stay here.' He had got to his feet, but she knew that all she had said had worried him deeply and that his glance had strayed a few times to the window through which several young people were to be seen clustered around a group of cars. Rupert would not be easy until he had seen Raymond Roche leave, and leave without his granddaughter.

It occurred to her, on the journey back to her convent, that Raymond Roche had a lot to lose if Sister Gertrude had uncovered the secret of his relationship with Sinn Féin. Apart from being the granddaughter of a very rich and highly respected man, Charlotte's father, also, had quite a fortune. A young man with expensive tastes, and no visible means of support, might do a lot to ensure that his secret would not be uncovered. Murder, she speculated as the chauffeur swung smoothly on to the Western Road, might come easily to one whose moral fibre was undermined by the use of drugs.

TWELVE

St Thomas Aquinas
Quia parvus error in principio magnus est in fine
(Because a small mistake in the beginning is a big
one at the end.)

The Reverend Mother was in her room with poor Kitty O'Callaghan, a former pupil, when Dr Scher arrived in answer to her summons. Sister Catherine had been so distraught on that morning that eventually the Reverend Mother had decided that bed was the best thing for her and then reluctantly telephoned for Dr Scher.

'I'm so sorry to trouble you,' she said when he arrived. She took him into one of the parlours but did not offer the usual refreshments. Her mind was on Kitty who needed her help. She did not want to leave the poor woman alone for too long. 'It's Sister Catherine. She became quite hysterical and just will not stop crying. These young girls are such a responsibility,' she said and was conscious of a fretful, impatient note in her voice. 'She is talking about suicide. She is convinced that Sister Gertrude's death can be laid at her doorstep.' Odd, she thought, how Sister Catherine, in her mind, was a young girl and Kitty O'Callaghan a woman. And yet they were of the same age. She remembered the day, fourteen years ago, when Kitty had come to school, running in through the gates ahead of her two elder sisters. A pretty little girl then, full of life and fun.

'Suicide!' Dr Scher raised a sceptical eyebrow. 'Does she say why?'

'She weeps when I ask her. I'd be grateful if you would see her.' The Reverend Mother gave him a hasty nod and rang the bell to summon Sister Mary Immaculate to escort him to the novices' dormitory before going back to Kitty. She saw his face look somewhat surprised at her abruptness and knew that he had noted the lack of sympathy in her voice. And, of course, her voice, she recognized, mirrored her inner feelings. She was not sympathetic towards Sister Catherine, although she tried to be understanding. Sitting in her room at the moment was a woman whose twin boys had died that morning of measles and who wanted the Reverend Mother to tell their four-year-old sister what had happened to her baby brothers. That woman, too, had been weeping, but her efforts to control herself, her thought for the little girl had wrung the Reverend Mother's heart.

'If you could just tell her,' had said Kitty, between sobs. 'You'll do it better than I can. You'll make a nice little story out of it, tell her about Baby Jesus and about the angels in heaven. I can only think of my two babies being put into the wet earth, and, and, and what happens next . . . I know I'd break down and upset her. Poor little mite. Don't mind me, Reverend Mother, and don't sympathize with me. I can't bear anyone to say anything to me now. I can't even face my own daughter. Give me an hour or two and I'll be myself again.'

These were her words, and the Reverend Mother was not surprised to find her room empty by the time she returned. Kitty had not wanted sympathy for herself, had thought only of her daughter, had entrusted that task to the Reverend Mother and now she had gone back to the dead bodies of her two little boys. Nineteen years old. The Reverend Mother remembered her so distinctly at the same age as her daughter was now, could picture Kitty O'Callaghan coming into the same classroom, being taught by the same nun. She had left less than ten years later, become pregnant, had hastily married and then been deserted once there were three small children to look after. The Reverend Mother sighed to herself, gathered her thoughts and then went in search of the remaining member of poor Kitty's family.

She had told her story, seen the little girl happily ensconced with a few best friends, drawing a picture of her baby brothers playing with a prettily crowned Jesus, using Sister Philomena's special crayons, while one friend undertook to do the angels and the other, having said modestly that she was no good at drawing faces, had promised that she would do enough clouds for them all to bounce upon. By the time that she left the children, Dr Scher was back downstairs again, standing in the hallway, talking with Inspector Cashman.

The Reverend Mother's heart sank. This was an official police visit. A young girl, in her care, had died and it did appear as if her death were connected with the convent.

'Go in, Patrick,' she said. 'I just want a word with Dr Scher.' One matter at a time, she told herself as she turned an enquiring face towards him. 'How is Sister Catherine?' she asked, doing her best to keep a note of exasperation from her voice.

'I've given her a mild sedative,' he answered. 'She seems very upset, but it's hard to know with hysterics. It is often an attempt to gain sympathy. Once she's had a sleep, I'd try to get her out of bed. Send her out to dig the garden, something like that. No praying or thinking about her sins, no discussing her feelings or having people be sorry for her.'

'I don't think that she would appreciate being made to dig the garden,' said the Reverend Mother with a wry smile.

'Convent life doesn't suit everyone,' said Dr Scher. To the Reverend Mother's ear, he seemed to be picking his words with care. 'Girls of that age, well, if you look at your young friend Eileen, out strolling on the quays with her young man, buying herself pretty clothes, riding her motorbike, having fun . . . Perhaps you could build a tennis court for your young novices. Get them some fresh air, some fun.'

'I've enough urgent causes on which to spend my money,' said the Reverend Mother curtly. Her thoughts went to poor Kitty O'Callaghan. Children got measles, it was part of childhood. Her cousin Lucy's children and grandchildren had measles, she seemed to remember that all had measles, round about the same time, picked up at a children's party. But none of them died of it. They were all attended by a doctor, given medicine, put to bed in warm rooms, cared for. The children of the poor did not have those privileges and yet, why not? Why should life and death be decided by the contents of a purse? Her heart hardened. Yes, Dr Scher was right. Convent life did not suit everyone. The problem that Sister Catherine posed would have to be faced sooner rather than later. The novice had no interest in the work that they did, shrank from dirty children, expressed open disgust for their unwashed smell, had little desire to teach; shuddered at caring for the sick old geriatric nuns, fainted at the sight of blood and so was quite unsuited to a nursing life. I'll have to have a strong word with the bishop, she thought, mentally practising the phrase used by Dr Scher: *Convent life doesn't suit everyone, my lord. Our medical attendant feels that Sister Catherine is not suited to our kind of life. Perhaps a contemplative order. But in the meantime, an interval at home to allow her to regain her health and her spirits.* Cheered by that decision she turned to Dr Scher.

'Let's join Patrick,' she said. 'I know that you are dying to poke up my fire and Sister Bernadette has left you some specially brewed tea.'

As soon as the two men were supplied with refreshments, she wasted no time in procrastination. If this crime was to be located in the convent, she needed to know all of the facts as soon as possible.

'How many hours between Sister Gertrude's death and swallowing this poison, Dr Scher?'

'It depends,' he said cautiously. 'She may not have swallowed it all at once, and she did have a good meal which complicates matters, but I'll stick to my first guess. I'd say not earlier than about five o'clock on the day before her death, probably later.'

The Reverend Mother thought about this. It was as he had first said. It seemed to pitch the ingesting of the poison firmly into something eaten in the convent, or else during the session at St Ita's School, during the Gaelic League classes.

'Perhaps you could give me an outline of Sister Gertrude's last day, Reverend Mother?' Patrick had seen the significance of Dr Scher's answer. He had his notebook out and she did her best to remove the thoughts of poor Kitty and the two little dead boys from her mind for the moment.

'Sister Gertrude spent most of the morning in here with me, sorting out my accounts, checking balances and doing something called a Standard Cost Accounting Sheet for the bishop's secretary,' she began. For a moment she could hardly go on. The girl had been so cheerful, so competent, so full of life and youthful energy, joking about the bewilderment that the bishop's secretary would experience when faced with a medley of accountancy jargon. 'Efficiency variance, budget variances, overheads variance, reconciliations, we'll hit him with some of that sort of stuff and he won't have a word to say,' she had said and the recollection of the alert face and confident voice brought the loss home to her with an unexpected poignancy. 'She ate dinner with the rest of the congregation,' she continued when she had control over her voice. 'After dinner she did a spell of teaching in one of the classrooms, and then, when school was finished, her sister came to see her. They walked in the garden together for half an hour. I saw her again for just a few minutes after her sister left.'

Odd that the sister, Betty, had not been to the convent since the news of the death, had not come to enquire about funeral arrangements. This thought suddenly popped into the Reverend Mother's head and she frowned a little. Perhaps she was too upset, but it was a little strange. Was there some bad feeling? Was the husband's excessive display of hysterical grief enough to cause jealousy, even of the dead, in his wife?

'And what time did her sister leave the convent, Reverend Mother?' Patrick's quiet voice interrupted her thoughts and she cast her mind back to that day.

'It would have been about four o'clock,' she said. 'The four novices had an early supper. Sister Joan, Sister Brigid and Sister Gertrude had to be at St Ita's School for their Irish lessons by five o'clock and Sister Catherine had her supper with them.' What did Sister Catherine do while the other three went off together, she wondered then? Prayed, probably. She should probably have insisted that she joined in with her fellow novices, but originally it had just been Sister Joan and Sister Brigid. Sister Gertrude had been a last minute addition, a sop to their Mistress of Novice's scruples about unchaperoned young girls in the company of young men. Sister Catherine, she had thought at the time, would merely be another compli-cation. 'Yes,' she said aloud. 'They had their supper at about four o'clock and then they walked through the city. The classes

finished at around seven in the evening and then they came
back here.'

'Did they have anything else to eat when they came back?'
asked Patrick.

'Not officially,' said the Reverend Mother, 'but I did notice
one evening before prayers that the three of them emerged
from the kitchen and that Sister Joan had traces of chocolate
around her mouth. I suspect that Sister Bernadette may have
had a mug of cocoa for them after their walk.'

Dr Scher grinned appreciatively while Patrick solemnly
made another note. Cocoa, of course, was sweet, if well
sugared. Not as sweet as treacle, she thought then. She
wondered whether to send for Sister Bernadette, but decided
to leave the matter unless Patrick brought it up again. And if
he did so, she would suggest that he popped into the kitchen.
It would be best if he interviewed Sister Bernadette on her
own territory and without the presence of her Reverend Mother
and then she could remain officially unaware of this use for
the cocoa which was supposed to be solely for the comforting
of aged and senile nuns in the convent's sick ward. She waited
for him to finish his note and braced herself for the next
question.

'Do you know of anyone who might have had a motive to
kill Sister Gertrude, Reverend Mother, or even to wish harm
to come to her? Was anyone in the community angry with her,
jealous of her, or afraid of her in any way?' Dr Scher, too,
was looking at her, but she did not answer Patrick's question
straightaway. Should Sister Catherine's absurd self-recriminations
be introduced at this stage?

'You see,' said Patrick apologetically, 'I usually start thinking
about who might have profited from a death, but in this
case with Sister Gertrude as a nun, well, she would have no
money, that's right, isn't it, Reverend Mother?'

'That's right. If a nun, or even a novice, inherits any money,
then that becomes the property of the order to which they
belong. On entering the convent, the postulants take a vow of
holy poverty,' confirmed the Reverend Mother, thinking, once
again with a tinge of regret, of what half of Mr Donovan's
'tidy sum of money' could have meant to the convent.

'"There is no art to find the mind's construction in the face",' she said eventually. 'You ask about emotions. Well, I can only tell you that despite the wimple and veil, we are ordinary women here and there may have been jealousy among the novices at the perceived privileges that Sister Gertrude had by working in here so closely with me. In addition, Sister Catherine . . .' And here she paused, feeling somewhat disloyal. She looked towards Dr Scher thinking that he might finish her sentence, but then remembered that he would be bound by some oath not to reveal what a patient had said to him and so she continued, 'In addition, Sister Catherine reported that Sister Joan and Sister Brigid had threatened to kill Sister Gertrude if she told me of how they had got involved in some Sinn Féin, anti-treaty activity. Sister Catherine feels guilty that she did not bring all of this to my notice . . .' The Reverend Mother tailed off her sentence, thinking how very strange all of this was, in connection with a convent and its demure set of novices and then she thought of Mary MacSwiney. Anger lent her fluency and so she continued. 'These are the facts, Patrick. Unfortunately, one of my novices, Sister Joan, fell under the spell of Miss Mary MacSwiney, who I understand is, during the absence of Eamon de Valera, now the head of Sinn Féin and at her bidding I understand that my two novices were despatched by her, supposedly collecting funds for the Foreign Missions, but in reality delivering letters to some who were under surveillance from the army and the police.' She saw Patrick give a sudden start, but continued her story to its end. 'I gather that Sister Gertrude found out what they were up to, threatened to tell me and in turn was threatened by them. The words were "I'll kill you", but I don't suppose,' said the Reverend Mother, hoping that she was right, 'I don't suppose that they were meant literally. Schoolgirls and -boys say that sort of thing all the time.' She looked across at Patrick. 'This means something to you, does it not, Patrick?'

'Eileen MacSweeney asked me about the surveillance of houses of men under suspicion,' he answered and she nodded, but did not comment. She wouldn't tell him about Eileen's information to her but he might well guess. Could Sister Joan and Sister Brigid possibly have carried out that schoolgirl threat? They were not schoolgirls after all, she reminded herself thinking of poor Kitty O'Callaghan, but grown women.

'There is somebody else, whose name I should mention. Somebody else who might have been alarmed at the authorities hearing of this threat,' she said, mentally sending an apology to Lucy's granddaughter, Charlotte. 'There is a young man called Raymond Roche, a young man who attends these Gaelic League classes at St Ita's. I have heard that he leads the life of a very rich young man, but is a person who has little visible means of support. He is known to visit London very frequently and a source tells me that drug-taking is suspected.' She added dryly, 'And the question is where does he find the money to pay for these visits, for his drug habit and for the yacht that he keeps moored in Cork harbour.'

'Yacht!' Patrick looked up alertly. 'He owns a yacht.' He lifted his pencil and held it poised aloft for a few moments. 'This Spike Island business. You've seen about that in the *Cork Examiner*. Some men landed on the island and set fire to an immense amount of ammunition. It was a miracle that nobody was killed,' he said slowly, his face very concentrated. 'And, of course, a yacht would have been a good way of dropping some men off at Spike Island. Especially if Mr Raymond Roche was in the habit of sailing around in that area. I wonder where he moors the yacht.' He made a quick note on a different page of his notebook and then sat back. 'Do you know,' he said thoughtfully, 'taking that in conjunction with the possibility that your novices had delivered letters to get a gang together, I think, Reverend Mother, that we might have a much better motive than schoolgirl jealousies. These people who carry out atrocities are utterly ruthless. Murder is nothing to them. As to the young man, well, I've heard a mention of Raymond Roche's name before. Just a mention. I must interview him.'

'Belongs to a very good family, of course. Property everywhere. Trabolgan, Kinsale, Rathcormac, connected with many other good Cork families, of course. The Newenhams, of course and the . . .' The Reverend Mother stopped herself abruptly. It was probably good for Patrick to know a little about the wealthy background to Cork's merchant princes, but he didn't need all of this just now. Let him do the practical work of investigating Raymond Roche.

'But how could this Raymond Roche have given Sister Gertrude anything which would make her die from alcohol poisoning?' asked Dr Scher. 'He'd have needed to give her something to eat or something to drink. No matter how liberated your novices are, Reverend Mother, I don't suppose that they would dare stop at a public house to have a drink with a young man. I'm afraid that it does look as though whatever killed Sister Gertrude was administered to her in this convent.'

The Reverend Mother thought of the tin of treacle found beneath Sister Catherine's bed, but pushed it to the back of her mind for the moment.

'There is another possibility, Dr Scher. I did notice,' she said slowly, 'that there were three decanters of fruit cordials on the sideboard of Miss Mary MacSwiney's sitting room. I observed them very carefully. All three were labelled in ornate copperplate lettering; her handwriting, I'm sure, as I noticed the same hand on the labelling of some drawers. The bottles were labelled Raspberry Cordial, Cherry Cordial and the third was Elderberry Cordial. The decanters matched exactly, except that the red liquid in the raspberry cordial and the cherry cordial reached right up as far as the stopper, but the purple syrup in the third decanter, the elderberry cordial, was barely at the shoulder of the glass container. Now fruit cordials are non-alcoholic drinks, normally made in the summer when there is a glut of such berries and then allowed to come to maturity and be served up several months later. Sister Bernadette makes them to serve to the community and their guests on Christmas day. They are non-alcoholic and, to my taste, almost unbearably sweet. The sugar, I suppose, acts as a preservative.'

'And so would be the perfect substance to conceal that ethylene glycol,' said Dr Scher enthusiastically. 'But how could this young Raymond Roche tempt Sister Gertrude into having some of the MacSwiney fruit cordials?'

'It could be done fairly easily if the mistress of the house was in on the conspiracy,' pointed the Reverend Mother and saw Patrick make another quick note before he shaped a large question mark on the top of his page. He sat back, chewing the end of his pencil for a moment and then said, with a decisiveness which surprised her, 'Well, here is a possible list of people who might have had a reason to kill Sister Gertrude: Mr Raymond Roche; Miss Mary MacSwiney; Sister Joan and Sister Brigid.' The most likely, of course, is Mr Raymond Roche, possibly in conjunction with Miss MacSwiney, but perhaps not. I shall go to see Miss MacSwiney. I can see a possibility where Mr Raymond Roche might have come into the room and poured a cordial for Sister Gertrude and managed to slip some poison into it without either of the women seeing it.'

Unlikely, thought the Reverend Mother, though she did not want to discourage him. These fruit cordials, if not yet used, were probably, like the convent's supply, designated for some modest Christmas festivities. In any case, from what she knew of Mary MacSwiney, she was not the type of woman to allow a young man to take liberties like pouring drinks without been bidden to do so.

'Could a possible murderer lay hands on this ethylene alcohol easily?' she asked aloud. 'It isn't the sort of thing that one could go into a shop and ask for, is it?'

'We don't know whether the murderer planned on using this particular stuff. But most tins that have poisonous content have the word "poison" on the back of them. You'd get it in lots of furniture polishes, shoe polish, window cleaners and paint thinners. Just something that was labelled "poison". I'd say that this might have been a random choice,' said Dr Scher and Patrick nodded his agreement while the Reverend Mother thought once more about the stolen tin of treacle from the store cupboard in the convent kitchens.

'And the sister left at four o'clock, too early, according to you, Dr Scher. And, in any case, the sister would have had no motive, would she? No inheritance, that's right, isn't it?' Patrick looked across enquiringly at the Reverend Mother.

'The father's entire fortune was left to Betty, Betty Kelly as she now is.' The Reverend Mother made the statement but she said no more. There was a question mark at the back of her mind, an uneasiness that was aroused by the excessive outpouring of grief from Denis Kelly. Surely too much grief. After all, Sister Gertrude was only a sister-in-law. Nevertheless, she did not feel justified in mentioning it now. No doubt she would see Betty once the funeral was arranged by the convent and then, perhaps, a few questions would help to make up her mind about the matter. 'No, not a penny was left to Sister Gertrude, and, of course, even if it were, her death would not benefit her sister in any way.' She added those words in an absent-minded way. It was, of course, completely possible for Sister Gertrude to leave the convent. The noviciate period was an opportunity for both convent and novice to have a change of heart. And it was not at all unknown for a young man to walk out of a marriage and take the boat to England. Did Betty have some fears about her husband's fidelity and did she wonder whether he might prefer her sister. The Reverend Mother wondered, in a cynical way, whether a blissfully happy young wife, in the first halcyon years of marriage, might easily have been talked into depositing her legacy into her husband's bank account. Girls and women, such as Betty, did not, as a rule, have their own bank accounts.

With an effort she averted her mind from this rather improbable line of enquiry. Let Patrick investigate Raymond Roche, this well-born son of a respected and affluent Cork family, let him inquire into the mooring berths of yachts at Cobh and other places within reach of Spike Island. Let Dr Scher return to lecturing the medical students at Cork University.

The Reverend Mother got to her feet. The interview was over and she was left with plenty to think about. She did not, as customary, ring the bell to summon Sister Bernadette to show the visitors out, but herself accompanied them to the front door. As she had expected, though, Sister Bernadette's quick ear had heard the sound and was at the front door before they could reach it, beaming a smile at her favourite, Dr Scher. The Reverend Mother waited patiently while they engaged in their usual banter. Her eyes were on Patrick. He was looking uncomfortable, she thought. His eyes travelled the length and breadth of the convent corridor and moved up the stairs to where there was a sound of nuns' voices. She had fobbed him off with Raymond Roche. That would be work that he was now competent to deal with, confident as well as competent. During his years of experience, Patrick had lost his awe of the gentry and was now quietly at ease while questioning them. Nuns, however, were a different matter.

And Dr Scher's professional evidence had made it highly probable that the murder had been committed within the hallowed walls of the convent. Patrick, like herself, had doubtless noted that, but she hoped that he would keep his attention on Raymond Roche for the moment.

The law of the land had to have precedence over the feelings of the cloistered, but, she told herself, it would be good for him to ascertain as much of the facts as possible before he was forced to turn his attention to the convent. She bade him farewell with a clear conscience and then lingered while Sister Bernadette picked up an errant paper bag, scanned the cleanliness of the hideously coloured glass in the front door and gave a quick polish to the shining door handle with the corner of her blue apron.

As she guessed, Sister Bernadette went back to see to the fire in her room and the Reverend Mother allowed her to riddle and add coals to her satisfaction before saying in a fairly nonchalant manner, 'You did say something about Sister Catherine, did you not, Sister Bernadette? Something about how she was upset by teasing. I think you mentioned something about a threat to tell the bishop . . . something about some secret. Poor child, she is very sensitive and perhaps Sister Gertrude, who had such a very different upbringing, upset her in some way. Was that right?'

Sister Bernadette's face brightened with relief. 'That was the way of it, Reverend Mother. "Horses for courses"; that was what my father, God have mercy on him, used to say. A nice man, he was, always very good to us all. Didn't like the city much; was brought up in the country. Worked in a stable when he was a boy and he used to say that he missed the horses. Always made the best of it, though. Got jobs down in the docks as often as he could. Could give you good advice, too. "If you fancy the life in the convent, love, well you just go ahead and make the best of it," that's what he said to me and it was good advice. I must say that I've been very happy here. I think myself very lucky.'

The Reverend Mother bowed her head. There were times when Sister Bernadette made her feel very humble.

'We have all gained from your presence,' she said. 'Your father bestowed a treasure on us.' And then, as she noticed that Sister Bernadette looked embarrassed, she said, 'But you were telling me about Sister Gertrude and Sister Catherine.'

'Just a brooch,' said Sister Bernadette dismissively. 'Just a little brooch, keeps it hidden. Just a little memory of her child-hood, I suppose. A bit scared of Sister Mary Immaculate, poor little thing. Got it inside that willow tree down by the river. Hiding it in a little hole, just like a little squirrel! I've seen her there with it some of the times when I've gone out to see if the washing is getting any dryer. She'd be holding it in her hand and letting the light flash from it.'

'I see,' said the Reverend Mother. Now she had got the information that she had sought. 'Now tell me, Sister Bernadette, how our stocks of potatoes are going. Now that we have got the children used to having a baked potato in the middle of the day, I would be very loath to run out of them when the worst of the winter weather is still to come.'

'Don't you worry about it, Reverend Mother, we had a great crop. Mr Twomey was ever so pleased. I went and checked them the other day and they're all sound. We've got them laid out on shelves in the back pantry where it's nice and cool. The only trouble is that more and more children are asking for them now that we started putting a lump of butter in them, or even a boiled egg. I was thinking that we might get a few leftovers from the market on a Saturday evening when they are cleaning up the place for the weekend. I'll have a word with the messenger boy. Just try to save our potatoes for as long as possible. I wouldn't like to deny any child of them. You never know what goes on in homes, do you, Reverend Mother. Sometimes the poorest can be looked after better than in families where the mother drinks and doesn't bother giving breakfast to the children. Well, it takes all kinds, doesn't it, Reverend Mother. Not for me to judge. We must just do the best we can with the potatoes, and perhaps a few turnips, as well.'

And Sister Bernadette took herself off happily while the
Reverend Mother remained standing absent-mindedly by
the fireplace and gazing out into the garden, once the haven
of sterile clumps of Victorian shrubs, but now laid out in neat
mounded rows, ready for the new crop of potatoes which
would be, by tradition, planted on St Patrick's Day in the
middle of March. The gardener was vigorously digging in a
wheelbarrow load of hen droppings and she watched him in
an absent-minded way as she turned over the matter of Sister
Gertrude and Sister Catherine in her mind. The rule was very
strict. When a novice took her vows, all property that had
belonged to her in secular life was completely renounced.
Somehow, though she was less shocked by Sister Catherine's
surreptitious hiding of some childhood relic than she was at
the revelation of another less pleasant aspect in Sister Gertrude's
personality. There was a whiff of bullying about it, a victim-
ization of the weak by the strong. Nevertheless, now that she
knew about this concealed brooch, it was her duty to deal with
the matter. The rules of the order had been laid down by the
sainted founder and it was not for her to bend them in any
way. The matter could be dealt with in private and might well
be a means of probing the state of mind of this troubled girl.
With a deep sigh, she decided to visit the invalid in bed.

'Good news, Sister Catherine,' she said cheerily as she came
into the novices' dormitory. 'Dr Scher is quite happy about
you and now that you've had a rest and a little sleep, he would
like you to get up and join your sisters again. Make haste now,
child, or you will be late for dinner.'

'I don't want any dinner,' said Sister Catherine.

'Nonsense,' said the Reverend Mother bracingly. 'Get up
now, my child, come downstairs and when dinner is over,
come into my room and have a chat about what might be
worrying you.'

There must, she thought as she went slowly down the stairs,
be a kind way of ending Sister Catherine's self-imposed
martyrdom without doing her any permanent harm. Or perhaps
before the girl did permanent harm to the community which
had to witness the pious giving-up of the world for the sake
of some dream of sainthood.

So long, of course, as her crime had only been something childish like concealing a brooch. If it were murder, well then . . .

Was there any possibility, she wondered as she paused at the window at the head of the flight of stairs that led up from the hallway, that the balance of Sister Catherine's mind was disturbed, that her self-accusation of the murder of Sister Gertrude was a figment of a disordered imagination? The thought comforted her. Saints, she had often thought, while listening to a reading about the lives of medieval martyrs, were often quite strange people and someone as straightforward and practical as Dr Scher might be relied upon to find some illness of the mind which might have driven a pious girl to some terrible action.

Suddenly the Reverend Mother began to feel ashamed of herself. Her patron saint, Saint Thomas Aquinas, had been quite unequivocal about murder and about what should happen to a murderer. She shuddered slightly at the recollection of the terribly harsh phrase: '*laudabiliter et salubriter occiditur*'. *Occiditur*: she was no great Latin scholar, but the word sent a shiver down her spine. It was, she thought, a terrible word. Cut down, felled, removed from life.

Almost mechanically she began to walk down the last flight of stairs. 'Father, if thou be willing, remove this cup from me: nevertheless not my will, but thine, be done,' she prayed.

THIRTEEN

W.B. Yeats
'What a man does not understand, he fears; and
what he fears, he tends to destroy.'

Eileen stopped for a moment, but then she walked on. She needed to gather her courage. I don't need to be involved in this, she thought, but she knew that long-term obligations, old affections, former assistance – all of these things were at the back of her mind. She owed the convent gratitude for an excellent education and she owed the Reverend Mother affection for the deep interest that she had taken in Eileen, encouraging her in her studies and not even losing that interest when Eileen did not take her advice about trying for a university scholarship, but instead, left school in order to join the Republicans.

The Reverend Mother, she reflected, was more worried-looking than she had ever remembered seeing her and it was important to help her to solve this strange murder. Particularly since Eileen herself had suspicions about the death of the young nun. She knew where to go for information, but she needed leverage. Rory was not the type to be impressed by her former service to the cause. Rory was a hard man, but a man who was determined to survive. No romantic business of hiding out in derelict houses, Rory ran a successful corner shop in St Mary's Isle, served cigarettes to treaty and anti-treaty supporters and kept his politics to himself. Soft talk wouldn't impress him. Only a threat would work with Rory and he was shrewd enough to evaluate a threat for what it was worth. She had to appear capable of delivering a threat to the man's security.

And for that reason she walked on briskly down Barrack Street, and then stopped when she was just outside the headquarters of the police force in Cork city.

'Oh, Patrick,' she said girlishly as he came out from the barracks. 'Isn't it a lovely day? I'd nearly forgotten what sun looked like. Are you off duty, Patrick?' She had carefully made sure that was the case, but even to her critical ear, the words sounded careless and unpractised.

He smiled down at her. Not a bad-looking fellow these days, she thought critically. He was very spotty when he was growing up and desperately shy, but now his skin had cleared and he had, oddly, even grown another inch or so taller. Or perhaps he was just holding himself so much straighter.

'And you?' he asked. 'Your half day, isn't it?'

Must be keeping an eye on her, she thought with a flicker of amusement.

'Going to treat myself to a few sweets and a visit to the cinema,' she said.

'I'll walk down with you,' he said. Very cautious type, Patrick. He would see how things went before venturing to suggest that he went with her to the cinema or anything like that, but she beamed happily at him and went back instantly to their shared memories about the convent school that they had both attended. He was laughing at her story of a prank that she and her nine-year-old friends had played on Sister Mary Immaculate, when they crossed the road to where Rory Duffy's corner shop was situated. The man himself was outside his shop, rearranging some cabbages. A favourite ploy of his when he wanted to have a word with some of his Republican friends. Messages could be passed, information exchanged while Rory removed the odd flabby leaf, or pulled an especially stout hard-hearted specimen to the forefront of his display or tied a piece of string around a job lot of cabbages, putting the best vegetable in the foremost position. He ignored her and she ignored him. She knew better than to greet him as an acquaintance when she was in the company of Inspector Cashman so she concentrated her attention on the window display.

'Oh, Patrick,' she said loudly and enthusiastically, 'look at those toffee caramels. I just adore these. Don't you love the way the runny stuff is inside the shell of the hard toffee.'

'I don't think that I've ever tasted them,' said Patrick after a moment's concentration on the window. He had not looked at Rory and so she guessed that he didn't know about him. Rory kept a very low profile and was one of the most secret of the undercover men and because of that one of the most valuable to Tom Hurley.

'Never tasted them! Oh, Patrick, Patrick! What are we to do with you?' She laughed into his face and squeezed his arm. 'Where have you lived? Well, you must have one before you are a day older!'

He bought the box, of course, paid a subservient Rory and went back out of doors with her. She made a point of opening the box at the doorway and popping the sweet into his mouth. Rory, she was certain, missed none of that intimacy, though he was now pretending to sweep the shop floor with great energy. She tucked her hand into Patrick's arm and walked away with him. As they stopped to cross the road at the bridge, she looked back. Rory was outside his shop, holding his sweeping brush idly in one hand, and his face was turned in their direction.

He was ready for her when she came back a couple of hours later, standing outside on the pavement and looking down the street. 'Enjoy the afternoon?' he asked, one bushy eyebrow raised in a quizzical fashion. He removed a 'BACK IN HALF AN HOUR' notice from the front door, and slipped it under the counter. No one else in the shop. She could do her business with him without being overheard.

'Oh, so, so,' she said carelessly. No point in trying to pretend that she was madly in love or anything. Power was what mattered to men like Rory Duffy. He would respect her if he thought she had the ear of powerful men. Otherwise, he would just throw her to the dogs.

'Very great with that policeman, aren't you? I hear you were in school with him, lived in the same street as him, before he joined the Peelers.'

So Rory had been talking to Tom Hurley. Otherwise he wouldn't have known all of that. He was not a Cork man, himself, had moved down when his native town in Monaghan had become too hot to hold him. Now she knew the reason for the 'Back in Half an Hour' notice. He had popped out to see his master. She didn't show her thoughts, though. Best to play the innocent for the moment.

'That's right; he was not so dishy, then,' she said with a giggle.

'Dishy! Him! Long string of misery. You can do better than him. You're not a bad-looking girl, you know.'

'Well, it's something to have a man who will do anything for you,' she said carelessly and gave him a minute to absorb that piece of information, while she ran a finger along one of the shelves and then dusted off the finger of her glove.

'Well, I still feel that you could do better. Clever girl, too. I was talking about you to someone the other day. "Yon one could mind mice at a crossroads"; that's what I was saying about you.'

'Really!' She laughed as he had expected her to. 'I must tell my mother that one! She's always saying that I would forget my head if it wasn't tied onto me. I like the idea of minding all those little scuttling mice, shooting off in different directions. I never heard that expression before.'

'It's a saying that we have in Monaghan for someone that has their eye on the ball all of the time,' he said, but he didn't smile, just watched her intently. 'So you're determined to stick to the long-faced policeman, are you? Not telling him any little secrets, are you?'

She ignored that. Let him wonder.

'What's a girl to do,' she said with a careless shrug. 'Not too many fellows around who have a good job these days.'

'What about that fellow Raymond Roche? Pots of money in that family. I hear that he's keen on you. You could do very well for yourself with a man like that. Lots of nice little presents, drives out into the country in that Bugatti of his, spins around the harbour in his yacht . . .'

He had given her an opportunity, probably deliberately, but she seized it quickly. 'Oh, I'm keeping away from him,' she said with a shudder. 'That business with the young nun. You've heard about that, haven't you? Wouldn't want anything to do with him.'

'Is that a fact?' He raised his eyebrows and his Monaghan

accent became very strong. His eyes were intent upon her. 'The one that was murdered. Read about that in the paper.'

'Haven't you heard then about Raymond; didn't they tell you,' she asked injecting a note of surprise into her voice and saw him wince. These fellows were all very insecure. Not one of them liked to be in a position where they were not kept informed. To be excluded from information meant that you were doubted. And from being doubted meant that you were only a couple of steps from a tribunal and then perhaps a bullet in the head and a lonely burial in some remote bog, or in the corner of a field. She could see him scan through his mind for information, weighing up facts and impressions. He had come straight from Tom Hurley, had checked on Eileen. Surely something should have been mentioned about the death of the nun.

'You knew about the two dupes, didn't you? The nuns with the Foreign Mission collecting box?' She saw a flicker of humour in his eyes and knew instantly that he had been informed of this. 'And, of course, the other one, the third nun, well, she found out all about it. Was going to put a stop to it.'

'Heard that from your policeman friend, did you?' He said the words with an ugly sneer, but she didn't deny it, just allowed a smile to pucker her lips. She was playing with fire; she knew that, but it gave her an oddly exhilarated feeling.

'Well, have to find something to talk about down the Mardyke on a dark night,' she said carelessly. The Mardyke was well known as a place for courting couples who would walk down the tree-lined path beside the dyke that drained the western marshlands and kiss and cuddle in the darkness there.

'I wouldn't believe everything that he says to you.' He was thinking hard; she knew that. 'Not Raymond. Not his style at all,' he said after a minute. 'Tom Hurley wouldn't use Raymond Roche for something like that. He's in the top class in this city. Courting the granddaughter of Mr Murphy, the solicitor in South Mall. Now that's a man with influence. If Raymond manages to marry the girl, then that might be a useful link. No, Tom Hurley is a cute hoor, as we say up

north. Can't see him using a fella like Raymond for delivering
death notices. He'd prefer to keep him in reserve, keep him
for the showy stuff.'

'Would he then?' She said the words in the manner of one
who knows better and he frowned again. Unsure, but uncon-
vinced of the possibility that Raymond might have been guilty
of a murder.

'The business was done, you know. There would have been
no point.' More talking to himself, than to her. She knew what
he meant. After all the letters were delivered and had done
the job required. She knew that. The men, contacted by those
letters, had responded to them and travelling by different
means, had turned up in Cobh, had boarded the yacht, one by
one, dressed as deckhands. Once moored beside the pier at
Spike Island, they had swum ashore and that night had blown
up the ammunition. They had not come back with Raymond.
She knew that because Raymond and she had returned to Cobh
and he had driven her home almost straight away. Some other
boat, a fishing boat, perhaps, would have picked the men up
some time in the darkness of the night. So Rory Duffy was
right. Tom Hurley was saving Raymond for the showy stuff,
like landing the men while he, and she, kept the officers busy.
She was beginning to be convinced that Raymond might not
have known anything about the murder of the third nun. He
was a plausible fellow, though, and he knew Sister Gertrude
from the Irish lessons. There was a possibility that he gave
her something with poison in it. Malachy had seen them
walking off together. Could have bought her a bar of chocolate,
or something like that. Something that she put in her pocket
and ate later on.

'I'll be off then,' she said, endeavouring to convey the air
of one who is taking her business elsewhere, to more well-
informed sources. 'See you, Rory,' she said jauntily and
walked straight to the door and had closed it behind her
before he thought to say a word. She gave a scornful glance
at the cabbages as she passed them. She had promised her
mother that she would buy something for their evening meal,
but she wasn't going to buy that rubbish. Rory's shop was
more a cover for other business. He certainly didn't take

too much trouble in stocking it with fresh and attractive produce.

When she returned from the market she went straight back to his shop. She made no effort to conceal the shopping bag full of food. She knew how to manage men like Rory. Show him that she did not care a fig for his opinion, that she did not regard him as a person of importance. He knew that she had access to Tom Hurley and now he had seen an example of her familiarity with a police inspector. He would wonder about her, would be unsure, and, she was fairly certain, would be anxious to conciliate her. And that was good. She could perhaps get out of him whether he felt Sister Gertrude was murdered by Raymond without instructions. Nothing would be said straight out, of course. Eileen knew how to do this sort of thing, how to ask for and how to receive information that was so wrapped up in irrelevant words that it would be hard for a bystander to pick up what might be going on. She would be quite safe in doing this, she thought. She knew how to play these dangerous games.

That's if no one from Tom Hurley's mob had decided that she could be a spy. In which case, Rory would play her along and she might find herself in custody. She cast a quick glance at the door and then at a barrel of turnips standing in the middle of the floor. If he showed any signs of approaching her, she would start firing the turnips and empty the barrel in his face and be out of the door before he had recovered from the onslaught of hundreds of these hard round vegetables.

'Been thinking about what you said.' He opened conversation the minute that she came into the shop. Abrupt. But that was the Northern style. 'You might be right.' Now he was talking as much to himself as to her. 'Not too pleased with your posh friend. I got that impression. He might be finding himself a bit short of the readies in the future. *Them above* not too pleased with him. They don't like any private enterprise.' He gave a nod towards the ceiling. Might mean he had someone upstairs, but it might also mean someone high in the hierarchy. These Northern men used one word where a Cork person used ten. Anyway, no one could call Patrick 'posh' so he must be talking about Raymond. Was Raymond out of favour, then, she wondered. And if so, why? Tom Hurley didn't mind murder but he didn't want his men showing any private enterprise. Was that it? Was the murder of a nun a step too far for Tom Hurley? Something that had not been authorized. Or had Raymond simply outlived his usefulness to the organisation. The regiment on Spike Island must be a bit stupid if they did not wonder about a connection between his visit that afternoon and the blowing up of the ammunition a couple of hours later. They might keep quiet, but they would have put two and two together.

'I'm always right,' she said smugly. Keep him guessing, that would be the way to handle him. She was still unsure, though.

'I suppose that you might know,' he said slowly. 'After all, you were in the centre of things. Good as a play to see you; that's what I heard, anyway.'

'Well, I'd better be off,' she said. 'Got all those mice at the crossroads to see to.'

'You'd be a match for them,' he said grimly, but made no attempt to detain her.

'Just going to pop around to see Eamonn, Mam. Think there might be something wrong with the old bike,' said Eileen carelessly. She had walked down to the pub where her mother worked and had escorted her home. From now on, she told herself, she had to be very careful, careful of herself and careful of her mother. At least her mother was home safely and so tired-looking that she would probably fall asleep in front of the fire after she had her supper. Eileen could leave her with a clear conscience. There would be nothing wrong with seeing Eamonn; she did so at least once or twice a week, but she wouldn't put it past Rory Duffy to have someone watching her. It wouldn't do for her to go straight to the convent after a conversation with him about the murder of a nun.

And so she decided to stay for a couple of hours with Eamonn and leave her bike with him. She would be less conspicuous walking, she would blend with the evening crowd, going to the pub or *doing Pana* as Cork people called spending a few hours walking up and down Patrick Street with a crowd of friends, meeting and greeting other friends. She could pick up her bike tomorrow. Her mother, the most unsuspicious of women, would not question that. Eamonn had been the original owner of the bike and was supposed to know all about its idiosyncrasies.

'I'll walk up with you,' said Eamonn when she rose from the table after consuming one of the huge suppers which Eamonn's mother, delighted to have got him back from the clutches of the IRA, invariably cooked for her darling only child. Eileen was glad of his offer. It would distract attention from her if Rory Duffy or any of his spies were around. Eamonn's parents' house was on Western Road and it was a normal routine for the two of them to stroll along through the busy shoppers in South Main Street and to stand looking down into the river from the bridge and chat idly. Eamonn was worried about a coming examination. His years as an active member of the IRA, hiding out in a safe house, south of the city, had made him fall behind with his studies and now he had to work twice as hard in order to catch up. Eileen volunteered to wheedle out of Dr Scher his impression of how Eamonn was doing and they argued a bit about that until Eileen turned the conversation.

'Does *your man* ever trouble you these days, spy on you, or try to get you to do jobs for him?' she asked. Eamonn would know who she meant. Tom Hurley was always '*your man*' to them.

'Not a peep nor a sound to be had from him,' said Eamonn. He gave a quick glance over his shoulder. 'I keep away from him and he keeps away from me. That's the way that I want it. And that goes for you, too, Eileen. You'd want to keep away from all of that. Let the police do the job that they're paid to do. The trouble with you, Eileen, is that you always want to be managing everything.'

'I feel sort of responsible. I should have guessed that something was going on. Those two stupid young nuns.' Eileen, also, looked over her shoulder. One of the enormous Beamish and Crawford's horse-drawn wagons was about to cross the bridge. This would be the opportunity to slip away. If anyone was watching her from a doorway across the road, then their vision would be blocked and she knew a few good shortcuts to the convent.

'Bye,' she said in his ear and saw him mingle with a crowd of slightly drunken sailors steering an unsteady way towards The Castle Inn on South Main Street. She briefly attached herself to the nearside of a fat woman with an overflowing shopping basket and then slipped away down a small alleyway. It was second nature to her to walk on the dark side of the street and to keep looking over her shoulder. She took even more care than usual. If Tom Hurley thought that she was frustrating him in any way then he might still carry out his threat to her mother. Somehow, though, she felt sure that Tom Hurley now would have lost interest. Eileen had served her turn. Had acted as a smokescreen, kept the regiment occupied and amused, allowing the yacht to remain moored for an hour at the pier and given the opportunity for the raiders to slip ashore. The daring raid on the ammunition in Spike Island had taken place and had been successful. Raymond, she thought, might well be sacrificed. She doubted whether he had enough information to pose any danger to the IRA. But if so, he would be shot. But, in any case, it would be unlikely that he would be used again as a decoy in a high-profile affair. Tom Hurley would be finished with him, now. There would now be another plan generating in that active brain.

When Eileen reached the side gate of the convent chapel she knew that she had timed her visit well. The nuns were streaming out. The evening service was over. Eileen waited behind a thick-leaved Portuguese laurel until they were followed by the elderly priest who ministered to this convent of nuns. The Reverend Mother, she knew from past experience, had taken on herself the task of locking up the chapel in the evening. She would go for a little walk around the grounds first; that was her custom. Eileen watched while the elderly nun came out, walked down the path and then bent over a neatly heaped row and pulled out what looked like a turnip, gleaming very white in the moonlight. She did not start at the appearance of Eileen, but shot a quick glance around the garden to make sure that no one else was present.

'Go into the chapel, my child,' she said quietly. 'I will join you in a minute.'

When she came in, two minutes later, the turnip still dangled from her fingers. With her usual composed manner, she laid it on the bench and dusted her fingers free of the damp soil that clung to them.

'We're growing these to close the gap between one season's potatoes and the next; I hope the children like them,' she said to Eileen. 'Not sure whether they are ready yet. What do you think? Are they big enough?'

'I've seen bigger,' said Eileen cautiously. Her mind went to the barrel of turnips in Rory Duffy's shop and she gave a giggle when she remembered her plan to fire them at him if he became troublesome. 'I'd leave them a bit longer, Reverend Mother.'

The Reverend Mother heaved a sigh. 'I'm afraid that gardening is not my forte,' she said. 'I'm too impatient, should have left that in the soil. Now tell me, my child, what brings you here.'

'I wanted to talk to you about the murder of Sister Gertrude,' said Eileen and watched the elderly face in front of her tighten and pale a little. 'I've been poking around a bit, Reverend Mother. I know someone who went to the Gaelic League classes, a fella called Malachy. He was the one who dropped me a hint about what was going on. Well, he was talking about Raymond Roche, and how he walked home with her, with Sister Gertrude, that evening when the two younger ones had gone off doing that job for Mary MacSwiney. I've been poking around a bit, because I thought that you would like to know.' Eileen stopped and eyed the Reverend Mother uncertainly. She didn't appear to be offended, though. Seemed to be thinking, staring ahead at the altar, her head bowed and her hands tucked into those big wide sleeves.

'Yes, indeed,' she said after a minute. 'Yes, I would like to know. We have to know, don't we? The Bible tells us that not even a sparrow will fall to earth unheeded. A violent death cannot go unremarked and unsolved. We must know. No matter what the consequences,' she added and Eileen noticed how much the elderly voice hardened on the last words and how the

Reverend Mother raised her head and looked at her former pupil with a very direct gaze.

Eileen nodded. 'That's what I think. That's what I thought you would say. You have to know.' She hesitated for a minute, wondering if that seemed a bit of a cheek on her part, but the Reverend Mother said nothing and seemed to be waiting.

'I know Raymond Roche. Don't like him much, don't think much of him,' said Eileen rapidly. She would not relate to the Reverend Mother the part that she had played in the attack on Spike Island, she thought, and so she continued rather hurriedly. 'I wasn't sure whether he had killed Sister Gertrude, done it for the man in charge, done it to get money.'

'To get money,' repeated the Reverend Mother.

Eileen ignored this. 'I was talking to a fella in the know, a spy, not Malachy, a fella from the north of Ireland, from Monaghan. He spies for the man in charge of the local unit, and I thought that he would know all about it. He didn't, but I could see that he didn't think that Raymond would have been given a job like that.'

'Why should the Irish Republican Army be interested in killing Sister Gertrude?'

'Perhaps to stop her interfering,' said Eileen uncertainly. 'You know what I told you, about the Mary MacSwiney business. The two young nuns were being sent off, supposed to be collecting for the Foreign Missions, but really delivering letters. I got wind of it and sent a message to Tom Hurley, but I think that Sister Gertrude had tackled them also. My friend Malachy said he heard them arguing.' She saw the Reverend Mother nod and guessed that there might have been some arguing or quarrelling at the convent as well.

'And you thought that perhaps Raymond Roche might have been entrusted with the task of removing Sister Gertrude,' said the Reverend Mother. 'And so you went to talk to a spy. I would not have wanted you to put yourself in any danger, Eileen. It might have been better just to talk to the police. I'm sure that Inspector Cashman would treat everything you said as confidential. The police, the Garda Siochána are here to protect us, you know.'

Eileen suppressed a smile as she thought of the part that

she had made Patrick play. It had helped, she was sure. Rory had respected her as someone who had a finger in two very different pies. She would not, she thought, explain all this to the Reverend Mother.

'Well there are all sorts of ins and outs, Reverend Mother,' she said vaguely. 'But after I had talked with this fella,' she continued, 'I had the feeling that he was pretty sure that Raymond Roche would not have had anything to do with it. I couldn't be certain, Reverend Mother, but that's just the feeling that I picked up. And that if he did do it, I wouldn't say that it was official. I mean that he wasn't authorized in any way.'

'Would he have murdered a nun for his own reasons?' asked the Reverend Mother, thinking what a strange world that they were living in when a young nun's death could be ordered, like a request for a chicken.

'It's possible.' Eileen considered the matter. 'But I don't see why. It doesn't make sense. The only reason why Raymond would do something dangerous like killing a nun would be if he were very well paid for it. Drug addicts are like that, Reverend Mother. They would do anything for money. He'd have nothing to get out of it unless he had been ordered to do it. Unless, of course, that something was going on between them and she became a bit of a nuisance.' That idea, she thought, would not be a welcome one to the Reverend Mother, but she considered it for a moment and then shook her head.

'I wouldn't think so, Eileen,' she said.

Eileen nodded. The Reverend Mother, she thought, would have a good idea of what was going on in the convent. She had always seemed to know everything, even about what the girls got up to out of school. She could accept her word about Sister Gertrude. And then, with a little curiosity, she said tentatively, 'What was she like? My friend said she was a bit bossy, a bit full of herself, one to speak her mind, that's what my friend thought of her.'

The Reverend Mother seemed to think for a moment. A slight frown, more of concentration than of displeasure crossed her face.

'Yes,' she said reluctantly after a minute. 'I think that could be true. I saw one side of her, but no doubt others, especially those younger, and perhaps those inferior to her, saw another side.'

'My friend said that she was a bit nasty to the young one, Sister Brigid, made her cry one day by saying something in her ear.' Eileen saw the Reverend Mother wince and decided to go back to the topic for her reason for her visit.

'Raymond's not too bright, you know. Out of his depth, I'd say.' She gave a look at the Reverend Mother. 'He's supposed to be courting the granddaughter of Mr Murphy, you know. Tom Hurley is pleased about that. He likes power. Would like to have power over someone like Mr Murphy. I was thinking that I should tell Mr Murphy about Raymond, warn him, tell him that he takes drugs, you know, but then I thought that perhaps you would be better at doing that. He might think it's a bit of a cheek of me and he's been very kind to me, allowing me to borrow books. I only found that out today,' she added. She would say no more, she thought. The Reverend Mother had not replied, though she appeared to be thinking hard.

'So, Eileen,' she said, 'you think, on the whole, that although Mr Raymond Roche is an unsuitable person for my cousin's granddaughter to plan to marry, nevertheless, you don't think that he was the one who killed Sister Gertrude.'

'I can't be sure,' said Eileen cautiously, 'but that's my feeling, Reverend Mother. For one thing, I don't see someone like Tom Hurley trusting a drug addict to murder someone at his orders. Tom is very cautious. He would think that someone who takes drugs might well take them on that day, even if he had sworn not to. And then he could make a mess of things.'

'Very true,' mused the Reverend Mother. 'Yes, I think if I were Tom Hurley I don't think that I would trust a difficult and dangerous job to a drug addict.'

With a flash of inner amusement, Eileen watched the revered and well-esteemed Reverend Mother of her youth making an effort to put herself in the position of a man with a large price on his head, a man who ordered murder and arson without a moment's compunction. She kept silent though, recognizing that possibilities were going through the mind of the woman opposite to her. Did nuns get used to wearing the wimple that must constrict their foreheads, those long robes that would impede walking and making running almost impossible, did they ever get fed up with living in a convent and seeing the same people all the time and never having fun. Why had someone like Sister Gertrude, with a good job, and good money – Ford's had the reputation of paying very good wages – why had someone like that entered the convent? Not particularly pious, either, had said Malachy. Had laughed at a joke that one of the lads had made. Something that he wouldn't have expected her to understand.

The Reverend Mother, she saw, noted the startled glance that Eileen gave her, but had then turned her mind back to the problem.

'You said "for one thing". Is there another?' she enquired.

'Yes.' Eileen thought about it for a moment, thought about how to explain matters. 'I think,' she said slowly, 'that Tom Hurley is a very good judge of different temperaments, different degrees of commitment. I know that when we, Eamonn, myself, Aoife and the other lads were in that house south of the city, we were never asked to do anything that would involve a real killing. We were always back-up people, the troops that swept in to do a raid, or things like that, the ones that drove a lorry, made a lot of noise. He wasn't sure of us, you see. He was watching us, training us up, I suppose. Seeing how far that he could push us. It would be the same thing with Raymond Roche, you know, Reverend Mother.'

'I must say,' said the Reverend Mother, rather tartly, 'I would not have thought that Mr Raymond Roche would have been an idealistic patriot.'

Eileen smiled a little. The Reverend Mother had a gift for summing up a situation in a very succinct manner.

'Raymond is a playboy,' she said, 'a man without ideals. Tom Hurley could get him to do things. *Amadán*s like myself and Eamonn, well we would do things for the love of Ireland and for the hope of gaining Ireland's freedom from Britain. But, of course, Raymond Roche wasn't like that. He was a playboy from a rich family who wanted to get the money for drugs and for visits to London. You wouldn't believe, Reverend Mother,' said Eileen emphatically, 'just how much all of that sort of thing costs. And so Raymond got trapped by Tom Hurley. He needed the money that he was being paid for his services. But anyway, when I talked with this man, a spy for Tom Hurley, he seemed to think that Raymond would be used just for the showy stuff. He didn't see him murdering a nun, and I must say that I don't see him murdering a nun, either. Always possible, I suppose, but somehow I don't see him doing it.'

Eileen sat back, leaning against the unforgiving rigidity of the bench. There was something about the Reverend Mother's face which disturbed her, a mixture of worry, apprehension and the look of one who is being forced to confront an unpalatable conclusion.

'What is it?' she asked after a few moments and the elderly nun bowed her head wearily.

'It's a problem, Eileen,' she said quite simply, speaking, Eileen thought, as though they were friends and equals. 'It's a terrible problem. You see, if it were not an outsider like Mr Raymond Roche who murdered Sister Gertrude, then it may be something, someone, connected with our convent here.'

'I see,' said Eileen. Her mind went instantly to the other two young nuns. The thought of the fuss and the scandal that would come of something like that would kill the elderly woman, she thought.

FOURTEEN

St Thomas Aquinas
Ita tamen quod si ex observatione talis voti magnum et
manifestum gravamen sentiret . . . non debet homo tale
votum servare.
(Yet should a man find that without doubt he is
seriously burdened by keeping such a vow . . .
that man ought not to keep it.)

The Reverend Mother stood in front of the ancient willow tree beside the river. She had been thinking about what Eileen said on the evening before, but now she turned her thoughts back to the tree. Over the years, perhaps even over hundreds of years, people had tried to curb its growth; had tried to cut back the exuberance of its branches, had tried to confine it to being just a decorous part of the riverside scenery. It had been chopped of its limbs, but had retaliated by producing sprouts of verdant growth. Small sockets had been formed in the trunk, not injuring the tree in any way as new bark healed the wound with a smooth protective surface, but forming intriguing little hiding places. She remembered trees like that from her childhood, in her father's house in Blackrock beside the River Lee as it went on its way right out to Cork Harbour. She and Lucy had loved to put little messages to each other in among the burgeoning twigs and branches. Now, almost without thinking, she went straight to the centre of a sprouting mass, found the hole, disguised by pale green twigs, fumbled for a moment among the bushy growths and then felt something hard at the bottom of the hole. She closed her fingertips over it and drew it forth.

Yes, Sister Bernadette had guessed successfully. A small cube, a box wrapped in a square of waterproofed gabardine, green as its surroundings. She knew what it was before she unfolded the material. Egans of Patrick Street. The lettering was just about distinguishable. No piece of rubbish, then. Egans were a high-class jeweller where the prices would mirror the quality of their goods. The Reverend Mother pressed the tiny knob and the lid jumped back with the ease of almost daily use. It was a brooch. A brooch, indeed, but not some sentimental memory of childhood, or not just solely that, amended the Reverend Mother, telling herself that she had no right to judge. But this brooch was, she thought, very, very valuable indeed. It was a beautiful brooch, a diamond-studded bar, from which hung a couple of coiled straps gleaming with jewels. There was no doubt about the stones. Even in the dim fog-filled air, they shone with an undoubted quality. The price of a house, she thought, and coveted the brooch for all that it could afford for the poverty-stricken children in her care. Resolutely she tucked the box into the capacious pocket of her skirt and turned back towards the convent. The community would now have finished their dinner and she would send a messenger to fetch Sister Catherine to her room.

The brooch was on the table by the window when the girl came into the room. The room was gloomy and little light came through from outside. Nevertheless Sister Catherine's eyes went straight to it, as rapidly and as directly as though attracted by a magnet.

'That's mine,' she breathed, her pale face flushing to a healthy pink. With embarrassment? No, not embarrassment. With interest, the Reverend Mother decided the expression on the novice's face was downright anger. She allowed the words to stand for a minute and then said gently: '*Ours*'. It was a standard correction for new members of the community, rather pointless, the Reverend Mother always thought. Surely it was natural for humans to have possessions, even if they were kept to the bare minimum. But, of course, a valuable diamond brooch could never belong to someone who was vowed to poverty and to community living.

'Tell me about it,' she invited, making her voice gentle. Sister Catherine had crossed the room, picked up the brooch and was holding it clasped within the shelter of the palm of her hand.

'It's mine,' she repeated. 'It was given to me by my godmother, at my christening. I've had it all of my life.'

'And you don't want to be parted from it,' murmured the Reverend Mother. Who was the girl's godmother? That was a very expensive gift. A useful one, too, if it could be used to convince Sister Catherine that the communal life of a nun did not suit her, then it would be worth every penny of those valuable stones. She waited for an agreement; even a reluctant admission of the impossibility of giving up all of her worldly goods would be a valuable step forward at this stage. Nothing came, though, just a heavy frown, rather ugly on the child-like face.

'It was Sister Gertrude who told you, I suppose. I knew she would.'

'Told me about the brooch?' The Reverend Mother inserted a note of query into the words.

'I knew that she saw me. She had eyes in the back of her head. Pretending to be talking to her sister!'

'When you were looking at your brooch. The day Sister Gertrude's sister visited.' That had to be the day before the girl's body had been found in the hen shed, the day when, for some reason, Sister Gertrude had swallowed poison. Yes, it had to be that day. Visits from families were only allowed once a month for novices. That was in the rule book. A stupid rule, she often thought that it was. The choice to sacrifice the life of a wife and a mother, to sacrifice personal wealth and possessions such as a diamond brooch, that choice should be made with clear eyes and a careful weighing up of the implications.

'And, I suppose, as soon as the sister had gone; and I saw them sniggering together. She saw me, I know. She was saying to her sister: "Be careful, Betty, there's Sister Mary Immaculate's little pet over there and she will go tittle-tattling to the big white chief if we're not careful." They were laughing together, the pair of them. Laughing at me. And I suppose as soon as her sister was gone, she went straight to you to tell some lies about me. I heard her in your room. I heard her laughing. And you laughed, too. I heard you!'

'I see,' said the Reverend Mother. It would, she thought, be useless at this stage to try to explain the joke at which both she and Sister Gertrude had laughed. She didn't think that

Sister Catherine would appreciate the humour of those accountancy terms: efficiency variance, budget variances, overheads variance, reconciliations, and all those arcane words, planned to surprise and to bamboozle the bishop's secretary which Sister Gertrude rehearsed with such glee.

'Just like her. We all knew that was what she was like. She was the one who went running, running to you, with every little piece of tittle-tattle. You can't deny it. She was in here all the time, talk, talk, talk to you.'

'She had experience in managing accounts,' said the Reverend Mother mildly. 'I find accounts difficult and appreciated the help that she gave, based on her experience in working in the accounts department at Ford's. Did you know that she had worked there?'

'Yes, of course I did.' Sister Catherine's cheeks were now scarlet. 'She was the one that accused my uncle, my mother's only brother, my poor uncle, she was responsible for getting him dismissed. He had a very good job there in Ford's. Used to be in charge of the sales department. And then that Patsy Donovan had to go poking into his expenses. Making a big fuss. He was just doing what the manager before him did. No harm in it. The Fords are rolling in money. Would never miss a few pounds.'

Well, well, well, thought the Reverend Mother, so there was a prior connection between the two novices. Nothing surprising in this. Always wheels within wheels in the city of Cork, had said her cousin Lucy on one occasion and she knew Cork inside out. Sister Catherine's father had seemed an ordinary sort of man, over-protective of his darling, but that was to be expected. The mother had spoken with what, in Cork, would be deemed a 'posh' accent. And the mother's brother had fiddled his expenses, been found out by the efficient Sister Gertrude or Patsy Donovan, as she was then. When had that come to light? Had there been an argument? Bad feeling? The novices were very strongly discouraged from talking about their past life; something that often came as quite a difficult trial for natives of Cork city, who always liked to trace relationships. Nevertheless, the rule was enforced quite strictly. The novices were told that this was a new life and that all which belonged to the past should be put aside, not talked about, nor, if possible, thought about very much. It was always a good test of how stable their vocation was likely to be.

'Did Sister Gertrude know about your feelings?' she asked, but was not surprised when Sister Catherine shook her head.

'She wouldn't be interested. She wasn't interested in any of us. She was just interested in spending every second that she could in here with you.'

It was probably true, thought the Reverend Mother. Sister Gertrude was a good four years older than the other three novices, and she had little interest in those around her. A true mathematician, figures rather than people were of importance to her. Any discrepancy in the accounts would be anathema; and the sin rather than the sinner would be of concern. She probably had no personal vendetta against Sister Catherine's uncle, but if the figures were wrong, then the man would be condemned.

But did all of this have any relevance to the poison which killed Sister Gertrude? Perhaps now was the moment to ask the question, distract attention from that spectacular brooch for a few minutes.

'By the way, Sister Catherine, I hear that a tin of treacle was found beneath your bed in the dormitory. Could you explain to me what it was doing there?'

'Treacle! I don't know what it was doing there. Where did it come from?'

'From the kitchen, apparently,' said the Reverend Mother. 'And as it was under your bed, I should have thought that you would have noticed it when you swept beneath it?'

She coloured up then, but that could have been guilt about neglected housekeeping. 'Well, I certainly didn't put it there. I don't even like treacle.'

'Nor do I,' said the Reverend Mother. 'But perhaps you intended to give it to someone else?'

'Well, I didn't.' There was something very obstinate and belligerent about the girl this afternoon; quite unlike her usual childlike and pious demeanour, but perhaps that was to do with the prospect of a battle over the brooch.

The Reverend Mother shelved the matter of the treacle for the moment and turned back to the immediate problem.

'I'm afraid that I shall have to ask you to hand over that brooch, Sister Catherine,' she said. 'I will contact your parents. As you are still a novice it may be handed back to them, or if they wish, it will be sold and the proceeds will go towards our work here.'

'No!' The exclamation came without a second's hesitation. 'No! You can't take it from me. I've had it all my life. I can't live without it. I need to see it every day. I need to touch it, to watch its colours. I need it! I can't live without it.'

Her voice had risen to an alarming pitch and now all the colour faded from her face and she confronted her superior, white-faced and large-eyed. She clutched the brooch, her fingers hiding it and her eyes blazed with . . . fear . . . no, not fear, anger. Yes, thought the Reverend Mother. It's anger. Something badly wrong with that girl. Not even the bishop, himself, was going to persuade her away from that view. She was not going to keep this particular novice. She would have to go.

'There is a third possibility,' she said evenly. 'You may, if you wish, leave this congregation of your own free will. You have taken no final vows and you are free to go. Your health has not been of the best since you joined us. I have noticed that your colour is poor and I'm sure that you have lost weight. Dr Scher, I know, would be very willing to explain to your parents why you found it necessary to give up your noviciate.' She watched a stubborn look come into the girl's eyes and her heart sank. 'And when you leave,' she said, playing her trump card, 'when you leave, you will, of course, take your diamond brooch with you.'

For a moment she thought that she might have won. The girl was sitting directly beneath the gas lamp and from time to time she turned the brooch so that the stones caught the light. There was a batch of letters, turned upside down and awaiting envelopes, on the table in front of her and as the Reverend Mother watched, a perfect spectrum of colours, more gorgeous than any rainbow, splayed out from the brooch and onto the white page. The girl's face lit up and became starry-eyed, almost as though she were seeing heavenly visions, like the peasant girl at Lourdes. The battle was lost.

Or was it won? The Reverend Mother saw her way forward as Sister Catherine rose to her feet, shaking her head with a resolute air.

'No,' she said. 'It's mine. No one can take it from me. I won't let them.'

'Very well,' said the Reverend Mother calmly. 'I suggest that you think about this matter until tomorrow morning. But if by tomorrow morning at ten o'clock I have not received that brooch from you, then I will telephone the bishop, tell him that I do not consider you a suitable candidate for our community. In the meantime, and before your parents come to fetch you home, I would beg you to take the utmost care of that very valuable brooch and do not let it become an occasion of sin for someone who might be tempted to steal it from you.'

And with those words, the Reverend Mother picked up her pen and began writing a new letter. She kept her eyes fixed on the page, but heard the door click quietly as it was opened and then shut with great care.

She put down her pen, then, and stared at the wall. She had failed. But that was of small importance. She was used to failure and had learned to push it aside and to get on with the next project. What was troubling her now was the fanaticism showed, the worship of that object less than two inches in width. Beautiful. Perhaps. Probably not as beautiful as a rose if viewed dispassionately. And yet Sister Catherine had made no protest, had not offered to give up her trinket when faced with the certainty that by retaining it, she would have to give up her lifetime dream of becoming a holy nun.

There was something definitely unhinged about Sister Catherine. The Reverend Mother propped her chin on one hand and thought about the girl. She did not pick up her pen, but in her mind's eye she formulated a list, each point preceded by a neatly bracketed number.

(1) Sister Gertrude had been in the garden when Sister Catherine had been adoring her brooch.

(2) Sister Gertrude had pin-sharp eyesight. Would have been curious, certainly . . .

(3) Probably Sister Gertrude visited the hiding place later. Would have been clever enough to evaluate the quality of the object.

(4) What if she had tackled Sister Catherine? Told her that she had no right to keep the brooch? Threatened, said Sister Bernadette, to tell the bishop. Sister Bernadette was a gossip, but she was a very truthful individual.

(5) How would Sister Catherine react to that threat?

(6) In desperation, Sister Catherine thinks of poison. Goes to the store cupboard. Takes out a scoop of shoe polish, perhaps, and mixes it with treacle. Possibly intending death, or hopefully just a bout of illness.

(7) Sister Gertrude, loudly and unashamedly, informed the whole world of the convent about how much she missed sweet things, had discoursed freely on her love for sweets, chocolates and, on one occasion, had related in the corridor to the other novices of how she always stole some treacle when her sister was making cakes.

(8) What if she had been tempted by the treacle?

The Reverend Mother got to her feet. Her head ached and she felt as though a walk would do her good. The children were in their classrooms for another hour, all of her nuns were engaged in teaching or other duties. Sister Bernadette and her lay sisters were busy cleaning, polishing and washing linen. Her world was orderly. She could venture abroad.

The fog had lifted by the time that she walked along Sullivan's Quay. The river was, she thought, quite a beautiful sight in sunlight with the seagulls squawking and swooping, the sun glinting on the water and the noble ships waiting to be unloaded of their cargo. Only the immensely long line of men, all of them desperately hoping to be chosen for a job, broke into her appreciation of the scene. Freedom from England had changed little, she thought. Unemployment in Cork was just as bad as ever. Why did those men not have solid job offers? Why did they all not have contracts that said when they attended at the docks, they would get paid for a day's work? Couldn't some more industries be set up in order to employ the surplus men?

By the time that she reached Dr Scher's house on South Terrace, it was afternoon tea time. As the housekeeper opened the door for her, she smelled the fragrant incense of a well-made pot of tea and the hot flour aroma of freshly baked scones filled the air.

'I'm being a nuisance,' she said apologetically to the house-keeper and was conscious that it was a stupid thing to say. She had a vague feeling in the back of her mind that these mid-afternoon rituals between a hardworking man and his housekeeper should not be interrupted.

'Not – at – all, Reverend Mother,' said the housekeeper, her voice rising up the scale with the musical delivery of a typical Cork woman. 'Inspector Cashman is here. He'll be delighted to see you. They'll both be delighted. You'll be very welcome.' And with those words, having dispersed all of the visitor's doubts, she ushered her into the living room.

'Reverend Mother, Dr Scher,' she said and then closed the door behind her.

The Reverend Mother was indeed somewhat reassured by the welcome that she received and more so by the fact that, although the small table in front of the fire had been laid out for afternoon tea, nevertheless the snack had not yet been served up and she had probably not caused any major upset.

'Good evening, Dr Scher,' she said politely, and then, 'Patrick, I hope your mother is well. I saw her a couple of days ago. She told me that you had bought a new griddle for her. She was delighted with it, was singing its praises.'

And with that she took the proffered armchair by the fire and waited until tea was served and eaten before bringing forward the purpose of her visit.

'I'm very worried about Sister Catherine,' she said to Dr Scher, not addressing herself to Patrick, but conscious that he was listening carefully. 'We have had a death in the convent. A young woman died of poison, and it behoves me, as superior of that convent, to be very sure that this poison was not administered by one of my community, possibly some shoe polish concealed in a spoonful of treacle. Sister Bernadette told me that Sister Catherine had a tin of treacle hidden under her bed.' She looked from one to the other and saw, to her slight surprise, that Patrick was the one who gave her an understanding nod and a keen glance from alert eyes, whereas Dr Scher looked flustered and rather taken aback.

'That girl, little Sister Catherine,' he said. 'Well, surely, Reverend Mother, you don't actually believe that she had anything to do with Sister Gertrude's death,' he said.

'The girl was neurotic and unstable, obsessed with strange notions about her vocation, about her sacred immunity from all wrongdoing,' she said slowly. 'I must say that I was very worried about it when I talked with her on the day when I found Sister Gertrude's body in the hens' shed.' She looked at both men, felt that their eyes were on her, but still hesitated a little. It would be important to get things right, to be very sure of what the girl actually said. 'What was it that she had said?' She spoke those words aloud, more to be sure of her ground, rather than in an effort to convince them. 'It was something about the Holy Ghost?' she said. 'I think that this was it. "I've felt for a long time that the Holy Ghost has put a shield around me, that a mantle has descended from heaven and that it wraps around me; something that keeps me isolated from all evil and wrongdoing. No matter what was going on among sinful souls, I was kept protected from it".'

'Strange,' said Patrick, but his eyes were very alert. He had his notebook open, but had not made a note. Perhaps the metaphysical tone was a little too fantastical for him.

Dr Scher scratched the few remaining hairs on his right temple and raised an eyebrow. 'Well, I don't know much about your Holy Ghost, Reverend Mother, but I must say that he would be a very busy man if he has to keep rushing around the world and wrapping mantles and shields around neurotic young girls.'

'She is neurotic, isn't she?' said the Reverend Mother soberly. 'In some ways, I am pleased to hear you say that because it confirms my judgement and relieves me of faint feelings of guilt because, try as I can, I find her very hard work and I would be sorry to think that I just called her neurotic because I just don't understand her type of religion. But . . .'

'But . . .' prompted Dr Scher.

'But if she is neurotic, if she is dangerously out of touch with reality, then, of course, there must be a possibility that she would have killed someone because they threatened her choice of a lifestyle, because they, in her view, were frustrating the will of God.'

'I wouldn't have thought that she had the gumption to do it, myself,' said Dr Scher.

'I think that you underestimate the power for evil that can fortify religious people,' said the Reverend Mother. She suppressed a smile at Patrick's expression. He looked greatly taken aback at her words. 'Look back into history, Dr Scher. Think of your own people and how they have been persecuted and all in the name of a Christian god. Think of Spain and the Inquisition, think of the great wars of religion. As for whether she had the gumption, well, remember that poison is death at one remove. Sister Gertrude was not killed by being shot with a pistol, being strangled, being stabbed with a sword or a knife, by being burned alive by the flames of fire – all of these methods would require that the murderer would subdue all feelings of humanity, of compassion and of fellow-feeling. No, death by poison would, in comparison, have been a very easy process for a murderer. The victim administers the fatal dose to themselves. It's all removed from the murderer. A pleasant taste. The dose is swallowed down. The agony and the death come, of course, but they come later on when the murderer is no longer around, and can no longer be made to feel remorse or compunction for their action. It is, I think, an ideal death to be inflicted by one who considers himself or herself primed by the Holy Ghost.'

'And you think that it is possible that Sister Catherine might have felt herself so moved. But why now? I gather that they had already spent several months, a year, isn't it, living together in the convent.' Patrick glanced through his notes.

The Reverend Mother nodded. 'Well, there had been developments. Sister Gertrude, I gather, had found out that Sister Catherine had, utterly against all rules of the convent, retained a very valuable diamond brooch. She knew that it was completely forbidden to keep personal possessions like this and so she hid it in a hole in the bark, high in the trunk of an old willow tree beside the river in the convent garden. Sister Gertrude, it appears, did notice her communing with her treasure, and so aroused suspicion that she would report the matter to me,' said the Reverend Mother, conscious, as she spoke, of the immensely juvenile sound of the whole business.

'And that would be enough to trigger a murder! Surely not!' Dr Scher, certainly, sounded extremely sceptical. Patrick, however, continued to write. How did one note down words such as 'Holy Ghost' in shorthand, wondered the Reverend Mother. She waited until her erstwhile pupil had finished, waited until he had closed his notebook, tucked it and the pencil back into his pocket before she spoke.

'What do you think, Patrick?' she asked and was conscious of a tremor of uneasiness in her voice.

He didn't rush to answer. She could see how the different aspect of this case of the poisoned novice nun shunted through his mind, could sense how he weighed up the facts as they were known. She liked and appreciated him and was proud to see how the little barefoot boy from a fatherless family had turned his life into such a success. Nevertheless, she often wondered whether he was able to appreciate the inner complexities of many of the minds involved in these murder cases.

'I can see why you are worried, Reverend Mother,' he said after the length of a couple of minutes. 'On balance, though, I would feel that this is probably a Sinn Féin, Anti-Treaty crime. I'm afraid that your two young nuns, Sister Joan and Sister Brigid, were meddling with very dangerous matters when they accepted the task of taking those Foreign Missions collecting boxes to designated addresses, and of course, delivering letters to men who were being carefully watched, and, I may tell you in confidence, that the routine is that all of their correspondence was read at the post office before it was delivered. So the Sinn Féin leadership had to find an alternative motive of getting in touch and of conveying orders. And, of course, poor Sister Gertrude was meddling even deeper when she endeavoured to stop them. I think, Reverend Mother, we will find that the poor lady's death was, in all probability, tied into the Spike Island assault. That was going to be a most successful piece of propaganda for these fellows. In one stroke, all that ammunition in Spike Island destroyed without the loss of a single life or liberty for any man fighting the Republican cause! Your Sister Gertrude, unfortunately for her, suspected that something was going on and she was known to be aware of the plot. These people, Reverend Mother, are no respecters of youth, religion or innocence. Once she crossed their path, once she threatened their security, well then, and I am very sorry to say this, Reverend Mother, and it doesn't mean that we won't do our utmost to find her killer, but I am afraid that once she was seen to be a threat to the enterprise, well then, her life was not worth a penny's purchase.'

And with that Patrick sat back, looking almost faintly surprised at his own eloquence. The Reverend Mother gave him an approving nod.

'Thank you, Patrick, that's very clear. You may well be right and if you are, well, it would be a weight off my shoulders.'

Once she was back in her room in the convent, though, she sat very still and considered the matter. A phrase lingered in her mind. Silly, school-girlish, it had just irritated her when she heard it first and had prompted a desire to talk to the bishop about setting the age of entry to a minimum of twenty-five years old, but now it came back to her with added significance. The reported words of Sister Gertrude to her sister, Betty Kelly. 'Be careful, Betty, there's Sister Mary Immaculate's little pet over there and she will go tittle-tattling to the big white chief if we're not careful.'

What were the two sisters doing that could have been reported to the Mistress of Novices? She put aside a letter that she had begun and began a quick note.

'Dear Mrs Kelly,' she wrote, 'Do forgive me for not writing before now to share our grief at the death of your sister and ours. I would like to see you and to discuss the funeral arrangements. Would it be possible for you to call into the convent? I shall be here all of tomorrow and the next day.'

She signed her name, put the note in an envelope, and summoned Sister Bernadette.

'Perhaps Sister Imelda could be spared from her duties to pop this into the post office in Bishop's Street,' she suggested. The post services in the city were very efficient and she would, she hoped, receive a visit from Betty Kelly tomorrow morning.

FIFTEEN

Thomas Aquinas
*Lex quaedam regula est et mensura actuum, secundum
quam inducitur aliquis ad agendum, vel ab agendo
retrahitur, dicitur enim lex a ligando, quia
obligat ad agendum*
(The law is a rule and a measure of acts, whereby
man is induced to act or is restrained from acting:
for 'lex' [law] is derived from 'ligare' [to bind],
because it binds one to act.)

Betty Kelly arrived at an inconvenient time, just when the Reverend Mother was in the middle of an English class with her older girls. For a moment she thought of keeping the young woman waiting, of requesting Sister Bernadette to ply her with tea and cake and hand her a copy of the *Cork Examiner* to keep her occupied, but remembering the small baby at home, she cancelled that hasty thought. She set the class an essay, put the oldest girl in charge and swept down the corridor, thinking with irritation that it would not have hurt the woman to send a message. She clearly remembered seeing a post office across the road from the house in Turners Cross. A letter posted there yesterday afternoon would have been delivered to the convent that morning. And then she could have certainly arranged her timetable in order to be able to meet and greet the bereaved sister of her late novice.

Nevertheless, as soon as she opened the door she repented of her impatience. Betty Kelly's face was dead white and there were black bruises under her eyes as though she had not slept well. Of course, the poor girl had lost a father and sister during the last month. Once she saw the Reverend Mother, she jumped hastily to her feet and stuffed a handkerchief back into her handbag, standing awkwardly with one hand on the back of the chair, as if for support.

Feeling somewhat contrite, the Reverend Mother swept
forward with hands outstretched. This, after all, was the nearest
relative of the girl who had died so very unexpectedly in the
noviciate belonging to her convent. As such, Mrs Betty Kelly
was entitled to all possible attention and commiseration from
the Reverend Mother whose motherly care had failed to save
her sister from death by a poisoner. The Reverend Mother
winced when she thought of that. Could this death have been
foreseen? Should she have banned these Irish classes from
the start? The bishop, she thought, would have been sure to
remark that they were, surely, a possible source of novice
contamination. She should, doubtless, have first ascertained
who would be present and then used all her connections in
Cork in order to ascertain whether it would be a suitable venue
for the novices under her care. She had long thought that it
was good for novices to use the noviciate time to make sure
that they were not misled by a pious impulse, but had a true
understanding of all of the implications of community life
and of what they were giving up from a life in the world
outside. These Irish classes, she supposed, were in the nature
of an experiment. And perhaps it was this experiment which
had led to the death of Sister Gertrude.

Or was it?

Her interview with the aunt of the two girls had caused
certain questions to arise in her mind. What was it that the
woman had said? *Not too close. Bit of jealousy between them.
Patsy had known him first. Brought him home for tea.* And
then the prettier of the two sisters had taken the attention of
the handsome young man. And the other sister had fled to a
convent, not even trusting herself to attend the wedding. Surely
Betty would have had some suspicions after this had happened.
How had the marriage gone since? An immediate pregnancy
and then birth and all of the strains that the care of a very
small baby could place on a young couple may well have
turned the young man's affections back towards the sister he
had known first. All these were the thoughts that came to her
mind as she held out her hands.

'My dear Mrs Kelly, this is a very sad moment for us both.
Your sister will be an immense loss to us all. You must be

devastated.' The Reverend Mother pulled forward a chair, but the woman didn't stir, just stood there, looking defensive. Strangely unalike, the two sisters. And not just in appearance. Sister Gertrude, the former Patsy Donovan, plump, squarely built, plain, had been self-confident and socially at ease. Confident in her brains and in her ability, she had deemed herself the equal of any whom she had met. Her sister, Betty, pretty in face, slim and graceful in figure, was, nevertheless, gauche, awkward and very much at a loss for words. She stammered something, dropped her handbag, picked it up, sat down once more at the Reverend Mother's bidding but fidgeted uneasily. The Reverend Mother braced herself for questions, but none came. Odd, she thought. Of course her aunt would have told her what she knew, what the Reverend Mother had revealed on her visit, but it almost seemed as if the girl consciously avoided any further reference to that untimely death of her sister and showed no inclination to make enquiries about how Sister Gertrude, the once-named Patsy Donovan, had been poisoned. She listened docilely to the Reverend Mother's funeral plans but contributed nothing to the suggestions; she had no idea what was her sister's favourite flower for the convent's wreath. Questions about a favourite prayer or a favourite hymn met the same shake of a head and a muttered 'dunno'. She almost seemed impatient with the talk of the funeral, as if she were waiting apprehensively for the conversation to turn in a different direction. In the end, the Reverend Mother decided that straightforwardness was needed from at least one of them.

'You will, I'm sure, be wondering what happened to your sister,' she began.

'My aunt said that she was ill, that she got sick.' The young woman leaned forward in her seat and looked intently at the Reverend Mother.

'That's right. She vomited straight after the meal.' And then as the girl seemed to expect more information, the Reverend Mother added, 'She appeared dizzy.'

'Wobbling?' queried Betty.

'That's right.'

'Panting? Did anyone take her pulse?'

'It was 116, I think.'

Betty nodded. 'That would be it.'

There was, thought the Reverend Mother, an unexpected shrewdness about Betty. Her eyes were intelligent, weighing up the matter. Perhaps she was just as clever as her sister, but early on their roles in the family had diverged. Patsy, the plain, plump girl became the intelligent one, while Betty, the pretty one, became the empty-headed one of the pair. The same thing had happened during her own youth when she, the plain one, had developed an obsession with education, had coaxed her father to supply a teacher for Latin, another for philosophy and, as her ambitions grew, a third for Greek; while her motherless cousin, Lucy, pretty as a picture, played the part of an empty-headed beauty. It was only in later life that she had realized how shrewd and clever Lucy really was. Now she looked across at Betty with interest.

'And her speech slurred, just like she was drunk?'

The Reverend Mother nodded. 'Well, Dr Scher, the convent doctor, who knew Sister Gertrude well, tells me that she was poisoned.'

'Seems strange.' The girl was pondering the words.

'He is not sure exactly what poisoned her,' added the Reverend Mother, 'but he thinks that it was some sort of alcohol.'

That got a reaction. The girl jerked up her head and stared with frank and unmistakable astonishment.

'Alcohol!' Oddly there was almost a note of relief in her voice. Astonished, but relieved. What had she expected? Not that, obviously.

'That's right.' The Reverend Mother decided that she would go no further. Patrick should not be hampered in his investigations and mentioning shoe polish and window cleaner and such like substances at this moment could jeopardize the finding of evidence. She sat very still and watched her visitor carefully. After a minute, though, the frightened, worried expression came over the girl's face again and she shook her head.

'Patsy didn't drink,' she said. 'Never. Not even at Christmas. She was a pioneer. She always wore the pioneer pin. She used to go to their meetings and all that. My father used to take the odd drink of whiskey when he had a cold coming on, or if he were very tired in the evening, but Patsy wouldn't ever touch a drop or let me, either. She was dead against whiskey. She wouldn't have touched it. It must have been something that she ate.'

'No one else was ill at the convent,' said the Reverend Mother quietly. 'And that was the only place where she had a meal,' she added and saw the girl look uneasy, almost as though that was not welcome information.

'She was going to those Irish lessons, wasn't she? She said something about it when we were talking, the day before she died. I remember her talking about them.' Still that air of unease about her. Still that impression that she was trying a little too hard to find an explanation for her sister's death.

'Yes, she did go to Irish classes, up in St Ita's School on Wellington Road. I suppose she talked to you about them. What did she say about them?' asked the Reverend Mother. Could Sister Gertrude have confided in her sister the doubts she had about her fellow novices.

'Not much,' said Betty. Her manner now was easy and relaxed. 'Said she found them a bit of a bore. Said she didn't know why anyone bothered learning Irish since hardly anyone spoke it. She didn't like the crowd there, either. Thought that they were stupid. Don't remember her saying anything else.'

'I see,' said the Reverend Mother. If only those wretched accounts had not taken up so much of her time, she could have probed a little as to the use of those Irish classes. Sister Gertrude, she thought, was probably shrewd enough to have guessed, quite early on, that more than drilling in nouns and verbs was going on beneath the surface. She would have seen the effect it was having on the susceptible and enthusiastic Sister Joan. Still, that was over and done with now and hopefully no further harm would come of it. The death of Sister Gertrude was another matter. That had to be solved, no matter what the cost. 'But she ate nothing there,' she said aloud. 'They did not provide a meal or even refreshments. Sister Gertrude, Sister Joan and Sister Brigid had their dinner here before they left to go up to Wellington Road.'

'Perhaps someone gave her a bottle of whiskey to drink

if she was hot and thirsty after the walk up that steep hill,'
suggested Betty. 'They might have pretended that it was orange
squash or something like that and she would have drank it
unbeknownst what it was really.'

Not a drinker, herself, thought the Reverend Mother digesting
this without any outward reaction. Betty, she thought, must
be quite a naïve young woman. No one who had ever touched
whiskey would imagine that it could be passed off as orange
squash. She suppressed a smile at the memory of her cousin
Lucy and herself sampling her father's whiskey, almost sixty
years ago, and how they had coughed and spluttered and felt
dizzy after a couple of teaspoons of the liquid. It would have
been utterly impossible for Sister Gertrude to swallow enough
whiskey to kill her, without being completely sure that it was
not anything harmless. And probably not, she added to herself,
without being hardened to the alcohol by months or even years
of heavy drinking. Most unlikely, almost impossible if she
were openly a member of the Pioneer Association. No, the
likelihood was that neither sister had ever touched alcohol.
Now that she looked more closely at the woman she could
see the tiny round pioneer pin nestling in the lapel of her
bouclé wool jacket.

'I'd say that if the man who did it to her were to put a few
spoonfuls of sugar in it, she'd drink it down,' continued Betty.
'You know what she was like, Reverend Mother. Mad for the
sweets, always. "You'll be a fat old woman once you stop
riding that bike", that's what I used to say to her when she
talked about getting a car one day.' Betty's voice sounded
more relaxed now, almost as though finding that the consump-
tion of whiskey might be a solution to her sister's untimely
death had relieved some of the feelings – were they of anxiety
or of sorrow? The Reverend Mother asked herself that question, but was unsure of the answer.

'The man . . .?' She put a query into her voice.

'Man, or woman,' Betty said hastily. 'I wouldn't know.'

'So you'd have no idea then who might have done something
like that to your sister, no suspicions, no guesses,' stated the
Reverend Mother.

Betty looked a little undecided then, almost as though

seeking a possible name and then came up with the usual solution for the times. 'It would be one of the Sinn Féin, that IRA crowd, wouldn't it?' she said. 'Aren't they behind most of the murders in this city? Did you read that article in the *Cork Examiner*, Reverend Mother? It's a sin and a disgrace. But that's who it will be. You mark my words. It will be them, or else one of the other crowd. The Treaty fellas. They're one as bad as the other, that's what I say.'

'And what about your husband? What does he think happened to your sister?' asked the Reverend Mother idly. The vision of the sobbing young man came back to her. What was the relationship like between husband and wife? Though she was filled with guilt for the part that she had inadvertently played in the death of the older girl, she would, she thought, hold back a little, make enquiries and hold the results within her until she was a step nearer to guessing the identity of the person who had cut short the life of the most promising novice that she had known for many a long year.

'Oh, he wouldn't have anything to do with either pack of them,' said his wife dismissively. 'He's never gone in for politics. He's got his head screwed on the right way.' It wasn't quite an answer to the question that had been put, but the Reverend Mother decided not to probe too much. Betty looked quite recovered now from her earlier unease and so the Reverend Mother thought that she could move onto another affair. She hesitated for a moment, wondering how to put the matter tactfully.

'You remember your last visit here, Mrs Kelly, when you came to see your sister, the day before she died, I wonder whether you remember what you talked of.'

The Reverend Mother's mind recalled vividly the words that Sister Catherine had spoken. What had the two sisters been talking about? Why had Sister Gertrude expressed resentment that they might have been overheard, or overseen? It would be interesting to see what Betty's explanation of the conversation was.

A momentary look of trouble crossed the woman's face. Perhaps that was understandable, given that it was the last meeting with her sister. However she soon rallied.

'Mostly about our father,' she said. 'The house is to be sold so I've been down there sorting out all of his things. I was telling her all about it. The job that I had! Patsy, Sister Gertrude, had left her room cleared out, and there was nothing in there. Don't think that he even opened the door once she left. He was that upset! But the rest of the place! He had a woman in to do for him, but you know what they're like. Never do much tidying up, just push a broom around and wash a few floors. Alright when Patsy was around. She'd be one to have a sharp word, but once she went into the convent, well, that woman would just skimp through the work. Not that I blame her too much. Easier to clean than to tidy, I suppose. He was a great hoarder, my father. Would keep a matchstick if he thought it might be useful for something. Terrible job to get him to throw out half-eaten food or even a half-eaten bar of chocolate. Very generous, mind you. Just brought up poor and never forgot it, even after he started making a lot of money. Waste not, want not. That was his motto. But, my word, it meant that the house was full of junk.'

So Betty and Patsy, the two sisters, met on the day before Patsy's death. They shared affectionate memories of their father. Talked about the contents of the house and the clutter that had to be cleared up. The Reverend Mother thought about the words that Sister Catherine had recollected, the words that Sister Gertrude had said to her sister: *'Be careful, Betty, there's Sister Mary Immaculate's little sneak over there and she will go tittle-tattling to the big white chief if we're not careful.'* Perhaps she had found the reason for them.

'Did you think that Sister Gertrude would like some memento, something to remember her father by? Something you found when you were clearing out the house.' It would, she thought, be only natural that Betty might bring something to her sister, perhaps a pen or something else. It would, strictly speaking, be outside the rules and Sister Gertrude who had a clear mind and an excellent memory for detail would know that. On the other hand, she was a pragmatic individual with a healthily sensible attitude towards rules and regulations. If Betty had brought something practical like a pen or even perhaps an accountancy book, then she could just imagine that

Sister Gertrude would decide that no harm was done to the spirit of the rule and would tuck the object into one of the capacious pockets which were set into the skirt of the nun's regulation habit. She would, however, be conscious of Sister Catherine in the distance, mooning over her treasure. And who knows, the threat about telling the bishop about the brooch which Sister Bernadette overheard might well have come as a tit-for-tat measure. That made sense and was more acceptable as a defence against tale-bearing rather than just a gratuitous piece of ill-natured bullying.

'So you brought Sister Gertrude a small memento from your father's possessions,' she said after she had waited for a space of time for an answer to her question. Sometimes an assertion is easier than a question. It requires a mere nod of confirmation. She made her voice sound absolutely neutral with not a shadow of blame or reproach in it.

'No!' There was a definite note of alarm in the voice. 'No, no, I gave her nothing. No, you've made a mistake, Reverend Mother. I didn't give her a thing.'

Odd, thought the Reverend Mother, but there was no contradicting this vehemence, not on such scanty and unreliable grounds as an implication from Sister Gertrude's words as repeated by a hysterical young nun. The atmosphere in the room, though, had definitely changed, now the young woman was uneasy, fidgeting; anxious to be off, perhaps. She got to her feet and stood fumbling her handbag and looking ill-at-ease. The Reverend Mother remained seated and looked at her appraisingly.

'I was wondering whether you would like me to pack up her clothes and things,' suggested Betty after a moment's silence. 'Denis can get the loan of a van from Ford's and then he'll pick them up tomorrow or the next day. Will that be all right by you?'

'Certainly,' said the Reverend Mother. She was quite taken aback. Beyond question, it was the right of Sister Gertrude's family to take away the possessions which she had brought to the convent, but it was unusual in the least. These clothes, toiletries and shoes had all been bought by the family of the girls who entered the convent, and provided in sufficient quantities to last them for at least three or four years. However, it was most unusual, in the case of a death, for the family to suggest taking them back. Or even on the frequent occasions when the girl herself was leaving the convent. Most were glad to abandon the unfashionable shoes, the heavy stockings, the unflattering underwear, Victorian-style nightdresses, along with memories of a mistake made, or even, sometimes, acute feelings of failure and embarrassment.

However, the woman had right on her side. The Reverend Mother instantly got to her feet.

'Come with me up to the novices' dormitory,' she said forcing herself to sound cordial. 'This would be a good time to go through the clothes as all of the novices will be busy around the school. We should,' she said, dragging her watch from her pocket and consulting its round face, 'be well finished and out of the way when the end of the school morning comes and the novices come up to their dormitories to get ready for dinner.'

She would be reluctant to intrude upon their ten minutes or so of liberty. It was, she thought, a valuable time for novices who were so watched and supervised through the normal routines of the day that it was important that they were allowed some such small breaks to chatter together even if the ostensible reason was to give them time to wash before their meals. She would, she thought, make sure that they were out of the way before then.

In silence, she led the way up the stairs and into the novices' dormitory. Why on earth should Betty want her sister Patsy's underclothes? They were of such a totally different shape and size that it was impossible to think that they would be of any use to such a smartly turned-out and well-dressed young lady. And the nun's clothing would be useless.

Sister Gertrude's section of the long clothes press which spanned one side of the room was in perfect order. Three items of outside clothing and five of underwear was the rule for families to provide for novices entering the convent. A spare full-length black dress, and a black winter-weight cloak hung from hangers. Pegged to another hanger were the spare wimple and veil, each carefully folded. Underwear and petticoats filled the shelves at the side, two pairs of well-polished shoes stood on the bottom floor and beside them two laundered and neatly folded towels. Betty efficiently dragged the trunk from under that section of the press and put it onto the bed. It still bore the label, Sister Gertrude, and the Reverend Mother found it very poignant to see the square, firm handwriting once again.

She tucked her hands into her sleeves and stood immobile while ideas went through her head. What had killed that girl? An accident. Impossible, she thought. There was no way that she could have eaten or drunk this alcohol or ethylene glycol by accident. Suicide, she decided, was so unlikely as to be almost impossible. Sister Gertrude had enjoyed life, had found the work in the convent to be stimulating, interesting and challenging. And she was a sensible, mature individual who knew, quite certainly, that the door was always open for anyone who wished to leave.

No, her death had to be murder. Who had administered the poison and how had it been disguised? The Reverend Mother pondered the matter as she watched the removal of Sister Gertrude's belongings. What on earth use would this well-dressed young mother find for wimple, veil, nun's full-length dress and black cloak? Some poor woman in the slums, though, would have been delighted with a gift of that cloak. Old-fashioned, but made from the best quality wool and certain to last a good twenty years. And yet the sister of the dead woman went through everything with the greatest care, searching every shelf, removing each drawer and searching behind it.

The Reverend Mother watched impatiently as Betty packed everything into the trunk: shoes, underwear and then the folded towels. She frowned a little at these, took each one out, shook it slightly and then refolded it.

'Funny,' she said. 'I thought that there were three large towels. I remember her buying them. Ever such expensive towels they were. She got them in Dowden's.'

'That would be correct,' said the Reverend Mother. 'There should be three.' There was something rather shocking about this insistence on removing all of her dead sister's belongings. Not a poor woman, either. The Reverend Mother remembered the solicitor's words. A very tidy fortune and all of it left to one of the man's two daughters.

'There will be other goods, purchased originally by Sister Gertrude, missing, also, Mrs Kelly,' she said in measured tones. 'The clothes that she wore at the moment of her death, the dress, the veil, the wimple would all be at the mortuary. I'm sure that you will be able to collect them from there, but there should, indeed, be three towels here in the dormitory and I will make enquiries. Just a moment,' she added. There was a quick, light step on the stairs outside and the humming of a tune. It would be Sister Imelda, returning from feeding an early dinner to the invalids on the top floor of the convent. She went to the door and waited.

'Oh, Reverend Mother.' Sister Imelda was taken aback and she stopped in the middle of her tune. The Reverend Mother smiled at her. 'Come in, sister,' she said, noting that Betty, making a thorough search, had not only pulled out the drawer and opened the door of the small locker by the bed, but was now checking the waste-paper basket. She turned her attention back to Sister Imelda. The song had already died from the girl's lips, but the smile also faded when she saw the dead nun's belongings strewn across the bed or already packed into the trunk. She stood very still and looked from one to the other. There was a shocked look on her young face.

'I wondered whether Sister Bernadette may have Sister Gertrude's third towel still in the laundry,' explained the Reverend Mother. She had noticed that there were piles of recently washed and ironed clothes on each of the other beds, but nothing on Sister Gertrude's. Sister Imelda, herself, had probably put the articles belonging to the dead novice away in the clothes press.

'Yes, she has . . .' Sister Imelda hesitated, her eyes going diffidently from the Reverend Mother's to the woman standing with an armful of snowy towels. 'There was a problem . . . there was a brown stain on it. It didn't come out in the wash. Sister Bernadette was going to have another try at it.'

The towel should perhaps have been given to Dr Scher. The Reverend Mother thought of that immediately, wondering whether the dead girl had used it to wipe away traces of vomit. Too late now, though.

'Tell her not to bother,' said Betty impatiently. 'Just bring it up to me. I won't want the trouble of coming again and of getting someone to mind the baby. My husband has got some stuff for getting paint off; it sort of dissolves it,' she explained to the Reverend Mother. 'If that doesn't work, then it can do for rough stuff. Good quality, these towels.'

When Sister Imelda came back with the towel, it was slightly steaming, probably from a red-hot iron from the top of the range. It was carefully folded so that the stain did not show and the young lay sister took care to keep it tightly wrapped up as she handed it over to the dead novice's sister. Betty, however, was made of sterner stuff. She opened the bundle and displayed the brown stain, right in the middle of the towel. She appeared, thought the Reverend Mother, to have shed her diffident and sorrow-filled demeanour and now showed herself to be a tough housewife, staring speculatively at the stain and then scratching at it with a fingernail. The Reverend Mother looked also. Despite her inner shrinking from it she needed to know what had stained the towel like that. She would, she thought, ask Sister Bernadette. She would not like to upset Sister Imelda, who, despite her nun's regalia, was still, after all, not much more than a child. The chances were, she thought, fairly sure that the dead girl had vomited in it, before moving to the window in order to empty her stomach of the poison that she had eaten.

Sister Imelda, though, seemed relieved that the sister of the dead girl was taking the matter in such a pragmatic manner. 'Sister Bernadette soaked it in cold water first,' she said eagerly. 'It wasn't much of a stain, just like you see it there. It wasn't blood or anything, we didn't think, Sister Bernadette and me,' she said reassuringly. 'Sister Bernadette thought it might be chocolate, but there was no chocolate pudding or anything like that served up, not since Sister Philomena's feast day when her niece brought that lovely chocolate cake for everyone to have as a dessert.'

Possibly treacle, thought the Reverend Mother as Betty efficiently refolded the towel and placed it into the trunk. She went back to the press and took out a pair of slippers that had been neatly tucked into the space beneath the dressing gown hanger in the clothes press and made room for them alongside the spare pair of shoes. Brown slippers, noticed the Reverend Mother. Neat brown leather slippers, not soft fluffy ones like most of the novices wore. And when the tins of polish were taken from the toiletries shelf there was amongst the black, one tin of dark tan-coloured polish. A stain from that, rubbed on a towel, might possibly be taken for chocolate. Or perhaps the stain was treacle mixed with tan polish. The combination of those two different materials might have been something that defeated Sister Bernadette's stain-removing capabilities. It was, thought the Reverend Mother, a possibility and visualized Sister Gertrude hastily rubbing the treacle from her lips, probably meaning afterwards to clean her towel but then feeling too ill to tackle it. She had been sick during the night. Had vomited out of the window. Had still struggled to her feet for morning prayers, then gone to feed the hens and collapsed.

As the Reverend Mother escorted Betty Kelly downstairs, mechanically absorbing the promise that Denis would call for the trunk either tomorrow, or at the latest on the day after tomorrow, her mind turned over the possibilities. Once she had left the visitor in Sister Bernadette's hands, she walked briskly to the telephone in the back hallway and gave Dr Scher's number to the telephone exchange lady. He would probably be at his lunch, she feared, but she would not keep him long. And he did always say that he ate too much and should try skipping his midday meal so that he could eat his evening one with a free conscience.

'Oh, Dr Scher, you asked me to report on Sister Frances,' she said as soon as he came to the phone. 'Well, you were right. The medicine seems to have worked very well. The fever has gone and she is sitting up in bed and enquiring about her dinner.' When she reached the end of the last sentence she heard a click from the exchange phone. The telephonist had found nothing interesting about this conversation. No juicy piece of gossip to pass on to the other telephonist and to whisper about in the tea shops of the city. Nevertheless, she framed the next sentence to him with care, relying on his quickness and his knowledge, like her own, of how telephone ladies listened into conversations. 'Sorry not to have phoned you earlier,' she said, 'but Sister Bernadette waylaid me with a problem of a towel stained with a mixture of treacle and shoe polish. Would you believe that?'

She heard a startled exclamation, bitten off before the word was completely finished. And then a silence. When he spoke again, his voice had changed. 'Oh, yes. Yes, indeed. Quite a possibility,' he said in interested tones and then smoothly went on, 'now Reverend Mother, don't worry. You let Sister Frances have her dinner and if she feels like it she can get up for a few hours. It will do her good. Tell her to stay indoors, though. That's a very nasty fog out there. I'll pop in and see her some time tomorrow. Would that suit you?'

'That will be perfect,' she said and rang off before Miss Clayton in the telephone exchange decided that the Reverend Mother had been a long time on the phone to Dr Scher and that something interesting might have come up for discussion.

SIXTEEN

Conradh na Gaeilge (the Gaelic League) was founded
in 1893 by Douglas Hyde, Fr. Eugene Ó Growney
and other Gaelic scholars.
The aim of the Gaelic League was:
1) The preservation of Irish as the national language
of Ireland and the extension of its use as a
spoken language.
2) The study and publication of existing Gaelic literature,
and the cultivation of a modern literature in Irish.

Patrick made sure that he arrived at Wellington Road a
little earlier than six o'clock in the evening. He did not
drive the police car right up to the MacSwiney sisters'
school, but parked it at some distance from Belgrave Place
and then strolled along the pavement, surveying the tall houses
on Wellington Road, most of which seemed occupied by
doctors, until he reached the enclosed terrace of houses at
Belgrave Place. No trace of any school children around, but
small groups of young men and young women were making
their way to number five, chattering animatedly in the Irish
language. He allowed them to go ahead, but scrutinized faces
as they passed him. He recognized none, and, even more
significant, had a feeling that none of them recognized him.
In any case, no one bestowed a second glance at him. Unlikely,
therefore, that these young people were members of any banned
organization.

The evening Angelus bell was sounding when he knocked
at the front door. Although the others ahead of him had simply
turned the handle and gone in, he thought he would not do
this. He was here on official business and he was determined
that this would be no informal visit. And so he gave a sharp,
authoritative rap on the door knocker and it was almost immediately opened to him.

Mary MacSwiney, herself. He recognized her instantly. No demonstration, no protest meeting in the city was complete without the grim face, the scraped-back grey hair and the funereal blackness of the clothing.

'Yes,' she said, taking in his uniform, the badge on the cap which he had removed. Her eyes travelled from the top of his head to the toes of his well-polished boots and her expression said that she did not think much of him. He produced a card from his pocket and handed it to her. 'Inspector Patrick Cashman, Miss MacSwiney,' he said.

'So I see,' she replied. 'I do not, however, recognize the present so-called government so I cannot acquiesce to any request that a lackey of that illegal organization might make to me.' She stared contemptuously at him and did not move from the exact centre of the doorway. Patrick did not move either, but alternatives were spinning through his head. If she had been the owner of a disorderly public house, he would have put her aside, gently but firmly, and mounted the stairs to where he could hear voices speaking loudly in Gaelic. If it had been a woman spouting obscenities and threatening violence he would have dealt with her without hesitation or anxiety, but faced with the refined English accent his courage deserted him and he felt that he should try gentlemanly methods first.

'Can I come in, Miss MacSwiney,' he said, after a long moment.

'You *may*,' she said with a strong emphasis on the correct form. She looked him up and down in a disdainful fashion, pursed her lips and then moved back into the dim light of the hallway.

He stepped over the threshold, resolving in a shamefaced way never to make that grammatical mistake again. *Oh, forget it, remember you are an inspector! Ignore the rudeness. Ignore the anti-government speeches*, he told himself. When it came down to it, she was just a little elderly lady. Can't send for the police to throw me out: he made the internal comment and it restored his confidence and his sense of humour. He followed her into the hallway and looked around. Shabby and in need of a coat of paint. Didn't make too much out of the school. Or else she just didn't care. Polite but firm, he reminded himself as he stood courteously awaiting her as she carefully closed the front door. He remembered the Reverend Mother's account of her visit to this place. That's the front room, he thought, the place where the Reverend Mother had seen the three decanters, whatever a decanter was. And he hoped desperately that he would recognize a decanter when he saw one, but reckoned that it must be some sort of container made of glass.

Yes. His eyes had become accustomed to the very dim light. Not a big house. School upstairs, on the first floor, bedrooms on the second floor, just two rooms downstairs, each leading off from the right-hand side of the narrow hall. Drawing room and dining room, they would be, and a kitchen in the basement below. First things first, he told himself.

'I'm just going to go upstairs to talk to the students,' he told her firmly as he walked past her and mounted the stairs. Let her follow if she wished. He laid a silent bet with himself that she would and so she did, treading heavily on the steps behind him. He did not stand back for her, though. Instinctively he sensed that he had seized the upper hand by his abrupt action and he was determined to hold it now. There were two flights of stairs, as is usual in these terraced houses, where bathroom and cloakrooms and closets were built on to the back of the house when indoor sanitary arrangements became common. He did not hesitate when he came to the end of the first flight, but turned the corner and proceeded up to the next landing.

The door to the room at the top of these stairs was closed, but the alien sounds of a rapidly spoken Irish language came to him and he opened the door firmly and strode in, allowing it to stand open so that Miss Mary MacSwiney could follow him if she wished.

'I am sorry to interrupt the work, but I have a few questions to ask,' he said to the man standing in front of the class. He heard his own voice with pleasure. Even six months ago, he would have cleared his throat first; a nervous habit, which he had cured himself of by constant practice on a solitary walk on an empty road through farmland. He had astonished the sheep who had congregated to the fence to listen as he recited a poem he had learned in school. Silly, he had thought afterwards, in rather a shamefaced way, but it had been a very useful practice and had given him confidence. He looked over the class now, and mentally designated them as sheep. He took his badge from his pocket, angled it so that the instructor who stood facing the class could see it plainly and then replaced it. The man said something to him, something that he did not understand, but he ignored it. He had never learned Irish and he was not going to make any excuses or apologies. If they wanted to communicate with him, then they could certainly do it in English. He moved to the front of the class and stood with his back to the window and addressed them. By now he was used to this and had learned to be steady, unemotional and matter-of-fact, and not to try to make any efforts to conceal or alter the accent of the streets where he had been born, though he did make efforts to pronounce his 'th' sounds correctly, rather than using the flat 't' of his boyhood. He introduced himself briefly, once more producing his badge and allowing the students in the front row of the class to peruse it for a minute and then proceeded with a bald statement of the facts.

'There have been three young nuns, three novices, attending these classes. I would imagine that you were all present on the last night that they attended. You may, or may not know, the reason why they have not returned. One nun, Sister Gertrude, was ill on her return from the classes and she died early the following morning. The police surgeon found that she had been poisoned. Now, is there anyone here who knows anything about this?'

There was a dead silence. He had expected no more. Mary MacSwiney, standing at the back of the classroom, glared at him with icy dislike but he ignored her. Not a stupid woman. She had decided that there was nothing that she could do about his presence and so she said nothing while he continued, running his eyes along the rows of young people.

'If anyone does remember anything of significance later on, then they should come to me, either here, or at the barracks. Just ask for me, Inspector Patrick Cashman.' Seizing a piece of chalk from the rim of the blackboard, he turned his back on them and printed his name in capital letters on the board. There was a murmur of conversation from behind him and he deliberately dragged out the time by adding the name and address of the Garda Barracks, though he was certain that the location of the main police station in the city would be known to all who were present. His ears were very sharp and he was sure that he heard the word Raymond. Someone in the first row, almost directly behind him, had whispered the name.

And then he turned back to face them. Mainly women, he noticed and that did not surprise him. About six men, all of them sitting together as though for mutual protection in this girls' school.

'Is Mr Raymond Roche here tonight?' He didn't think so but there was no harm in asking the question. Heads were shaken and the students looked at each other beneath lowered eyelids.

'He went out with two of them, with two of the three young nuns, that night, did he not?' He allowed that to stand while they exchanged glances. No one contradicted him and so he added, 'Sister Joan and Sister Brigid were to undertake an errand for him, while Miss MacSwiney detained Sister Gertrude, the oldest of the three nuns, in her room, downstairs.' He left a silence after that statement and then said rapidly, 'Which of you knew what was going on?'

He directed his question to a girl in the middle row, directly in front of him and she reacted with alarm.

'I don't know anything about it,' she said and now he was quite sure that she was the one who had mentioned Raymond's name. Pretty girl, he thought. Enormous brown eyes and red-gold, curly hair, worn quite long. She had a distinctive voice, quite husky, and very low-pitched for a woman.

He thought that he would let that go. He glanced at the clock on the wall. Half past six. The class had another half hour to run.

'Good,' he said briskly. He looked down at the desk. There was a register there and all of the names with addresses attached. He took out his notebook and copied in the name and address of Raymond Roche. Montenotte. Well, of course, that was where most of the rich of Cork city congregated, well above the sights and smells of the ancient settlement on the great marsh of Munster that was named Cork after the Gaelic word *corcaigh*, meaning a marsh. He returned the register to the teacher in charge.

'Please make me a copy of all of the names and addresses on this list,' he said and without waiting for an answer, he turned back to the class.

'One more question,' he said. 'Did anyone here notice whether Sister Gertrude had anything to eat or drink during her last evening here?'

That seemed to take them by surprise. There was a chorus of murmurs now. Heads were shaken firmly. Everyone was determined to disassociate themselves from any connection with a death from poison.

'A bar of chocolate, a bottle of Coca Cola, or ginger pop, anything like that lying around that she might have eaten or drank?' he asked, looking along the lines of faces, while making his suggestions.

'I don't encourage students to bring food here into the school,' said Miss MacSwiney from the back of the room. Her face had gone very pale. He ignored her and looked keenly at the girl in the middle of the first row. She was whispering to her companion. And then a movement from the back of the room caught his eye. Mary MacSwiney had moved towards the door, opened it and closed it carefully after her with the slightest of clicks.

Patrick took alarm. Had he made a mistake? Was there something that he should have done before coming upstairs?

'Well, thank you, everyone,' he said hastily and followed the woman out of the room and onto the stairs. She had moved very quickly. He heard the opening of the door downstairs when he reached the first landing. He turned the corner rapidly, swinging from the post at the top of this flight of stairs and then going down them as quickly as he could. He could hear the noise of his heavy boots thudding on the wooden steps. She would know that he was on her heels, but he couldn't help that. When he leaped onto the hall, skipping the last three steps, he could hear a sound, a creaking sound from the front room. By the time that he had opened the door, the draught of wet, foggy, river-smelling air met his nostrils and he subdued a curse. The window was wide open.

A quick glance at the heavy old-fashioned sideboard, described by the Reverend Mother, showed three glass containers still on it. Two completely full and the third about three quarters full. Just as the Reverend Mother had described. So why was the window open, and what had Miss MacSwiney thrown out of it? He sniffed hard. There was a smell of something, something that had been overlaid initially by the river smell that haunted the city of Cork but now rose slightly above the marshy, sour smell and in a moment he had identified it. Burning! Something had been burned.

Mary MacSwiney wore a long black cardigan over her black dress and one pocket of it bulged slightly. A box of matches – the oblong shape was unmistakable.

'What have you burned?' he asked and then went to the window, determinedly moving her to one side and leaning out, his elbows on the window sill and his eyes scanning the untidy muddle of overgrown pink flowers that were the sole occupants of the space. He saw it almost instantly. The fragment of a sheet of burned paper, resting upon one of the deeply scored green leaves of the plants. She made a movement as though to hold him back, but he evaded the skinny hand with ease and strode from the room. As he went through the front door, he took the precaution of clicking the catch into the open position. If she tried to shut him out, at least this would give him a few seconds with which to react.

In a moment he was in the flowerbed. Not raining, thank goodness, nor windy, just a steady damp fog filling the air with moisture. He bent over the scrap of paper, not daring to touch it, but doing his best to read it before a final disintegration took place. He took his notebook out from his pocket and tried to slide it under it, but it didn't work. The paper was too fragile. A list, he thought. Bending over it and then he knew a moment's disappointment. 'Tom' he read and then something after it that might have been the letter H. Even as he looked that part of the paper curled feebly and then dropped off. Some

Republican stuff, he thought. He wondered why she had bothered. The name of Tom Hurley was probably as well known
to the army and to the police in the city as was the name of
Michael Collins. There were more names. A list of them. Some
scorched beyond recognition. Something beginning with an
R, but then that too curled and died. He straightened himself,
put the notebook back in his pocket and then turned to face
the woman. For a middle-aged woman, he thought, she had
moved very swiftly, following him out of the house and now
was at his heels.

'I suppose you want to handcuff me and drag me off to
gaol, now.' She got the remark in before he said anything.

He ignored it. Some people always wanted to be martyrs. He
wondered whether, deep down, she remembered almost with
affection those days when she, like her brother, had gone on
hunger strike. In her case, being a woman, she had been sent
home every time she looked near to death and so had not died.
He had heard, though, that she had been just as stubborn, just
as resolved. And, of course, the world's press hung around
the prison, waiting for news of her decline and her near-death
episodes. And after that she had visited America, talking about
her brother, talking about her own experiences, dragging her
brother's widow with her, and she had collected large sums
of money for the sacred cause. He wondered whether her
present existence was boring and hum-drum to her after the
excitement of those tragic days. The present government had
taken the decision to ignore her, to turn a blind eye to her
decision to pay no taxes, to her determination to obey no laws
that they issued, and that decision had rather isolated her into
a position of meaningless protest. He resolved to follow that
example; not to allow her to feel victimized, and without any
comment he turned and walked back into the house, going
ahead of her into the front room in a pre-occupied manner
and allowing her to follow as she pleased.

'I said, I suppose you want to handcuff me and drag me
off to gaol, now.' Her voice was high-pitched and incredibly
posh. *North Main Street; that's where she comes from,* he told
himself. Not as poor as his own background, but not rich by
any means. Must have picked up that accent when she got a

scholarship to an English university. Cambridge, someone had told him.

'I hope that will not be necessary, Miss MacSwiney,' he said. He hadn't given a second glance to the burned fragments that lingered, just had led the way back into the house, and now stood stolidly beside the sideboard.

'I have authority here to search your house and to remove such items as might be of assistance to me in solving the crime of Sister Gertrude's death,' he said primly. He held out for her perusal a court order. The superintendent kept a small stack of them, already signed by a local judge, locked into the bottom drawer of his desk.

'I don't recognize the authority of the courts of this false government,' she said angrily.

'I'm sorry, Miss MacSwiney,' he said mechanically. It never hurt to speak softly, he had learnt that. 'There's been a death from poisoning of a nun who spent two hours here before falling ill and I understand that she stayed here, in this very room, in your company, while her two companions, two younger nuns, went home without her.' He took from his attaché case a small jar with a lid and carefully poured some of the purple liquid into it. This must be the elderberry cordial that the Reverend Mother had spoken of, though he was slightly surprised to see that the level was much lower than she had described. He wondered what it tasted of.

'Utter nonsense,' she scoffed. 'Do you think that I would poison that stupid girl? That elderberry cordial is perfectly safe. I drink it all of the time, myself.'

To his immense alarm, she took a glass from her desk, filled it to the brim with the liquid, her eyes challenging him all of the time.

Patrick knew a few minutes of acute anxiety. What if she dropped dead at his feet? He could just imagine the scornful headlines in the *Cork Examiner*, an enquiry from Dublin, the losing of his position; all these thoughts were racing through his head as she sipped the purple liquid, her rather watery eyes fixed on him, with what Patrick imagined to be a mocking expression. For a moment, it had crossed his mind that she might be committing suicide right in front of his eyes. After all, anyone who deliberately abstained from food for days on end, as she had, must have contemplated suicide, must have come to terms with the thought that the end result could be death. A mental image of the superintendent's purple face and his pungent comments if a suspect committed suicide while being interviewed by his inspector crossed his mind as Miss MacSwiney drained and then refilled her glass, before swallowing some more of the stuff.

But then he told himself, what would be the point? A hunger strike within a prison brought dozens, or even hundreds, of new believers to join the Republicans, and filled the party coffers with donations from rich Irish-Americans. Suicide in her own front parlour would do neither, only further deprive the Republicans of leadership.

'Would you like some, inspector?' she enquired, her voice full of undisguised mockery. 'I can assure you that the drink is harmless.'

'No, thank you.' He listened to himself critically. He had tried to make his voice sound neutral and felt that he succeeded relatively well. A thought had occurred to him. The fact that the drink in the glass container was innocuous meant nothing. The fatal poison might have been already in the bottom of the glass, already prepared, for the girl. Easy to conceal if the woman stood with her back turned to Sister Gertrude as she took a glass from behind the doors of the bottom part of the sideboard. On an impulse, he took a torch from his attaché case, dropped to his knees in front of the old-fashioned piece of furniture, opened its two doors and shone the torch into the dusty interior. Nothing much of interest, he decided after a few minutes spent moving jars of pickles, bottles of various liquids, some small glasses, discoloured by age and lack of use and a few odd pieces of china, fragile with age and cloaked in dust.

'I may be back,' was all he said when he got to his feet. He should, he thought, thank her for her cooperation and apologize for having disturbed her, but in the face of her openly mocking expression he felt like doing neither and contented himself with a nod as he strode from the room.

He lingered outside, though. A glance at the clock in her

room had shown him that the class would be over shortly. He took out his starting handle and leaned against the bonnet, twirling it idly in one hand and gazing down over the city and its two winding sheets of water. Odd to think of it once being a marsh, the great marsh of the province of Munster. And then the colonization of the two islands and the gradual spreading of houses and shops along the banks of the streams. And then his ear caught the sounds of young voices; he couldn't distinguish the words, but knew from the lilt that they spoke in Gaelic. He straightened himself, gripped the starting handle and walked around to the front of the car. There was a right and wrong way of starting the Ford's engine and he chose the wrong way, inserting the handle only about halfway up the slot and turning it in a lackadaisical way. A few croaks came from the engine and nothing else. Encouraged, he waited until they streamed through the door and then he tried again. The engine spluttered a bit this time and hastily he ceased, just in case by accident he got it going. He straightened himself, passed his wrist across his forehead and looked at the Gaelic League scholars who were coming down the steps.

'Anyone any good with a starting handle,' he called and the appeal, as he knew, was always irresistible to young lads.

'I'll have a go if you like,' offered one and Patrick thankfully passed him the starting handle.

'You'd think they could invent a better way of getting them going,' he said to the girl who had sat in the front row, the girl with the brown eyes and the red-gold hair.

She smiled at him. 'You would, indeed,' she said shyly and a little colour stole into her cheeks. He felt a little embarrassed. Perhaps he had shown his admiration a bit too openly. He could feel a warmth in his own cheeks.

'What does Mr Raymond Roche look like?' he asked trying to make his voice sound casual. Luckily the young fellow was having trouble with the Ford. He had banked on that, had learned by experience that it was always best to walk away from it, once you had messed up the initial attempt. For the moment, all the attention was focused on the car and he could chat without arousing any hostility.

She shrugged a little in response to his question. 'He's all right, I suppose,' she said.

'Funny thing to walk home with that nun, wasn't it?' He asked the question in a very casual fashion and she shrugged again.

'Well, the other two nuns had gone off early that night and I suppose he thought that he should escort her.' She giggled a little. 'Took her to Thompson's Bakery, too. You wouldn't believe that he'd do that with a nun, would you? I saw him coming out. She had waited outside the shop for him but I saw him give it to her. He had bought her one of their Swiss rolls!'

'Did he, indeed!' Patrick did his best to laugh in an amused fashion. 'I wouldn't have thought that a nun would be allowed to eat in the street.'

'Oh, she didn't eat it. It was one of their small ones. I saw her put the little box into the bag where her books were. I suppose that she had it later on for her supper. Lucky her! I love them, especially the ones with raspberry jam and cream between the layers.'

'So do I,' said Patrick. He sounded very fervent, he thought, and hoped that she would put it down to the fact that he had a very sweet tooth and found cakes irresistible – it was the truth, anyway. He too loved that mixture of jam and cream, but he was even more excited by the information than the thought of one of Thompson's Bakery's famous Swiss rolls. Raspberry jam and cream. Delicious.

And bound to disguise any sweet-tasting poison. What was it Dr Scher had said? A couple of spoonfuls would be enough to kill.

'Got it!' shouted the young fellow with the starting handle. The splutters and silences had now turned into a steady chug, chug. Patrick decided that it was well worth a shilling for a drink for them all. That had been a very valuable piece of information that he'd extracted while they were all busy at the noisy job of starting up his car.

So Mr Raymond Roche had bought a Swiss roll for Sister Gertrude. And she had waited outside the shop. That meant that he could have done something to the cake before handing it over to her.

He smiled happily at the girl. Pity he was a policeman on duty. Otherwise he would take her to the Thompson Bakery, only a stone's throw down the hill from where they stood. And he would buy her as much Swiss roll as she fancied. With some sweet lemonade. He liked the way that she allowed her curly hair to grow down over her shoulders and he liked the full skirt of her dress that went below her knees. He didn't like a lot of the girls these days with their shingled hair and their terribly short skirts. His mind went briefly to Eileen MacSweeney. Perhaps she and Mary MacSwiney shared a common ancestor a hundred years ago. Some rebel, he guessed and then put them from his mind, resenting the memory of how Miss MacSwiney had mocked him while drinking that elderberry cordial. Raymond, he thought, would be a more likely villain than the elderly schoolteacher, and he was glad about that.

'Thanks,' he said to the girl before he left her. 'Perhaps I'll see you again, some time.' Pity he couldn't take her for a snack, but it was important to get hold of Raymond as soon as possible and find out as much of the truth from him as he could possibly do.

Raymond Roche was at home when he arrived at the house in Montenotte. He had braced himself for the discovery that the bird had fled, but as he drove cautiously through the gates, he saw the man himself standing beside his car and looking down at an obviously punctured tyre with disgust. He was already all dressed up for a night's entertainment. He wore elegantly-cut black trousers, a black tail coat, made from finest wool and trimmed with silk braid, a stiffly starched and ironed white shirt with a white bow tie. The double-breasted coat was open and the evening wind caused it to lift slightly, displaying the elegant white satin of its lining.

Not an outfit in which to change a muddy wheel.

And yet he seemed indecisive, not calling imperiously for help, just standing there, peeling off his white gloves and dangling them thoughtfully by the fingers. Perhaps his parents were tired of him hanging around the house with nothing to do, making, by all accounts, no effort to get himself a job, or even do something like joining the army or the navy. Perhaps servants no longer took orders from him.

'A puncture, sir, bad luck,' said Patrick and saw the man turn to him with something approaching relief. Good-looking fellow. Tanned, well-groomed, fine-featured with beautifully barbered dark hair, he would certainly have impressed two unsophisticated young nuns.

Well, I'm damned if I'll change a tyre for him. The thought that he might be expected to do that had crossed Patrick's mind for a second, before he said smoothly, 'May I give you a lift, sir? I'm on my way back down to the city.'

Raymond wavered for a moment, looking from Patrick to his broken-down car, no doubt weighing up the possibility of getting another lift home at the end of the evening, with the stronger likelihood that he would have to pay for a taxi, but in the end he decided to chance the lift with the policeman.

'Very good of you,' he muttered and went around to the passenger seat of Patrick's car, sitting there, very stiffly, while Patrick reversed the Ford and then drove carefully back out through the elaborately decorated iron gates.

'What address, sir?' he asked aloud, just like a well-trained chauffeur. Call them 'sir' the superintendent had told him when he was first appointed. Call all of the toffs 'sir' and then you ask them what you like. They can't object if you stick 'sir' front and back of every sentence.

'The Imperial,' said Raymond. Grumpily. As if he had been forced to admit something.

Best hotel in the city. Expensive place for a man with no job, thought Patrick, not as if the Roches were particularly rich these days. Would have been in the past, according to the superintendent, but not now. If Raymond had a need for drugs, then he would have to get the money from some other source. So had said the superintendent, and the Reverend Mother, in slightly more discreet language, had said more or less the same thing.

'The Imperial Hotel, well that's no problem; I have a visit to pay in South Mall,' he said aloud. 'I can easily drop you off there. I wanted to see you anyway, sir, in connection with

the death of Sister Gertrude,' he continued as he took the car
at a slow pace along the narrow road.

'Who?'

That was a mistake, thought Patrick, feeling somewhat
cheered by the monosyllable. Of course, the man would know
that name. The whole of Cork was talking about Sister
Gertrude. It wasn't a city where the inhabitants kept quiet
about any piece of news. The *Cork Examiner* had written one
of its 'shock/horror' articles, implying that the affair was all
down to the IRA troops that lurked underground in the city.
Every shop and every public house in Cork would be discussing
the matter and doubtless the same could be said of the bars
and the restaurants of places like the Imperial Hotel and in
the clubhouse of the Muskerry's Golf Club. There would be
no chance whatsoever that Raymond Roche did not know of
that death. And, of course, he had actually known Sister
Gertrude, had for the last few weeks attended classes with her
at St Ita's School.

However, Patrick, seized on the opportunity. 'Of course,
you weren't present at the Gaelic League class in Miss
MacSwiney's school this evening, were you, sir? I've just
come from there. It was the subject of conversation there,' he
added and was glad to see a look of apprehension cross the
face of his elegantly dressed companion. Let him mull over
that, he thought, as he turned his attention to the steep hill
leading down from the genteel heights of Montenotte and onto
the Western Road. Raymond was in a state of nerves; he had
jumped when he heard that. 'Your name was mentioned in
connection with Sister Gertrude,' he added aloud as he negoti-
ated a steep corner.

'I knew absolutely nothing about Sister Gertrude,' said
Raymond angrily. 'Hardly said a word to her.'

'True,' said Patrick thoughtfully. He pulled in at a layby,
partly to allow a stately Daimler to overtake his humble Ford,
but mainly because he wanted to watch Raymond's face when
he delivered his next sentence. 'True,' he repeated. 'It was
Sister Joan and Sister Brigid that you and Miss Mary
MacSwiney concentrated your attention on, wasn't it?'

'I don't know what you are talking about!'

There was no doubt that Raymond's nerves were in a bad state. There was a twitch at the corner of his mouth and the long dark eyelashes were blinking rapidly.

'You recruited two young nuns to serve your purpose, or that of your master, Tom Hurley.' Another reaction to the name of Tom Hurley. This time a violent blinking. What a naïve young man if he didn't realize how the eyes of the police and of the army spies would be watching out for any connections to Tom Hurley.

'The plan for Spike Island would not work unless you got some trained men, trained with explosives, secretly onto Spike Island. They did a very good job, must have been experienced. It takes a steady nerve and a lot of training to handle that amount of explosives and so you had to have the right people. It was important to get letters out to these men without any suspicion being aroused. What could be better than recruiting some innocent young nuns? Was that your idea, Mr Roche?' Patrick injected a note of admiration into his voice. It didn't work though. Not a good enough actor, or else Raymond was a tougher proposition than he had hoped for.

'I don't know what on earth you are talking about,' he said angrily. 'Now, if you don't mind, could we get on? I do have an eight o'clock appointment.'

'You can always say that you had a puncture and it would be the absolute truth,' said Patrick mildly. 'Indeed, far more truthful than you saying you don't know what I am talking about. Yes, you do know what I am talking about and I want to know all of the details. A young nun, Sister Gertrude, has been murdered and I can tell you, Mr Raymond Roche, that your name features on my list of suspects.'

'Why should I kill that nun?'

'Because she was getting in the way of your plan. The two young innocent and easily-led sisters were a godsend to the plot. Mary MacSwiney did a good job in recruiting them.' Patrick thought fleetingly of what Eileen had said to the Reverend Mother. Clever girl, Eileen. He was sure she was right in her surmise of how the young nuns' feelings had been worked on by that woman. Sister Gertrude was a different matter. She might have met the two with their collecting boxes and then informed the authorities once she got back to the convent. 'You gave her some poisoned cake, didn't you?' he said aloud. 'You thought that she would eat it straight away, but that did not quite work out as she refused to eat it in public. Popped it into her bag so that she could eat it later. Spoiled your plan, didn't it? But didn't save her life.'

'I don't know what you are talking about!' Raymond put his hand on the door handle. In a moment he had opened it and swung his long legs out. Patrick sat very still. He was satisfied about the way that the interview had gone, but now was the time that everything was put on a more formal basis.

'I'd like you to attend the barracks for further questioning tomorrow afternoon at four o'clock, sir,' he said. Then as the man turned an angry face towards him, he said evenly, 'Please do be on time, sir. I would hate to upset your parents by having to send a constable to escort you.' And with that he eased in the clutch, moved the gear and drove off just as Raymond slammed the door shut. Best to leave it at that, he thought with satisfaction. This business of asking questions in a car was not a good idea when you are dealing with a man who may, who very likely had, committed a murder.

SEVENTEEN

St Thomas Aquinas
. . . bonum unius hominis non est ultimus finis,
sed ordinatur ad commune bonum.
(. . . the benefit to one man is not the ultimate end,
but is ordained to the common good.)

Sister Bernadette had the trunk ready in the back hallway by first thing on the following morning. She had, noted the Reverend Mother, put the keys in a neatly labelled envelope which she had left on the desk of her superior so that they were kept safe until the brother-in-law of the late Sister Gertrude arrived. The nuns, filing in for breakfast after the morning service, all cast a glance at it, and a low murmur rose up from amongst them. News spread fast. No doubt the three remaining postulants had spread the news that the trunk had been removed.

'Will you want to see him, Reverend Mother?' Sister Bernadette was always punctilious about ascertaining the Reverend Mother's views on visitors before she even attempted to announce an arrival and she accosted her on the way back from the chapel.

'I don't think so,' said the Reverend Mother. She had nothing to say to the young man that she had not said before, and she had no desire to have any more hysterical scenes re-enacted in her room and taking up her valuable time. 'Come and collect the key when he arrives. Tell him that I am busy, if he enquires for me.'

He was at the door punctually at ten o'clock in the morning. The Reverend Mother heard the doorbell peal and the sound of Sister Bernadette's rapid footsteps. There was a pause then and after a few moments a discreet knock on the door. The Reverend Mother reached into a drawer, took the envelope with the keys from it and called an invitation to enter and hesitated for a moment. Did she want to see the young man again, she wondered? This was a moment when she could change her mind. However, she could not think of any particular reason to do so and handed the keys silently to Sister Bernadette.

She searched through the drawer for one of the bishop's letters. Something about a meeting, one of the numerous meetings with which his lordship beguiled his time and kept a close eye on the workers on the marshlands of the city. She didn't find it and hoped she had not put it hastily into the nearest bin, but then another envelope caught her eye. She had deliberately not filed this one, but had kept it in her own private and locked drawer. She remembered when it came that she had determined that it should not fall to the eye of Sister Gertrude, at that time efficiently creating a muddle-proof system of filing in the Reverend Mother's office. Now she took it out and read it again. It was from the solicitor who had made the will of John Donovan, very shortly before his death and he had enclosed a copy of the will itself for her perusal and with a hint that perhaps, as Sister Gertrude's superior, she would divulge the contents rather than hand over the will itself. She had agreed with him heartily. Sister Gertrude had shown no interest. The money would not have benefited her in any way, of course, but would have gone into the community's coffers. It was just as well that she did not read what her father had said, though. The will had been worded with a bitterness that was surprising.

> *Since my older daughter has abandoned her father and her home in order to pursue a way of life that would deny her of a child and her father of a grandchild, then no portion whatsoever of my goods, chattels, shares in Ford's Company and money, whether in the bank or . . .*

The Reverend Mother stopped reading and stared into space. Why had Mr Donovan reacted so strongly that he had needed to cut his older daughter completely from his will and with such venom? He had not shown any very noticeable signs of grief or of anger when his daughter, the late Patsy Donovan, had decided to enter the convent. He had not wept, but then he was not that type of person. His attitude, she seemed to remember, was one of a man who had, to a certain extent, washed his hands of the enterprise. 'She's old enough to know her own mind.' He had definitely said that, but he had said it philosophically rather than bitterly. And the will, she noticed once again, as she perused the solicitor's letter, was not made at the time when Sister Gertrude had taken her first vows, but quite shortly, just a week or so, before the man's death, when a year had elapsed since his daughter had left the family home. He had visited throughout that year. Punctually once a month, she thought, still puzzling over the matter. Never said much, quite unlike the parents of both Sister Catherine and Sister Brigid, who had been full of anxious questions and pieces of information to convince the Reverend Mother of the unique and sainted nature of the delicate souls that she had taken under her wing. Sister Joan had been the eldest of a large family, whose parents lived in north Cork, quite near to the border with Limerick. They visited less frequently and their time at the convent always seemed to be studded by shouts from her lively young brothers and sisters; and cries and squawks from pursued hens. A lively lot, said kind Sister Bernadette, but most other nuns drew in a sigh of relief once they had left the premises.

Mr Donovan's visits, however, had been short and almost unnoticed. The Reverend Mother had praised the work that his daughter was doing on her recalcitrant accounts and filing system, but he merely nodded and said, 'That would be no bother to her.' He did not seem to be very interested. He appeared, she thought at the time, to be one of those rare breed of parents who felt that it was up to their daughter to make her own decision as to how she wished to live her life. She had heard the two of them laugh together as they paced the garden paths. His visit was friendly, sociable and soon over.

But the will told a different story and had shocked her when she read it first. There had been real anger in the words that were written down, presumably at his dictation. He had, it appeared, bitterly resented his daughter's decision to enter the

convent and deprive herself of children and her father of
grandchildren. Was it because of that attitude that Sister
Gertrude had fled to the convent before her sister's wedding
could take place? With a sigh she tucked the envelope away
and returned to her task.

It was about half an hour later when Sister Bernadette gave
her distinctive double knock on the door.

'Come in, sister,' called the Reverend Mother.

'Just wanted to check on your fire, Reverend Mother.'

There was, of course, nothing wrong with the fire. It had
been well set, and well banked up and was glowing in a well-
behaved manner. Sister Bernadette fussed a little with the
damper, managed to add another few coals and then made
movements of one who was about to leave the room, but who
wanted to relieve her mind before doing so.

With an inward sigh, the Reverend Mother put down her
pen, and waited for what was to come.

'Raining again, I see,' she said. A remark about the weather
would give Sister Bernadette permission to engage her in
conversation and after a perfunctory 'never stops, does it!' she
launched into her grievance.

'He's gone. He's taken the trunk away, that Denis Kelly.'
Sister Bernadette's voice was abrupt and the very use of the
word 'that' was enough to show the Reverend Mother that the
young man and his manners had not been approved of.

'That's good,' she said and waited for what would come
next.

'Don't know what he expected,' said Sister Bernadette with
a toss of her head. 'Don't see why he should have thought
that we had any interest in keeping anything belonging to
Sister Gertrude. For my part, I have enough rubbish around
this place. It's twenty peoples' work to keep it all dusted and
clean and tidy.'

'Yes, indeed,' said the Reverend Mother sympathetically.
'Why, did he think that we had kept something?'

'Wanted the trunk opened,' said Sister Bernadette. 'Would
you believe it? Blamed the wife, of course. Said that she told
him to do it. Took the keys from my hand. Not so much as a
by your leave, just reached over and took them. Unlocked the

trunk, threw the lid back. Standing there and staring into it. Asking me if there was anything missing, asking it before the trunk was even open. Saying that his wife told him to check it before he went off with it. That towel again. Would you believe it! A stained old towel with more than a year's wear taken out of it. Wanted to make sure that there were three towels in the trunk. Involved the young girls into the questioning, too. Asked poor little Sister Imelda if everything was in there. I didn't let him get away with that, though, Reverend Mother. Counted out the towels. Told him fair and square. Faced up to him. "What is it that you are looking for, Mr Kelly?" I asked him. Of course, his father was just a coalman. Still a nice man, the father. Wouldn't have given his son any ideas above his station in life. "Just tell us what might be missing, Mr Kelly." That's what I said to him. He had the trunk open by then. Didn't even answer me. Just stood there staring into it. Too much trouble for him to even answer. After all the business of unlocking, didn't even thank me when I pulled up the lid. Didn't worry about all of the clothes, everything that was in the trunk, all of the stuff that his wife, Betty, had put in there. Didn't even pick up a single thing. I was the only one that touched anything. Showed him that the three towels were there. You'd think that he would be embarrassed. Well, he wasn't. Not a bit of it. Well, he looked a bit strange, but not a word out of him.'

'Was he happy, then?' asked the Reverend Mother, puzzled as to where this saga was leading, but Sister Bernadette disregarded the question. There was more still to come.

'You'll never guess, Reverend Mother,' she said dramatically, 'but there on top of all the clothes, just under the lid of the trunk, there was a box of chocolates. Well, not a box of chocolates, exactly. An empty cardboard box. All squashed up it was. Nothing in it. Don't know why on earth the woman put it in. "Who put that in there?" That's what he said. "Your wife," says I. "She's the one that packed it. You don't think any of us would put a piece of rubbish like that into the trunk." I'd have taken it and thrown it into the waste-paper basket, but he slapped the lid back down and was off before you could say Jack Robinson. Just took the trunk, grabbed it by the handle and then off with him. No manners, no manners at all. Still, it's not for us to judge, is it, Reverend Mother?'

Sister Bernadette, having talked out her indignation and hurt pride at an insult to the establishment, now began to back her way out of the room, swabbing some damp from the window that was weeping in sympathy with the weather outside and then running a quick finger along the length of the top of the bookshelf to make sure that it had been well-cleaned that morning. She was leaving an opportunity for something to be said, but the Reverend Mother said nothing.

When she had gone, the Reverend Mother put down her pen, pushed away the writing pad and stared ahead.

A box of chocolates. An empty box of chocolates.

A sweet tooth. What was it that the girls' aunt had said about the remaining sister? *Always nice and slim. Didn't have a sweet tooth, not like Patsy. Funny child, she was; Betty, I mean. The only child I've known that wouldn't thank you for a sweet.*

And Sister Catherine's remark: *Be careful, Betty, there's Sister Mary Immaculate's little pet over there and she will go tittle-tattling to the big white chief if we're not careful.*

'Be careful.' Not 'hush' which would indicate an incautious word. 'Be careful' would assume that there was something to hide. Something handed over. She had thought of a memento, like a pen or something like that.

But what was it that Sister Gertrude had cheerfully confessed that she found the most difficult aspect of convent life? Giving up sweets, of course. Unlike her sister Betty, Patsy loved sweets, loved chocolate; would, her sister had remarked, get extremely fat if she ever gave up riding a bike.

A box of chocolates. Those new chocolates. Her cousin Lucy had tried to tempt her with one on the occasion of her birthday. She remembered it clearly. It had had a solid chocolate shell and, according to Lucy, a sweet liquid sealed within its covering. Easy enough, perhaps, to make a small hole in the top and to inject poison, a sweet-tasting poison, into the chocolates.

The box had been completely empty. Squashed flat. Probably hidden behind some clothes. So the chocolates had been consumed and it was easy to guess who had consumed them. Patsy Donovan, the girl who could never resist a sweet. But would she have eaten the whole box?

The Reverend Mother sat and thought about this for a while. It was a very long time since she had eaten chocolate or sweets of any kind, probably well over fifty years. Nevertheless, it would, she thought, be unlikely that a whole box would be consumed surreptitiously after lights were out in the novices' dormitory.

But even putting that aside . . . What would be the point?

'But why?' she said quietly to herself. She got up from her chair and paced the length of the room. Why should Betty poison her older sister, Patsy? That question went around and around in her head.

Jealousy?

Fairly unlikely.

After all, the younger sister had come away with all the prizes. Had the man; safely married to her. No chance of him marrying her sister. Had a baby son. Had all of the money left by her clever and industrious father. A lot of money.

'A considerable fortune!' That's what she had been told. A substantial bank balance, shares in Ford's, best shares in the country, according to the solicitor. New house, new car. A good education for her son. It was all in her lap. Why should she be jealous of her older sister, now immured behind the walls of a convent?

Once again, she took the will from the drawer, the last will and testament of John Donovan. A hardworking, shrewd man who had accumulated a fortune and then left it all to one of his two daughters. She went through the will, reading it with care. It did not enlighten her. And then she started again, struck by something that she had not noticed before, or if noticed, had not pondered upon.

The puzzle was, she thought, in the tone of the will, the rancour; the anger. None of that had shown on his monthly visits – one of them only two weeks before his unexpected death. Had someone worked on him? Had the younger sister, Betty, a new mother of a baby boy, roused feelings of anger against her older sister, purely in order to ensure that she got her father's entire fortune?

It was possible.

Mother love, she understood, was a very strong emotion, something that would very easily surpass the vague and tentative emotion aroused within her for the sister with whom she had grown up.

Would Betty put the future of her son before the present welfare of her sister? A girl who, she probably thought, had made her bed and should now lie upon it.

It took her less than a minute to peruse the details of the will once more. And then she sat back and pondered whether Sister Gertrude's death could have benefited her sister in any way. No, Sister Gertrude's death could not have benefited her sister. She could not come up with a single valid reason. A nun has nothing to leave, even to her nearest and dearest. If she had been left a fortune, then it would have gone straight into the coffers of the convent. Even if she had lived for another seventy or eighty years, she could never have touched the money that her father had bequeathed to her. It would all have disappeared long before her death.

But another matter intruded itself. She looked at the date at the top of the will. Made just one week before he died. A week after his last visit to the convent. Her mind was clear on that. She remembered Sister Gertrude's bewilderment. *'It's only two weeks since I've seen him and he was perfectly well then. I never knew that he had anything wrong with his liver. He hardly missed a day's work all the time that I knew him.'*

'That,' she said aloud, 'is very interesting.'

'Never went to the doctor, much. Never missed a day's work, anyway. He just fell ill, was vomiting and then, he just died. A terrible shock for the girls. They sent for the doctor down at Turners Cross and he came and said it was his liver.'

And there was something else interesting lurking at the back of her mind.

If a man had a bad liver, would he not visit a doctor, need to take days off work when he felt ill. And were not the symptoms of his death very similar to those that occurred to Sister Gertrude: sickness, vomiting, death.

Beyond a coincidence, she told herself that.

It was just the question of the motive that made her hesitate.

And then a sudden thought came to her. She sat very still, very upright in her chair, staring out at the grey sky and thick mist outside. Her mind went back to Dr Scher and his explanations and softly she said to herself, 'Of course! I've been blind and stupid.'

She got to her feet decisively and walked rapidly down the corridor and lifted the phone.

No response. No crackle. No sound whatsoever.

The phone was out of order.

EIGHTEEN

Garda Siochána Act 1924
'In the event of a rule being broken, it shall be lawful
for the Commissioner, or for any other officer of the
Gárda Síochána nominated for that purpose by the
Commissioner, or for any person nominated for that
purpose by the Minister to hold an inquiry and to
examine on oath into the truth of any charge or
complaint, of neglect or violation of duty preferred
against any member of the Gárda Síochána, and also
by summons under his hand to require the attendance
of any witness at such inquiry.'

Patrick sat back in his chair and stared across his desk at Eileen MacSweeney. Nothing in his training, nothing in his studies had prepared him about how to respond to her demand. An elderly woman, a very elderly woman, had sent him a message through this girl, not a very respectable girl, but one who had been involved with rebels; a girl who had reputedly broken into Cork gaol in order to release a prisoner, who had been subject to police surveillance and who had mixed with some of the most notorious Sinn Féin outlaws in the city. And now she came with instructions for him, a police inspector.

And the instruction was based on a theory, not on any hard facts. She had told him to enter a house, something that required a court order, had told him that he needed to arrest someone. And all without a shred of hard evidence. He cleared his throat and wondered what to do.

'Come on, Patrick,' said Eileen impatiently. 'The Reverend Mother is terribly worried. The convent phone is out of order. That's why I am here, otherwise she would have asked you to come and see her and would have talked to you herself. But now time is getting on. Something might happen. That's

what she said. She says that you must go there immediately.
She's trying to get hold of Dr Scher, also. The lay sister who
came to find him went on to find me. That's what the Reverend
Mother told her to do if she couldn't find him. She said that
she had never known Reverend Mother Aquinas look so
worried. You must do what she says, Patrick. I went to the
convent straight away as soon as I got the message and she
explained everything to me.'

Left her work, just like that, thought Patrick, feeling almost
distracted with worry. All right for her, he supposed. Some
people could get away with murder.

'I can't.' He tried to explain it to her. 'I'm in charge. I can't
leave here. I'll send Joe and get him to ask if everything is
all right.'

'And what happens if he gets no answer? Or what happens
if the answer is that everything is fine? What does he do then?
Go away with his tail between his legs.'

Patrick felt himself flushing hotly at her scorn. She just
didn't understand how these things worked. 'And I can't get
a court order until the superintendent comes back,' he said.
'And he has the Ford, so how can I get up to Friars Walk?'
he finished.

'Oh, for heaven's sake, Patrick! Come on. I'll give you a lift.
My bike is faster than that car of yours. Come on, Patrick! If this
gets into the papers; that you knew and you did nothing . . .'

He flushed angrily, but he knew that she was right. He
could just imagine the newspapers. He lifted his phone. 'Joe,'
he said, 'could you come in here, please, for a moment?'

'I'll wait for you outside,' said Eileen and he let her go.
While he scribbled down the name and address for Joe and
added a brief note for the superintendent, with the heading,
'Acting on Information Received' he could hear her revving
up her bike. A glance through the window confirmed that she
had taken the bike out through the gates and for a moment,
oddly, he panicked in case she had gone without him. But no,
she was still out there on the street, that motorbike of hers
puffing out steam into the fog-laden air. He would do without
his coat, he thought. He could imagine how it would stream
out behind them like a sail.

This is ridiculous, he thought, as they sped through the streets. Nevertheless, he had to admit that Eileen was making a good job of it. Either she had good directions or knew the area well. She never hesitated, never scanned the road names, placed high on buildings, but wove her way in and out of horses and carts, donkeys and carts, lorries and messenger boys on bikes until she pulled up in front of a smart newly built house in Friars Walk. Nothing parked outside. Everything looked quiet and normal.

'A fool's errand,' he muttered to himself. There was a post office across the road and without a word to Eileen, he crossed over to it. Empty of people. That was fortunate. A quick showing of his badge and then he was in the back room with the door firmly closed and a telephone in front of him.

'No, the superintendent is not back yet.' Joe sounded worried, suggested that he take a message to him. Patrick hesitated. Over the years he had come to know the superintendent well and now he could guess the reaction to this interruption. A refusal to take action on such flimsy grounds, to 'buy a pig in a poke' as he would put it. An angry command to return to the barracks. He would not be able to disobey that order from a superior. Perhaps the Reverend Mother was wrong, but she could be right. And if she were, well then . . . The thought was too much to dwell on. No, he couldn't risk it. The danger was too great.

'Leave it for the moment, Joe, but stay near to the phone, won't you?' He didn't wait for a reply. Joe was someone that he could rely absolutely upon. Once again, he wished that his assistant was with him. Somehow things were always easier to decide upon when Joe was standing beside and waiting, with a look of calm confidence for a command from his superior officer.

'Many thanks,' he said to the postmaster and strode out of the shop. Eileen was waiting for him, her face impatient.

'I'll knock at the door and make an enquiry,' he said curtly to her and wished that he was on his own.

'Have you got a gun?' she hissed and he gave her an impatient look before striding towards the front door. Everyone knew that the Gardaí Siochána, the guardians of the peace, were unarmed. He hoped that she didn't have an illegal weapon secreted in some pocket but he didn't really want to know. If only he had Joe with him instead of this girl. It would have been better to have taken Joe, even if they both had to use push bicycles. Friars Walk had not been too far from the barracks. Eileen had been up to the top of Evergreen Road almost before he knew it. Yes, he should have taken Joe. He should have known that the superintendent would be unlikely to be back before lunch time.

And then, just as he reached his hand forward towards the knocker, there was a sudden scream, the scream of a woman and the thin, high cry of a very small baby.

'Around the back, Patrick.' Eileen had the sense not to shout, but said it in his ear and he followed her past the small wooden shed, its door bolted. She neatly vaulted the padlocked gate between front and back gardens and he did the same, cautiously testing that it would hold his weight before he clambered across. The woman's screams had stopped before they reached the back corner of the house. Not cut off abruptly. He noticed that. No, there had been words said. Words that were not muffled by any wall or window.

Eileen had heard the words, also. Now she had flattened herself against the wall and was moving slowly and cautiously towards the corner of the house. The baby still cried, a shrill, alarmed cry, but nothing else. It was very loud for such a young baby, though. Only a couple of months old, he seemed to remember.

A window was open. He was sure of that. Once again he heard something beneath the piercingly high shrieks. Somebody had spoken. Spoken in a low voice. No words distinguishable. But he was confident that he had heard something said.

And now he was around the corner. Stepping out a little to avoid a prickly rose that clambered up almost to roof height, neatly tied to a solidly built timber trellis. He had been moving slowly and carefully, nevertheless he almost bumped into Eileen. She had stopped just beside a window frame and was standing, pressed closely to the wall, flattened against the trellis, her head turned sideways, tilted upwards.

Above them was another window. One of those modern

windows, not a sash window, but one that was hinged and both panes opened outwards like a pair of doors. A pair of lacy curtains, blown to and fro, dragged in and out by the wind, flew like sails, taking his eye as he looked up.

Then he heard words again. Just two words. '*Drink it!*' Almost a scream. More of a plea than a command. And a movement. Through the tangle of the curtains. Another piercing wail, a tempest of sound. A baby, bare legs, kicking the cold damp air frantically, a baby thrust out through the open window, chilled, shocked, seeking warmth and comfort. Screaming almost as though it sensed the terrible danger.

Something said from inside.

And then the cry, an angry scream more than a cry: 'Don't come any nearer!'

A few words from the woman, a plea, perhaps. The body of the small baby stayed where it was, poised above the concrete path, the curtains, wrapping and unwrapping themselves around the small body. No more from the first voice. A pause, a wait, waiting for something to happen. Eileen had replaced her pistol in her pocket and moved forward, going step by step, moving very carefully, keeping her back to the wall, with her head turned, looking up towards the body of the screaming child. Now she was directly beneath the window. Hands empty, arms slightly stretched forward. Waiting like someone ready to catch a ball. Then she glanced at him and he gave a nod. There could be no certainties, but somehow he was sure in his mind that he could depend on her. Now it was his turn. For a second, he touched the truncheon at his belt, touched it for reassurance, but did not remove it. With another quick glance upwards, he stepped slightly forward, skimmed past her, just avoiding touching her and then he moved on. Yes, there was a back door, there, leading from a kitchen to the small back door.

More words from the window. Another scream from the baby. A hasty glance upwards showed him that it was tiny, far too young to be aware of its peril; to be afraid for its life. It was just the shock of the cold air, the lack of reassuring arms holding it tight. The cold and the shock, he told himself and hoped that he was right. It wouldn't be the first injured and then murdered baby that he had come across since the time when he had entered the police force.

'Drink it down, every last drop,' now screamed the voice, high-pitched, almost unhuman. Patrick glanced back. Eileen was in position, hands slightly forward, turned upwards. Without looking, she was aware of him and he saw her nod. He waited no longer. Put his hand on the door.

Locked.

Patrick felt in his pocket. His penknife. No, not there. Nothing but a few coins. He had taken it out! He remembered now, had emptied his pockets to allow the tailor to clean his jacket. He could kick the door. It looked pretty flimsy. He could easily knock the glass out of the top section. Could easily climb through. He could do all of those things, but he could panic the criminal; he could cause the baby to be dropped. He glanced back at Eileen and she gave him another nod. Somehow it filled him with confidence and instantly he remembered. His trouser pocket, the hip pocket. That was where he had put it.

He slid the knife out, unfolded it. Yes, that was the blade. He had a moment's gratitude towards Charlie Mac, now serving a prison sentence for burglary. Couldn't stop himself boasting, that was Charlie. Just like a lot of them. Had to demonstrate exactly how he had got the door of the insurance office open without attracting the notice of a policeman on the beat. Had insisted on Patrick locking the door of the interrogation room and trying his hand with a penknife. Pointed out the right blade to him.

And it had been easy. Easy while a professional was guiding him and a comic relief at the end of a successful piece of investigation.

Not like now when it might well be a matter of life or of death.

Patrick slid the blade into the lock, shut from his mind the shrill, distressing sound of the frightened and cold baby, turned the blade with the twist of hand that he had been taught and then . . . nothing.

Once again, he said to himself. *Concentrate. Shut your ears. Eileen is there. That baby is tiny. No more than catching a ball*, he tried to tell himself.

The narrow, slim knife blade was in the keyhole now. *Don't rush it! Listen for the click!* Charlie Mac's words in his ears. Everything was now blotted from his mind. Absolute concentration.

And it failed again.

Third time lucky, he said to himself and the knife turned once more. No result.

This time no words came to his mind. He focused on Charlie Mac. Not the worst of them, Charlie Mac. Robbed the rich and gave to the poor. The 'poor' being himself, of course. But not a bad fellow all in all. He might drop in and see him some time. The thought made him feel relaxed. Charlie was a character.

Now just a calm feeling from head to toe.

Click. It was open.

Softly he depressed the handle, slipped through into the kitchen. Very tidy, nothing lying around, nothing but an opened jar of Bovril on the table. A tablespoon lying beside it.

The stairs. Nicely carpeted. New house. No creaks.

No hesitation, now. He had broken up enough late-night dangerous fights in public houses and domestic violence situations to know how to handle this. Terrible sound of retching from within. No time should be lost.

'Good morning,' he said as he opened the door. 'Sorry to let myself in, but I couldn't make anyone hear.' That usually worked well; not confrontational, nevertheless put a man or a woman slightly on the defensive. It worked, now. The figure holding the baby swung around, took a step towards Patrick, but said nothing.

'Oh, dear,' said Patrick. 'I can see that Mrs Kelly is not well. Should you get a doctor, or an ambulance? What do you think?'

The woman was vomiting into a basin on the washstand. He walked over towards her, very conscious of the tiny baby still in terrible danger. Not screaming too much now. Exhausted. Slightly warmer, too. Possibly even conscious of its mother's presence. When did they learn to recognize different faces? Patrick weighed up the consequences of any movement on his part. Desperation could do terrible things.

'Perhaps you should go across the road and phone for an ambulance,' he suggested without looking around. Anything to ensure that the baby was put down. No movement could be made, no possibility of an arrest until the baby was safe. At least it had been taken away from the window and the crying was less intense. Patrick stood very still, willing himself to make no sudden movement.

And then a sound from the window, a booted leg swung over the windowsill, tweed breeches, tweed jacket, hair concealed inside a leather helmet. Then she was in, the window slammed shut behind her. The catch engaged.

And the gas light caught a glint from the rim of a pistol. She held it very steadily, pointed it very accurately. The danger was minimized for the moment.

'Oh, Miss MacSweeney, could you take the baby, please.' To his pleasure, Patrick heard his own voice, as steady as a doctor giving orders to a nurse. He himself took the little wet, cold bundle first and then handed it over to her. No resistance.

One arm sufficed. She took the baby, but the pistol never wavered. For a moment Patrick's mind went to the official report that he would have to write. He knew instantly that no mention of this pistol could be allowed to appear upon it. Rapidly he produced a pair of handcuffs. They were on and snapped shut while he was still reciting the official warning. Only then did he relax and only then did he give himself a chance to look around.

Now Eileen had put the baby into its cot, warmly wrapped in a blanket. It still cried, but more quietly, almost hiccoughing now as though exhausted. The mother tried to go to it, but had to return to the basin. Badly poisoned, he thought. While the pistol still pointed at the murderer, he spoke over his shoulder.

'We need an ambulance, Miss MacSweeney. There's a post office across the road. Could you get one immediately, please. Mention my name. Say it is very urgent. A case of poisoning by ethylene glycol. Ask for the message to be passed to Dr Scher.'

She proffered her pistol before she left, but he shook his

head. He was quite happy with his truncheon and he had faith
in the handcuffs. Still swinging the truncheon, he went across
and locked the door, removing the key and putting it into his
pocket. No way of locking the window, unfortunately, but the
truncheon was heavy enough to fell the toughest of men and
he would not hesitate to use it.

His eye went to the mug on top of the chest of drawers.
Smelled only of Bovril. It was completely empty, even its dregs
had been drained. Only a dark stain remained around the rim.
He must remember to secure that for Dr Scher. It would be
part of the evidence.

The baby had stopped crying now. For a moment he worried
about it, took a step forward. Could it have been poisoned,
also? That crying had stopped very abruptly. Keeping the
truncheon poised in his right hand, he leaned over the cot and
moved the blanket with his left.

The baby was asleep, sleeping peacefully, dark eyelashes
on flushed cheek. Gently he put back the blanket and looked
towards its mother. She too seemed to be sleeping, slumped
on the bed. A strange snoring noise coming from her.

'I could give you a cheque for five hundred pounds. Just
take these things off while I write it.' The first words spoken
and he didn't bother replying. Funny the way criminals were
always so optimistic. Never gave up. Not even when the prison
door slammed on them. Always trying to pull some sharp trick.

A loud groan from Betty Kelly. Another violent attack of
vomiting. This time she did not manage to make the bowl on
the washstand, but vomited straight onto the mat by the bedside.
A white mat, now stained yellow with a crimson centre. He
looked at her uneasily. Vomiting blood. That seemed a very
bad sign. He waited. Nothing else that he could do, but the
time seemed endless until he looked at the small clock on the
mantelpiece. Less than five minutes.

And then Eileen was back. He heard the footsteps, coming
up the hallway, running up the stairs, banging on the door. He
went to it, unlocked it, but kept his eyes on the prisoner. And
just as she came in, he heard the siren of an ambulance.

'I'll go down and open the front door,' she said. 'Everything
all right?'

'The sooner the better,' he said with a nod towards the woman now slumped exhausted upon the bed. Her eyes went to the bloodstained vomit but she made no comment.

'I rang the barracks. Told them you'd made an arrest. Joe is on his way with a couple of constables and the van.'

'You'd better put that thing away before he arrives.' He indicated the pistol with a movement of his head.

'I'll go with her to the hospital and take the baby, too,' she said, ignoring him. 'That baby should be checked over. He's very young, poor little fellow.'

To his relief, she did put the pistol in her pocket before she scooped up the baby, keeping him well wrapped in his blankets and went toward the door, giving him, as she passed, a smile which he ignored.

'Tell them that she was poisoned with ethylene glycol,' he said and she gave a brisk nod which, somehow, annoyed him as much as the smile.

'Stand up,' he snarled to the prisoner. 'Let's make sure that you don't get any bright ideas about escaping.' Flexing the truncheon in his hand in a menacing manner, he took a cord from the dressing gown on the back of the door and bound the ankles together, just leaving room to hobble, but making anything faster an impossibility. The ambulance had gone. He heard the siren sounding and knew that they had recognized an emergency. He hoped that they would be in time and that Dr Scher was at the hospital. Still, even if he were not there, surely the hospital could cope. He was glad that Eileen had gone with the woman. She was not one to be backward. She would ensure that the stomach was pumped. And he could rely on her to remember the words, ethylene glycol. He had seen her lips move and knew that she had memorized the words.

And then another siren. A raucous one, this time. The Gardaí Síochána van. He recognized the sound of it. They had put the siren onto it because it often made a riot easier to break up. A surprising amount of people left the scene once they heard that siren. Rather unnecessary here, but the prisoner might be impressed by it.

'All right, sir.' And there was Joe, reliable as ever, always knowing his place, but ready to support and to ensure the success of his superior officer. Joe, thought Patrick, was a very good fellow.

'All right, Joe. Everything under control.' That could be a question, or an assertion. In any case, everything was going well. Joe and one of the constables hustled the prisoner into the van, himself at liberty to make a quick note of everything. Once he was back in his office, he would write up the whole matter. Eileen, he thought, could appear, very legitimately, as a concerned acquaintance of Mrs Betty Kelly. Nothing wrong with that. Everyone in the small city of Cork knew everyone. No strangers here, he had once heard a Cork person say that and he had recognized the accuracy of the remark.

'We'll take a statement as soon as we get back,' he said to Joe and hardly waited to see Joe nod. There was an admiring look on his face. I must do my best for Joe, thought Patrick. He was an ideal assistant. Mentally he began to draft his report for the superintendent as he followed the prisoner down the well-carpeted stair of the opulently furnished house. He would, he thought, make a mention of Joe and how supportive he had been. As for Eileen, well, she would not thank him for any account of the role she had played in the final arrest.

Poor John Donovan, he thought. One daughter murdered, another in danger of death from the same murderer and his little grandson only just rescued from having his skull split open on the concrete path below his parents' bedroom.

It just showed that you needed to be very careful about whom you trusted. He climbed into the driving seat of the van and waited for Joe to turn the starting handle. He himself, he decided, would be very careful to whom he entrusted that nice little bank account that was building up in the Cork Savings Bank when the time came for him to get married.

NINETEEN

St Thomas Aquinas
*Et ideo si aliquis homo sit periculosus communitati
et corruptivus ipsius propter aliquod peccatum,
laudabiliter et salubriter occiditur, ut bonum commune
conservetur, modicum enim fermentum totam massam
corrumpit, ut dicitur I ad Cor. V.*
(Therefore if a man be dangerous and infectious to the
community, on account of some sin, it is praiseworthy
and advantageous that he be killed in order to
safeguard the common good, since 'a little leaven
corrupteth the whole mass'. (1 Cor. 5:6).

'How is she, doctor?' The Reverend Mother had been on edge all of the morning. As Sister Bernadette closed the door softly leaving the doctor there, facing her, she rose to her feet and approached him. Several times during the previous afternoon and this morning she had found herself going towards the telephone, now restored to its crackling normality, and had then stopped herself. Dr Scher would let her know about Betty as soon as possible; she knew that. He was here now, in person, and she hoped that was not a bad sign.

'Recovering rapidly,' he said reassuringly. 'Don't worry. I wouldn't have left her if there were any concerns. We pumped the stomach. She's doing well. No liver damage. We'll keep an eye on her for a while, but she'll be fine. A healthy young woman. And the baby is fine, too. We kept him in overnight, but not a thing wrong with him, so her aunt took him home with her this morning. I've been to see Mrs O'Sullivan just now. She's very relieved. The little fellow was crying and I could see that she had been crying too. She told me that she had been sitting there, nursing him, thinking that he might be an orphan with his mother dead and his father in prison charged with the murder of his aunt.'

'Excuse me, Reverend Mother, Inspector Cashman would like a word with you,' said Sister Bernadette, popping her head in through the door less than two seconds after her knock. She had an air of suppressed excitement about her. There was nothing Sister Bernadette enjoyed better than the excitement of continual coming and going, of taxies being ordered, phone calls coming and now both Dr Scher and Inspector Cashman in the Reverend Mother's room.

'I'll bring the tea in two seconds, Dr Scher; Sister Imelda is laying out the trolley,' she promised with a beaming smile at the doctor, who was always her favourite visitor.

Patrick, thought the Reverend Mother, as they waited for the approach of the tea trolley, was looking well. Calm and purposeful. She had heard all about how he had arrested the man, slipped the handcuffs on, after a reading of rights. Eileen had told her all about it, had said that Patrick, once he had made up his mind, had been very decisive. They had met on the previous evening, had a meal together, apparently, and she had got out of him how he had turned the man over to Joe, how he had explained to his subordinate in an undertone that the charge would not be drafted until they received news from the hospital about the survival of the latest victim of poisoning. And, of course, how he had carefully sealed up the mug with its tell-tale stains of Bovril that had been left on the kitchen table.

Eileen, to the Reverend Mother's satisfaction, had been full of praise for Patrick and now, on the morning after the crisis, he looked thoroughly pleased with himself. The arrest of Denis Kelly, stopped in the act of poisoning his own wife, was from Patrick's point of view a satisfactory end to the affair. Just as well to have no IRA connections, or no connections with a wealthy family engaging a team of top-class lawyers to concoct a lily-white background for their client; no hunger strikes or anything like that, if it had been Mary MacSwiney. And, of course, any connection with a young nun would have been appalling and would have aroused strong feelings in the city and brought the bishop down on the barracks like a ton of bricks. Patrick had, thought the Reverend Mother, the look of a man who had satisfactorily wrapped up an awkward piece of business. With a few giggles Eileen had told her about the gun and how Patrick's face had showed how appalled he was and the Reverend Mother decided not to mention Eileen's presence to him. Let him celebrate the successful arrest of a murderer. He, unlike Eileen, had not been gifted with exceptional brains, but had made the best of lesser gifts such as tenacity of purpose, strong mindedness, complete concentration and the self-discipline to devote the necessary amount of work to a project, no matter how much it cost him. She admired him for this and allowed him to bask in the satisfaction until after he had swallowed his tea and demolished his slice of cake with two bites, before she said quietly, 'Of course, Patrick, Denis Kelly did not murder Sister Gertrude.'

They both swung around to stare at her.

'But you said it yourself,' said Dr Scher. 'You said that his wife Betty had known that he was guilty, had put the empty chocolate box on top of all the clothes in the trunk in order to show him that she knew.' He was frowning in a puzzled manner. It had begun to strike him that there was something wrong about this.

'Denis Kelly was indeed guilty of *a* murder, as well as the attempted murder of his wife, but he was not guilty of the murder of Sister Gertrude,' said the Reverend Mother. 'After all, Patrick, think about it. What could have been his motive? Her death would have been of no particular benefit to him. She had nothing to leave to him. His wife Betty had inherited the entire fortune from his father-in-law. I suspect that the birth of the baby, of John Donovan's grandson, may have prompted the will which left everything to the younger sister. John Donovan had, if the aunt is right, made an earlier will where he left to her a sufficient sum of money to recompense his sister-in-law for her care of his motherless girls, and presumably in that will the rest of his estate would have been divided between the two girls. Then when the elder sister entered the convent, he may have changed the will, again, but possibly not. The will I have seen was made just a few months ago, probably around the time of the birth of the baby son to Betty. But he may have made another will in the meantime, and I have known a case where this happened, that left half of his fortune in trust for the older daughter where she would inherit if she left the convent. You must remember that Sister

Gertrude had not taken any final vows and she would have been free to go at any moment if she decided that was right. But the birth of a grandson may have weakened the bonds between him and his favourite daughter and he may, like many men, have enjoyed the thought of bequeathing a good sum of money to Betty and her husband so that the little boy could be brought up in comfort and be well educated.'

'And so the last will left everything to the younger sister,' said Dr Scher.

'Yes,' agreed the Reverend Mother. 'That will of course was the important one. And that will was what brought about his death. The man was dead within a couple of weeks of making it. John Donovan could have lived for another twenty or even thirty years in the normal way of things. Denis Kelly did not want to wait as long as that. And so he bought a box of chocolates, injected ethylene glycol into them. I must say,' said the Reverend Mother, 'I did have him in my mind as a source of the deadly stuff. You said it yourself, doctor. Don't you remember? I remember your words very clearly. "It's a sort of syrup, thins out paint, and liquefies solids. They use it in lots of factories." I blame myself for not following up my first idea. But you see, we were all thinking of the death of Sister Gertrude. I, or any of us, I imagine, couldn't think why Denis Kelly should kill Sister Gertrude. In fact, if I am any judge of people, he was devastated by her death. Shocked and horrified. That was the reaction that I noted myself when I met him. Excessively so, I thought at the time.'

'Excessively so,' echoed Dr Scher, looking at her attentively.

'That's right,' said the Reverend Mother. 'I'd guess,' she went on, 'from something that the aunt said, that Patsy, Sister Gertrude, was his first love and then he was tempted for a while by the younger and far prettier sister, but afterwards, I think, regretted it. I saw the man just after he heard the news about Sister Gertrude's death and I would be quite sure that he was grief-stricken and horrified.'

There was a puzzled silence after she said that.

'So why . . . so who killed Sister Gertrude?' It was Dr Scher who asked the question, but Patrick looked at her eagerly, waiting for her answer.

'Her sister killed her,' said the Reverend Mother. 'Her sister gave her the chocolates which were injected with the ethylene glycol.'

'So you think her sister got hold of the stuff, got it from her husband. Of course, they probably have some sort of pump to squirt the stuff into the paint, to get it to the right consistency; they'd use it for undercoats as the undercoat would be thinner than the top coat. So that's what could have been used, injected into the chocolates. Let it stand for a few hours in a warm atmosphere and the hole in the chocolate would probably seal over.' Dr Scher pondered aloud over the matter while Patrick sat with a puzzled expression on his face.

'So Mr Donovan . . .' he said slowly and then stopped. 'I don't understand,' he said and then got up and paced the floor between the window and the fireplace. 'Why should she kill her sister? Was that why Denis tried to kill his wife? You think that Denis was in love with the older of the two girls, but married the younger. So it was what they call a love triangle. Betty kills her sister because she suspects that her husband loves her better. And then her husband tries to kill her in revenge. So love was the motive, is that right, Reverend Mother?'

'The older that I get,' said the Reverend Mother, popping her prayer book back into the drawer and closing it firmly. 'The older I get,' she continued, 'the more I realize the importance of money. It comes into almost every aspect in life. No, it was nothing to do with love, though I can see that there was an unhappy triangle between Denis Kelly and the two Donovan sisters. But, in the end, all that has nothing to do with the murder. And so we need to go back to the man who did have money.'

'John Donovan,' said Patrick slowly and the Reverend Mother gave him an approving nod.

'Yes,' she said. 'Once I found out that John Donovan died in almost the same way as Sister Gertrude, I realized that it was possible that he was murdered, that this was a crime, was *the* crime that needed investigating. After all, John Donovan was a very well-off man and all of his money was left to the one daughter, now Betty Kelly.'

'So she . . .?' Dr Scher looked from one to the other.

'Or he,' said Patrick eagerly. 'Much more likely Denis Kelly killed him using the same method. She, the wife, probably wouldn't know much about ethylene glycol, may not have known anything. Why should she? She had her household duties and her baby to look after. But he, Denis Kelly, he would. Safety regulations would make sure that he knew the stuff was poisonous. He'd have to warn the workers in the paint department.' Patrick was thinking hard.

'And why kill Sister Gertrude. That did him no good. The money, all of it, was left to his wife, isn't that right?' Dr Scher looked from one to the other.

'It wasn't he who killed Sister Gertrude,' said Patrick slowly.

The Reverend Mother nodded a cordial encouragement to him. 'That's right, Patrick,' she said. 'We must remember,' she went on, 'that something like a sweet tooth can be inherited,' she said. 'Sister Gertrude was very fond of sweets. She told me that what she found the hardest part of convent life was not being able to buy sweets for herself. Her sister Betty disliked sweets, liked things such as Marmite, according to the aunt that cared for the sisters after their mother died.'

'So the chocolates were doctored with ethylene glycol and given to John Donovan . . .'

'I was stupid,' said the Reverend Mother ruefully. 'I should have realized that what Sister Catherine told me was of the utmost importance when she saw Sister Gertrude with her sister in the convent garden. Something was being done that would be against the rules. She witnessed that, overheard them laugh about the possibility of her spying for Sister Mary Immaculate. When I asked Betty what she and her sister talked about, on that last afternoon before Sister Gertrude died, she told me, very readily, that they talked about their father. Betty had been tidying out his house, making it ready for a sale. Quite a task, apparently. According to her, he was a man who would keep a spent match in case it might be of use and she certainly wouldn't have been surprised to come across a half-eaten box of chocolates, and as she did not eat sweets herself, she brought them, in all innocence, up to her sister. And, of course, I should have guessed that it might be that something to eat was handed over, not a pen, not a memento such as a book, where, if I were asked, I would certainly have given my permission for it to be kept. But what if there had been some chocolates left in a drawer? After all, eating sweets and chocolates, well, that was poor Sister Gertrude's besetting sin. But, of course, I could not think of any reason why Betty should want to poison her sister. Not financial certainly: all of their father's money was left to her. She and her husband and her little son would be quite rich once probate was granted. I did briefly think about jealousy, but I didn't think it could be too strong. Why should Betty be jealous? After all she was married to the man, had borne his child and was now about to bring him what would have appeared to both of them as a small fortune. Her sister was happy in the convent. She really posed no threat to Betty who had always been the pretty one of the two sisters. Also, every time I thought of that last day when the two sisters were in the garden, hearing them talk and laugh together, well, there appeared to be a good relationship between them. No, the chocolates were given in all innocence. Betty wasn't to know that they had already killed her father. She did not live in the same house as he did, so she wouldn't have known that he had eaten some of them that night.'

'And then Sister Gertrude ate them in the dormitory, after lights were out, I suppose.' Dr Scher grimaced slightly.

'So the book of evidence against Denis Kelly will be that he poisoned his father-in-law, John Donovan, in order that the man's entire fortune would come to him, through his wife, of course, but that would be the same thing,' said Patrick. 'We'll have to exhume the body of John Donovan, Dr Scher, and you'll have to test it for traces of poison. And, of course, in the meantime we can hold Denis Kelly on a charge of attempted murder against his wife. The death of Sister Gertrude will be misadventure, I suppose. No blame will attach to the sister. But what made him attack his wife and try to kill her? And I'm surprised that she would eat and drink in his presence if she had suspected him of murdering her father.' And then Patrick contradicted himself swiftly. 'The baby, of course. I heard him myself. He forced her to drink the stuff or else he would throw the baby out from the window.'

'I wonder,' said the Reverend Mother slowly, 'whether poor Betty thought, by leaving the empty chocolate box on top of the trunk, she would give him an opportunity to escape. She had told him to open it in the convent, had told him to check whether there were three towels. She had put two and two together. I'd say. Guessed it was Denis. Both her father and her sister had died of what seemed like the same illness and one thing that they had both eaten was those chocolates, the chocolates that her husband gave to her father. It may have been a habit of his to bring little presents of sweetmeats to his father-in-law. When Betty thought about it, when she found the empty box among Sister Gertrude's things, well, she was probably fairly sure. She perhaps covered her consternation by making a fuss about a missing towel, but underneath she was thinking hard. She couldn't bear to be the one that sent him to the hangman, but she wanted him to leave, perhaps to go to England. To remove himself from her life and from her baby son. So she gave him instructions to check on the towels before he took the trunk away from the convent and I can only think that was because, when she found the empty chocolate box, she immediately connected her sister's death with her father's – the symptoms were identical. Perhaps Denis Kelly had betrayed himself earlier when he heard of the death of Sister Gertrude, when he found out that she had given her sister the half empty box of chocolates. That was something that could have been said in all innocence over the supper table. He could have raged at her, demanded why she did that. In any case, when she found the empty chocolate box, she knew that her sister had eaten the same chocolates as her father and she guessed that her husband was responsible for both deaths. She probably could not bear to live with him as her husband again, but she baulked, as I say, at condemning him to the gallows.'

'Understandable,' said Dr Scher with a sigh. 'I don't suppose that I could endure to do that to someone that I had once loved. I'd give them a chance to escape.'

'You would be wrong, Dr Scher,' said Patrick firmly. 'Once someone has murdered once, they will murder again. I've seen that before.'

'I wonder what she thought when he came home after all her efforts,' said Dr Scher.

'He probably took out the chocolate box and came home showing nothing, I suppose. She opened the trunk; the box wasn't there, she perhaps thought that one of the nuns had thrown it away before the trunk was locked. She may even have been half-relieved. But, of course, he knew that she had guessed the truth. I've tested that mug that had Bovril, Reverend Mother, and you were right. It did have ethylene glycol in it, a large amount. Very strong-tasting stuff, Bovril; it cloaked the sweet taste. And, of course, he knew that she wouldn't have taken a chocolate from him, but she had probably made the Bovril before he arrived. He could have asked her to get something and then slipped the stuff into the mug.'

'She drank it,' said Patrick in a low voice. 'She must have known, but still she drank it. I heard him shouting at her to drink it.'

'According to Eileen,' said Dr Scher, 'she was forced to drink it or risked having her baby thrown from the window. Mother love is a great thing. Poor girl. She just drank it down, drained it to the last drop. Anything to save her baby.'

'Well,' said Patrick, stretching his legs and luxuriating in the heat of the fire, 'well, it's all ended well. The baby is alive, the mother is alive and the world will not miss someone like Denis Kelly. No doubt that he will be convicted and hanged.' He had the air of one who is at peace with himself.

The Reverend Mother said nothing. Her namesake, the saintly Thomas Aquinas believed in capital punishment, but she was not sure that she did. She felt confused and ill-at-ease. She glanced at her two companions. Dr Scher, of course, was used to death. It must be something that he had inured himself against from the time that he had been a medical student.

Patrick, also, perhaps. His experience as an officer of the law would allow no room for external self-doubt and perhaps, by now that outward self-assurance which he had worn from the start of his career was beginning to be internalized. Just now he looked quite relaxed and completely at ease. Unusual to see him like that, but success was beginning to iron out the lack of confidence from his system and give him the poise and composure that would allow him to enjoy life. She was glad for him.

But for herself, she could not contemplate the deliberate killing of another human being without an inward shudder, a darkness of the soul. Could there be, should there be another way? Something that would keep the world safe from a murderer like Denis Kelly; that would allow him to live under guard, to have a chance to compensate for that evil impulse of greed which had induced him to murder his father-in-law and to attempt to murder his own wife. Her mind went to the prayer that had been recited at morning Mass in the chapel.

Sancte Michael Archangele, defende nos in proelio, contra nequitiam et insidias diaboli esto praesidium. Imperet illi Deus, supplices deprecamur: tuque, Princeps militiae coelestis, Satanam aliosque spiritus malignos, qui ad perditionem animarum pervagantur in mundo, divina virtute, in infernum detrude. Amen.

The Archangel Michael, she thought, did not kill Lucifer and the other rebels for their terrible sin, but banished them eternally from the presence of Almighty God. Could a solution like that prove an alternative to the brutal hanging of a murderer? Her mind went to the numerous islands that were scattered around the coastline of Ireland. Perhaps one could be made to accommodate criminals such as Denis Kelly where they could live out their lives making recompense for the evil that they had done by growing food to feed the poor of their native city.

And then she sighed. She had enough problems to solve in her own little world. She had grave doubts about that permanently leaking roof in the junior infants' classroom. The store of potatoes in Sister Bernadette's pantry, earmarked to make a nourishing lunch for hungry children, was diminishing at an alarming rate. And she still had to see the bishop in order to discuss the question of the pious Sister Catherine.

The Reverend Mother got to her feet. 'I must not keep you any longer; I know that you are both busy men,' she said as she rang the bell for Sister Bernadette.

'Rome wasn't built in a day,' she said to herself and tried to find some comfort from the thought as they both departed.

Lightning Source UK Ltd.
Milton Keynes UK
UKHW012109141119
353550UK00003B/52/P

9 781847 519061